Penguin Books
SUGAR AND RUM

Barry Unsworth was born in 1930 in a mining village in Durham. He attended Stockton-on-Tees Grammar School and Manchester University. He has spent a number of years in the Eastern Mediterranean area and has taught English in Athens and Istanbul. His first novel, *The Partnership*, was published in 1966. This was followed by *The Greeks Have a Word for It* (1967) and *The Hide* (1970). *Mooncranker's Gift* received the Heinemann Award for 1973 for its 'sheer beauty of writing and richness of experience'. He is also the author of *Pascali's Island*, which was shortlisted for the Booker Prize in 1980 and has recently been filmed, and *Stone Virgin* (1985), which the *Daily Telegraph* described as: 'A marvellous novel, beautifully written and compelling to read.' Many of his books are published in Penguin.

Barry Unsworth is a Fellow of the Royal Society of Literature.

SUGAR AND RUM

by

Barry Unsworth

Penguin Books

PENGUIN BOOKS

Published by the Penguin Group
27 Wrights Lane, London W8 5TZ, England
Viking Penguin Inc., 40 West 23rd Street, New York, New York 10010, USA
Penguin Books Australia Ltd, Ringwood, Victoria, Australia
Penguin Books Canada Ltd, 2801 John Street, Markham, Ontario, Canada L3R 1B4
Penguin Books (NZ) Ltd, 182–190 Wairau Road, Auckland 10, New Zealand

Penguin Books Ltd, Registered Offices: Harmondsworth, Middlesex, England

First published by Hamish Hamilton 1988
Published in Penguin Books 1990
1 3 5 7 9 10 8 6 4 2

Printed and bound in Great Britain by
Richard Clay Ltd, Bungay, Suffolk
Filmset in Bembo

For Aira, with love

Metaphor: The figure of speech in which a name or descriptive term is transferred to some object to which it is not properly applicable.

Shorter Oxford English Dictionary

PART ONE

Signs and Portents

1

This was a time of trouble for Benson, when he felt silence forming over him like a crust, when he couldn't work and couldn't sleep and spent a lot of time walking around the city in an ancient overcoat of grey tweed, talking to strangers, looking for signs, portents, auguries. Unhappiness made him superstitious; he saw clues everywhere, even in the vagaries of the weather.

In February the grip of winter eased for a short while, the temperature rose suddenly and there was a succession of sunny, astonishingly mild days. They began in the same way, with thick mist off the river; but by mid-morning the sun had licked this up and the sky showed through, pale and radiant, suffused with a soft, bright haze, as if the gorged sun were breathing out the surplus of the feast in vaporous exhalations.

Some of Liverpool's blackbirds were fooled into singing early; Benson heard them in different parts of the city, singing jubilantly in unlikely places. One afternoon, less than a minute before witnessing a suicide, he heard one in full spate on the parapet of the Yoruba Club in Croxteth Road. At sixty-three the arteries may be hardening but the mind is as soft as ever for impressions. This outburst of the deceived blackbird became linked with death in his mind for ever.

He had paused to look down the weeded driveway, past the fringe of sad birch trees, at the flaking, dilapidated club house, pale in the sunshine, with its incongruous verandah, the strange confusion of tribal and social in the name above the door. There was never anyone there when he passed, never any sign of life. What were the secret hours of the Yoruba? This afternoon he had felt – once again – some-

3

thing of the half-painful sense of mystery, the sense of a secret life going parallel to his own, that he remembered from childhood.

After this, he crossed the road so as to walk on the sunny side. He was approaching the tall block of flats at the beginning of Croxteth Road. The white railing round the top was half lost in light, half dissolved in the blank, milky-blue heaven of mid-afternoon. Casually glancing up into this bright zone of air, Benson saw the flash of the leap, heard a cry, but despite this thought at first it was a carpet falling, a red and blue carpet, because of the way it seemed to drift and sidle in the first moments, but then it went straight and fast and landed on the concrete forecourt with a sound a carpet wouldn't have made. Feeling slightly sickened, Benson strove to fix the sound of impact in his mind so that he could make a note about it when he got home – he still made notes. The man was lying on his back, motion-less, inside the forecourt but in full view from across the road. His face was turned aside, away from Benson, as if that mild sun were too bright.

A car had stopped farther down. A small man got out and walked towards Benson. He was wearing a black leather hat with a very narrow brim. "Somebody fell off the roof," he said. His eyes were bloodshot and sad. He looked across to where the man was lying. "He's had his lot," he said. "You can tell, can't you?"

"Looks like it. No one else seems to have noticed anything."

Which was odd, considering the sound, the fact that he had gone hurtling past windows and balconies. Benson too was sure that the man was dead. There was no sign at this distance of blood or damage; but he knew, he recognised, in a way at once obscure and definite, that quality of stillness, that semblance of ease. The man was strewn there, littered.

"We should do something," he said.

Two young black women emerged from the building. They were dressed to go out, in light, summery-looking clothes. Both were short-haired and slender and young, no

4

more than sixteen or seventeen, Benson thought. Their meeting with the body seemed unplanned, but then there was something ceremonious, accustomed, about the way they took positions, one at the head, one at the feet. Neither of them touched the man or stooped to look at him more closely. After a moment or two both girls clutched at themselves. Perhaps merely chilly, Benson thought – it had seemed to him when they emerged that they were too lightly dressed, that they had been misled by the soft and hazy sunshine. The gesture itself could have meant anything; even the presence of death was not enough for it to be construed with any certainty. Demonstrating the paucity of body movement available to humans in time of stress – he would make a note of that too.

"He's a goner," the motorist said.

There was no one else, no other cars had stopped, there were no passers-by. One of the girls went back to the building, leaving her companion on guard.

"Gone to phone," the motorist said. He glanced along the road to where his car waited. "Gone to notify the authorities," he said, more loudly and somehow demandingly. A warm reek of leather came from his hat.

Benson assented. He regarded the motorist's face, saw a relief similar to his own: there was no need to do anything, no need to cross over – the girl had gone to notify the authorities. He looked into the man's eyes, sad and moist and shifty under the mildly reeking brim of his hat, and felt for a sharp moment an impulse to embrace him. Instead he made a gift of words, presented a fragment of his experience. "I thought it was a carpet, at first," he said, "you know, from the way he fell."

He would have liked to enlarge on this, now that the need of action was over, to commemorate this death with at least a few minutes of conversation. But the motorist had already turned away and begun to walk back towards his car. Benson too, after a moment more of hesitation, moved on along the pavement. He noticed after some time that he had reversed direction: whereas before he had been proceeding

5

on a southerly course, towards Sefton Park, he now found himself walking back towards the city centre. This didn't matter. He had no particular destination. He had a client to see at 5.30, nothing before that. On this mild afternoon he was walking down Prince's Avenue, on the southern border of Toxteth, distressed by what he had just seen, lonelier for that lonely death, with a twinge of rheumatism in his left arm and absolutely no sense of where he wanted to go.

The avenue, in its straightness, its wideness, its long blank vista, seemed designed to add to his desolation. Many of the tall Victorian houses had slumped and cracked open, it seemed, gaping ruinous, eviscerated, spilling their rubble out onto choked gardens, or charred and gutted with arson. People, mainly men, mainly black, mainly out of work, were sitting on seats along the central strip, where stunted saplings grew at intervals in their cages of wire netting. Pausing at intersections, glancing to his left, Benson looked down wide streets of low houses, like streets in settlement towns, where space is plentiful and materials few. Figures in the distance moved slowly against the luminous horizon, were lost in the haze where the streets dipped down towards the Mersey. Stages, he thought. The man's fall had been a kind of paradigm, leap of birth, indeterminate motions of infancy, gathering gravity . . .

When he was nearing the end of the avenue, Benson saw a fattish, serene-looking, middle-aged negro sitting by himself on one of the benches, dressed in a raincoat and sneakers. He crossed over and sat down beside him. After a moment or two he began to tell him about the suicide.

"He jumped at the precise moment I was passing," he said. "Half a minute either way and I would have missed the whole thing." He leaned forward eagerly, moving his hand in gestures that were rapid but half formed and inconclusive. As always these days his own words impassioned him. "I see it as a performance, a kind of performance," he said. "Meant for me somehow. As if, you know, he was waiting up there. Here is Benson now, hoop-la! Over you

6

go. Just in that space of time." He shaped the duration of it with one of his sketchy gestures. "Then these two girls came out," he said, "that was a performance too. Then the thought came to me that the whole thing was like the stages of life."

The negro was looking at him steadily with a half smile. The smile was sleepy but the deepset eyes were bright with a sort of derisive appraisal, which Benson was aware of but too intent on talking to consider much. He began to explain what he meant; the leap, the floating, the plunge. His loquacity was not new, but nowadays, when he was on the brink of speech, there was a slight but noticeable convulsiveness about his lower jaw.

"In the floating there was also the crash," he said. "In my beginning is my end, as Eliot has it." That isn't it, he thought, with sudden discouragement. There was something else he wanted to say, but couldn't – something to do with the hush and blankness up there, the mild sky, the white railing half-melted, the leap, the cry. The man had jumped from the heart of silence. And those two black guardians . . . "That is the phase before personality is formed," he said, less certainly. "That would correspond—"

"No stages," the negro said suddenly in a soft blurting voice.

"How do you mean?"

"You telling me he jump off. You talking about stages. No stages there, man. When he jump off, that the end of the story."

The man's face glistened slightly in the sunshine. He was smiling still but Benson did not think he was very well. His pale lips were chapped and sore-looking and the whites of his eyes were discoloured.

A little girl and her mother came and sat down on the other side of them. They were waiting for the bus – there was a stop just opposite. The little girl was dressed for some occasion, in a pale blue coat and white stockings, and she

7

had white ribbons in her hair. She was eating ice cream from a carton, freighting her little plastic spoon with minute quantities and eating in a series of darting licks.

"Woman drown herself in a poddle," the negro said, nodding his broad face in the direction of Granby Street. "Last November. Three inches poddle water. My wife's cousin living in Antigua, cut his wrists but he didn't die."

"You don't want to get that all over your coat," the woman said. The little girl had started to eat the ice cream very slowly, to make it last, and it was melting and dripping.

"Policeman in Aigburth eat rat poison," the negro said. "It was in the paper. He's smoking his pipe, lean over the gate, say hello good evening like every evening, then he goes to this little shed he got in the garden and eat the rat poison. Where the stages there?"

"For God's *sake*, Sandra," the woman said. "I dunno why I got you that ice cream." She caught Benson's eye and smiled with resignation and pride.

The negro turned a softly blinking face away from Benson towards the cooling sun. There was a smell of vanilla and dry dogshit and warm dust. Feelings of sorrow came to Benson in this aftermath of shock, amidst these odours remembered from childhood. Something else from childhood too: he had been rebuked; he had spoken on impulse and been rebuked for being excitable, for being fanciful. He remembered the ironical patience on his father's face. "I'm not trying to detract from the man's death," he said, "you think I'm making a story out of it, don't you? But we can make analogies surely. You are only thinking of it one way. In my view nothing is accidental. The universe is a vast system of correspondencies, as Baudelaire said."

After a moment or two the negro sighed and lowered his head. "Police got their feelings too," he said. "But they buried deep."

Later, back in his apartment in Greville Street, Benson resisted the temptation to tell Jennifer Colomb the story of the death leap, mainly because she was waiting for his opinion of the new chapter of *Treacherous Dreams*, and was so tense about it that to raise any other topic at that point would have verged on sadism. Miss Colomb was a valued client. Apart from anything else she actually paid him his fee for the weekly consultation.

In happier days, when he was full of plans, before he was stricken with silence, while working on the closing stages of *Fool's Canopy*, his novel set in the Venice of the 1790s, and while at the same time beginning the research for his complex and ambitious new novel set against the background of the Liverpool slave-trade, he had hit upon the idea of supplementing his income by setting himself up as a literary consultant. *Have you got that manuscript in your bottom drawer?* his advertisement had demanded. *If so, now is the time to bring it out. Are you having technical problems with work in progress? Blocked? Stuck? Bogged down? Get expert advice from a professional writer on all aspects of the craft of fiction, style, narrative, characterisation. Also marketing. Fee by arrangement.*

The arrangement was five pounds when he could get it. Initial response had been good, half Merseyside was in a fury to write, it seemed, but now only a few clients remained to him. By an ironic reversal, in which under other circumstances he might have seen beauty, he had become the very bogged-down creature appealed to in the advertisement. He, the unblocker, had got blocked and more than ever talkative and progressively stranger. He was left now with those too innocent, unhinged or self-absorbed to be put off by the change in his manner, the growing lack of any real resemblance between this pale, gesturing improviser behind the desk and knowledgeable Clive Benson, the Literary Consultant of the advertisement and the sign outside the door. This heroic remnant he privately named 'Benson's Fictioneers'. They kept on coming, bringing manuscripts for assessment, more then ready to read extracts, avid for practical hints. In the nights of his insomnia he heard sometimes the crazed voices of their fictions whispering and crooning to him from reverberant wells.

Jennifer Colomb was of this company. She was sitting across the desk from him in jumper and cardigan of the same shade of lilac and pearl earrings, pale hands clutching the handbag in her lap. Silence gathered between them as he read the beginning of her new chapter.

"This burning sun of June is no friend to one of your fair and delicate complexion." Sir Reginald spoke in a tone between jest and earnest, keeping an easy grip on the reins of his gelding.

"Nay, Sir Reginald, I am tougher than I look."

"Ay," he said softly, his dark eyes intent upon her delicate profile, "I doubt it not, but I would not be the cause that you should put it to the test. For the sake of your beauty and my conscience," he urged her, still in that tone of honeyed jest.

"Nay then, an you list, let us ride into the coverts. I will not gainsay you. 'Twould be impolite in a hostess. You will not have cause to complain of your treatment here at Beaulieu Castle, and in my father's absence. Besides, it makes no difference to me as I have ever been a lover of the wildwood."

"Have you so?" The innocent gaiety of her words had touched him but abated nothing of his fierce purpose. The motto on his crest was 'I Will Repay', and in the dark history of his family it had always applied equally to a debt of honour or an injury. With a kindled look on his hawklike features, he signalled his retinue to retire a little farther off, while he led the Lady Margaret into the grateful shade of the trees.

Being in the wood was something like sitting on the inside of a green aquarium, the tens of thousands of leaves all round filtering out the unwanted blues and reds from the spectrum to leave a sort of green haze broken only by an occasional shaft of sunlight.

Benson raised his eyes from this to the fair-skinned, delicate-featured woman opposite; she was flushed and her eyes had an oddly beseeching look. It was a look he sometimes saw on the faces of all his clients, except on that of the dreaded Hogan, whose face was too rigid with depression to show much.

"Well," he said, "I think it's going along all right."

"Do you really?"

"Yes. I would cut out that first 'delicate' if I were you – you don't really need it. And I am not sure that you are quite getting the right consistency of tone."

"Where do you mean?" Miss Colomb had leaned forward tensely. Her hair was streaked blonde and permed in an elaborate style that swept it high off her forehead, giving her face a naked, exposed look. With this elaborate coiffure and her naked face and her pearls she always seemed to Benson like a person made ready for sacrifice. She was easily his most affluent client. She lived with her father in Kirby, in a house near the sea; her father was an antique dealer and Miss Colomb helped him in the shop – she loved beautiful things. There had never been mention of a mother.

"It's Lady Margaret," Benson said. "Sir Reginald always stays cool, bless him, but she keeps jumping out of the frame. I mean, for example, would a woman of her class and time say, 'I'm tougher than I look'?"

"She might," Miss Colomb said defensively. "I don't see why not. She is very unconventional. I've made that clear elsewhere in the book. She is a free spirit."

"She is, yes." Familiar weariness descended on Benson. Miss Colomb was using the argument of character against him, a ploy used by all his clients at one time or another. "She may be a free spirit," he said, "but that doesn't enable her to defy anachronism. We must remember that she is a character in a story. And a story is a world. It has its own laws, its own internal consistency."

"Yes, but she is a free spirit in the story. She defies the narrow conventions of the day."

"That may be so, but she can't anticipate the speech patterns of a future age."

He paused, smiling at Miss Colomb, for whom he felt considerable sympathy. He was conscientious in his dealings with his clients, making it a point of honour, even in

11

the midst of his own despair, to take their work seriously, try to offer what help he could. But there was not much point in pursuing this particular issue. He thought he knew why Lady Margaret, and only she, committed these solecisms. It had started happening since Sir Reginald Penthaligon had ridden into her life on his bay gelding and she had become the object of his dark designs. In fact, it was Miss Colomb's voice that kept breaking through, but he didn't think he could say this to her except indirectly. He didn't want to hurt her.

She was waiting. She was looking at him expectantly. He must say something. What sins have I committed, he wondered, that I must be plagued so now in late career? A little tact, Benson.

"Of the various attributes we fiction-writers require," he said, "one of the most important is detachment. Of course tenacity of purpose is the *sine qua non*, otherwise we'd never keep on with it for the year or two years or longer that it takes to finish the work. And we have to be a certain sort of egotist or we wouldn't want to make a display of ourselves, would we? But without detachment, without distance, there is always the danger of losing perspective, of getting enmeshed in our own fictions."

He paused, looking across the desk with a hope that quickly withered of some admission or acknowledgement. Miss Colomb's level grey eyes looked back at him steadily. Her mouth, which must have been pretty, did not make motions of speech. In her silence, on her face, Benson read the marks of the true fictioneer, saw his own abjectness, his own absurd obstinacy. Miss Colomb was in the prison of her invention and she did not want to be free. He thought in that moment of the man who had jumped. High up there, quite alone, he had clambered over the white bars of the railing. Benson knew now why the railing had fascinated him, knew what he had wanted to tell the man on the bench, but had been afraid to because the man was black. In the Liverpool shipyards they had fitted high rails on the slave ships to make it difficult for the slaves to jump into the sea.

"That description of the wood," he said, "it's a bit ordinary, isn't it? All you are saying is that inside the trees the light was different. And they are not sitting in an aquarium, they are sitting on their horses, they are moving. Couldn't you give it more atmosphere, more sense of movement away from the light? This is not just any old wood, is it? It is the fatal wildwood, it is the wood that Lady Margaret and Sir Reginald Penthaligon are entering together."

2

The cold came back but the memory of that February afternoon stayed with Benson, haunted his imagination, a lull of warmth and death sealed like a bubble in ice by the return of winter. The elements changed order but were always the same: the sunlit air, the flash of the leap, the guardians in their summer clothes, the premature song of the blackbird, the crash and sprawl. Trapped somewhere among these shifting images, there must be a meaning, as he pointed out to Dolores one dark night in the vicinity of the Anglican cathedral.

"Trouble shrinks a man in some ways," he said, "but the capacity for receiving messages is immeasurably increased, if you have the gift at all."

He felt himself to be a living proof of this. He had always had a delicate sense of correspondence; that is characteristic of the literary mind. But in those days of his affliction, when he felt somehow ambushed by his own past, he saw parallels everywhere. They bred in the silence of his life. This silence too he spoke about to Dolores on that same night. By this time it was early April and he had become a sort of specialist in silence and messages. And in a way he did not for a moment regard as accidental he had found in Dolores the perfect person for this type of conversation because Dolores never spoke and almost never moved.

"That this world is silent, I know," he said. "We both know it. This is a completely silent world in its essential condition. Sound is transient, sound is a pimple. Silence is the only unity that mortals know. Value judgements have got nothing to do with it, it makes no difference, no *essential* difference, whether it is a fart or a cantata. This silence has got nothing to do with peace either."

He peered gesturing through the darkness, opening his mouth softly, reverently, to let out the spirituous heat: he had drunk a fair amount of whisky on his way here. "That would be an elementary blunder," he said. "By God, I am not capable of it. What I didn't know is that it can take you over. Silence can take you over. And if it does—" He leaned forward for emphasis, despite the fact that Dolores was not looking at him. "If it does, you won't know who you are, you might as well be at the bottom of the sea with pearls for eyes. Of course, it isn't uniform. Well, perhaps in the final terrible phase, but we are not there yet, are we? It can be fine-spun or it can get thicker."

He could make out little of Dolores but the rigid and melancholy profile – all he ever saw, really: Dolores never turned to look at him and always sat at the extreme limit of the bench, always the same bench, which at least made him easier to locate than Walt or The Pilot, the two others Benson sometimes talked to in the Hope Street area – they were more peripatetic. In the course of his wanderings in this part of the city he had found three human creatures who would listen to him without offering insult or launching into rival monologues of their own.

"Miasmic sometimes," he said. "I may be dwindling at scalp and scrotum but I have got my powers of observation."

Not far away voices were raised, a woman's among them. There was a little group of inebriates sitting together on the ground; Benson could see the pale shapes of their faces. Here and there across the plateau of wasteland there was a sort of broken radiance, wisps and fluffs of light, random spores from the vast floodlit cliffs of the cathedral.

14

This colossal edifice, though several hundred yards away, filled the sky to the west completely, blotted out the stars. Once again, eyeing the monstrous bulk, Benson felt that all in its shadow must have indulgence of a sort, himself, Dolores, the drinkers and all other lurking souls there. A structure so insanely large condoned any excess, any degree of hyperbole or hysteria. Here if anywhere it should be permitted to stalk the stricken creatures and confide in them . . .

"Or don't you think so?" he said.

He heard the other give a sudden groaning breath. It was a sound Dolores made from time to time, as if at some stab of physical pain or some painful or oppressive memory. It was because of these sounds of pain, not out of disrespect, that Benson had privately named him Dolores. People have to be named. Sometimes he snuffled up mucus that had slowly gathered in his nostrils. Occasionally there would come the violent scrape of his heels on the ground before him. But he never actually said anything.

"Right then," Benson said. "Your own body is no barrier to it, get what I mean? Something about you tells me you may have made this discovery already, you are not a novice in the field. We come into this world equipped with a special membrane that separates our own silence from the silence outside. Mine has rotted away, that is the point I'm trying to get across."

He paused: the other man had made a sudden movement in the dimness; after a moment Benson recognised it for the first move in an unvarying sequence: Dolores was going to light a cigarette.

"Words hold it off," Benson said. "Words are magic. Talking. Singing. Trying to write. When you were a child you used to sing or whistle when you were scared. You might have thought it was to keep your spirits up, but it was to make a protective screen." He felt the beginnings of a headache. Suddenly he was weary of his own fluency, his practised, unreliable voice, not sticking anywhere, not really engaged with anything. Wretched spouter. And

15

speechifying to this poor Dolores . . . Once he had seen him in the daytime, only once, stepping short, arms pressed close to his body, head thrust back on the rigid stalk of his neck, picking his way along Huskisson Street as if it were a minefield.

"No," he said, "it's the gaps that are dangerous. You have to act. People talk about self-dramatisation as if it were a fault or an affectation, whereas it's a matter of life or death. This is *acting* I'm talking about, the fabricated self, non-authentic behaviour, *mauvaise foi*. I couldn't get through without it."

He heard the spurt of the match, saw the lowered face, curiously meek in the brief flare of light. He averted his gaze quickly. Someone is looking after Dolores, he reminded himself, to reduce the discomfort of his compassion. Dolores doesn't smell, Dolores has a warm-looking coat on. He is clean-shaven. Someone, somewhere, is washing his socks, cooking his dinners. Devoted mother? She makes sure he is wrapped up warmly when he comes out to sit here on his accustomed bench. A simple, god-fearing woman, she cannot understand why he should want to spend hours alone in the dark, why he should need to hold himself so rigidly and fearfully against dissolution, making no sound but snuffles and groans. No, she accepts, she does not question. One of the humble of the earth. Always in an apron. Dark-haired, a care-worn face, beautiful luminous eyes . . . No, it is his sister. Big-boned and gaunt, passionate, rather ungainly, incestuous mole on her cheek. She worships him. No . . .

"My life seems to have lost all direction," he said. "In small things as in great I am not aware of any operation of the will, any progression. One minute I might be sitting down, the next I am standing or walking. There is no sense in my mind of an interval between those two states, no moment of purpose or decision."

The drinkers had lit a fire; he could see the movements of the flames. That would bring the police on them sooner or later. When he had started coming here it was January and

16

still very cold. There had been quite a few fires at that time, in different parts; plenty of firewood then, sections of old fencing lying around and planks from sheds, left over from a building scheme on the wasteland above Duke Street. The work had ceased abruptly and had not been resumed and perhaps never would be, a situation common enough in these days of abandoned projects, derelict enterprises, boarded-up ambitions. Only the name of the contractor was left: Bentcock – mocking with its suggestion of poor performance the failure of any erection to materialise on the site. Homeless people used the wood for fires until in their own good time the police got together, came in some force and made them put the fires out.

Benson glanced up to where the remote battlements of the cathedral, escaping from the spent rays of the floodlights, merged into the night sky. He wanted to tell Dolores the story of the owl, which also involved a fire, but for some reason hesitated. "If I could sleep," he said. "But I won't take pills. Or if I could find a reason for what has happened to me. I still take notes. More than ever. I was always a great note-taker and researcher. Diligent Benson. Well, you have to be if you want to write historical novels. I have been reading about the Liverpool slave-trade for two years now. That was to have been my next subject. Perhaps I have told you this before? It was because of that I came to this city in the first place, three years ago now. You know, local archives, get the feel of the place. That was three years ago. I keep scrapbooks too, I am an inveterate scrapbook man. I have them going back to the last war. I thought they'd be useful – you have to know your own times, don't you? But the effect of looking through them now is appalling – a sort of thickening silence, like, I don't know, like shreds of death falling on you, death flakes. I know that's an ugly word."

He paused and at once Dolores uttered a series of groaning breaths, as if he had been politely suppressing them until the interval. "Yes," Benson said, "you have been through the mill yourself, you know how things are. Diligent note-

17

taker and researcher, scrapbook compiler *extraordinaire*, that is Benson. It isn't loss of faith in *words*. Words are magic. It isn't on the plane of ideas at all. More like an illness of some kind, something I contracted long ago. It has been lying dormant, chooses this time to come out. And in late career, when this happens in late career, I will be sixty-four next birthday, yes, I know I've told you this before, but bear with me, you worry that death will intervene. It would be just a slightly deeper stage of paralysis. You can't help it, you can't help worrying."

In spite of the whisky, in spite of his attempts to maintain a sort of facetious formality of speech, Benson found that his throat had tightened painfully. "I am getting lachrymose," he said. "What makes the whole thing deeply ironical is that I am also Clive Benson, Literary Consultant. Yes, I know I've told you this before. I advertise or used to. My name is up, outside the door. I comment on style and technique. I advise my clients on all aspects of fiction writing, I give practical hints on marketing. In *rigor mortis* myself, I tell them to loosen up. Through locked jaws I shrewdly analyse. I only have five clients left. I think you'll admit that the situation has a certain terrible beauty about it. But it is a tribulation of spirit to me and it is often quite impossible to get any money out of people, especially these days. Funds are low. I live from hand to mouth. My marriage broke up some years ago. You can't tell living people from people in books, she said to me. My wife, that is. She had a burnished look that day, the day she told me she was leaving. I wasn't expecting it. You don't know the difference, she said. I am flesh and blood, not someone in the book. You have taken my life, she said. She looked somehow lustrous, but not from triumph. She looked like a character in a book. Now, on top of everything else, my libido has been affected. I don't feel sexual desire when I am with someone, only when I am on my own. There's a certain dangerous beauty about that too. I don't sleep well and things get jumbled up together. Now trouble of this order makes a man sensitive to omens and I am convinced, as sure as I am sitting here, that this business of the owl means something. The beetle too."

And so it was that Benson finally began to tell Dolores the story of the owl and the beetle. He didn't tell the whole story on that occasion and in fact Dolores never heard it all. Nobody did. It was told in bits and pieces to a number of people, most of them complete strangers. But that he might have found a Muse that night he mentioned to nobody.

3

The day of the owl had begun rather badly, with a visit from Hogan. Hogan was a client, one of Benson's Fiction-eers, but he was in a category of his own, not being a writer in primal impulse, not buoyed as the others were by a sense – however groundless – of vocation. Hogan had never thought of writing anything until his doctor suggested it; he had suffered a nervous break-down followed by clinical depression and the doctor, who took an interest in psychiatry, on discovering that Hogan liked reading, had suggested that he might try writing something. A form of therapy, in other words. Now while all creative activity is therapeutic in some degree, or so at least Benson believed – were not his own miseries a living proof of the converse? – he still did not feel quite easy in his mind about Hogan's motivations.

This was the man who sat across from him now in the little room he used as an office, clean-shaven, blue-eyed, prematurely bald, briefcase in lap, dressed in his navy-blue suit and maroon tie – one of the several terrible things about Hogan was the drowning way he clung to appearances.

"What," Benson said, "you are going back to your childhood now, are you?" He had been dismayed to learn of this further regression. "I thought we had decided to begin with the adolescent love-affair." Every time they agreed on a beginning Hogan shifted the ground further back.

"I want to get back to my roots," he said now.

"Let's recapitulate, shall we?" Benson averted his gaze. He knew he had taken on something of a priest-like role with Hogan and it worried him. At the prospect of speech he felt his jaw start on its course of slight convulsions. "When you first started coming to see me," he began, "you had your ideas quite formed, as I remember. An autobiographical novel it was to be, but concentrating on your experience of the last few years. It sounded promising. What has happened to you has made you a representative figure in a way, hasn't it?"

He paused, aware, without needing to look, of the other's expectancy, the slow blue eyes, the stiff face – nearly all mobility had left Hogan's face since the break-down. He had plastered his hair with something, some lotion, so as to reduce the impression of baldness, and the sweetness of it hung in the air, troubling Benson, whose sense of smell had always been acute.

"Yes, well," he said at last, sighing. "Here you have a man in his prime." He wasn't sure it did much good in the long run but he knew Hogan derived a sort of solace from hearing recounted, in exact sequence, the events that had wrecked his life. It had become a saga, translated into the third person. "In his thirties," he said.

"Thirty-four."

"Thirty-four years of age, married, two small children, just started buying his own house, in Crosby, in a nice part—"

"Semi-detached."

"Semi-detached house in Crosby, well-paid job as an electrician in the shipyards."

"Electrical engineer."

"He bore in his own person the aims and aspirations of a generation."

"He did so," Hogan said, almost with animation.

"Then – stroke of the gods or as many would say owing to the brutal cost-cutting of a callous and shortsighted government, led by a woman who cannot hear the cries of the oppressed for the rattle of the cash-till, the yard is closed down on grounds of unprofitability, he becomes redundant, he can't find another job anywhere on Merseyside, which has one of the highest unemployment rates in the country, he gets into debt, his house is repossessed by the Building Society, his marriage falls apart, his wife divorces him and obtains custody of the children, he has a nervous break-down . . ." Benson paused for breath. "Have I left anything out? Now he is back in rented accommodation."

"Sub-standard."

"Sub-standard rented accommodation."

"That is the truth of it," Hogan said.

"The real truth would have been in the telling. But then you changed your mind. You said you wanted to go back to adolescence, to this love-affair with an older woman."

"I wanted to go back a bit," Hogan said. "Try to get back to my roots." He protruded his tongue slightly, as if it were momentarily too big for his mouth.

"Well, it is a pity in some ways. Your first idea had elements of Greek drama about it. There you are, ensconced in your house in Crosby. Let's say your wife is beside you on the sofa. Let's say you are having a well-earned light ale. You are pleased with the progress of your children. You talk about piano lessons. You have got holiday brochures there on your lap. You make plans for a holiday on the Costa del Sol."

"Costa Blanca."

"Costa this, Costa that," Benson said. "What about the costa to you? What about the costa to the bloody country? It's time the accountants who rule us looked up from their balance sheets and started counting the human costas."

This speech, which had sounded angry, was born of shame and compunction on Benson's part. He had felt the blood rush to his face. Glibly making up a story, turning this shattered man into a stage figure, seeking to shape a loss too raw to be shaped. And my offensive assumption of familiarity. Taking over his intimate life for purposes of

21

illustration. Why do I do it? No better than those who injured him. Far away, on another costa altogether, one that Hogan would never visit, people whose own jobs were not at risk had looked at columns of figures, met in committees, then proceeded to strip him of everything he possessed. Though not leaving the precincts of Westminster, though borne on no tide but bonhomie and Beaujolais, they had plundered Hogan just as surely as the Vikings, crossing the Irish Sea, had plundered his forebears a thousand years ago. The altars of Woden and Thor had been exchanged for those of more abstract gods, but for Hogan the result was much the same. Even his identity they had half wrenched from him. He was trying to hold it together with his briefcase, his navy-blue suit, his plastered, fragrant hair . . . Pity is not the answer, Benson thought. Pity is too easy. If I could summon rage, fire. He said, "You have been robbed, Michael, just as surely as—"

"Plenty of others besides me," Hogan said. "There was the slump in oil prices, giving rise to a world recession. We are seeing the results of market forces operating on a world-wide scale. It's a complicated matter. Not easy to under-stand at all."

"That is *their* language," Benson said. "You are using the phrases they use against you . . ." Abruptly he fell silent. He had seen what he ought to have seen before: Hogan would need to believe complex impersonal forces were responsible for his troubles, just as he would need to feel that large numbers of others were in the same boat. It helped him not to feel unworthy. It was the same assertion that he was seeking to make through the business suit and the briefcase. "You may be right," Benson said. "Anyway, that was the first scenario, wasn't it? Then you retreated from that. Your next idea was to go back twenty years or so, to your adolescence, to write about a love-affair with an older woman, ending in a return to your childhood sweet-heart. Now, once again, you have slipped back. Now you tell me you are going back to childhood."

Hogan had begun to fumble in his briefcase. "I've been

doing some research," he said. He took out what looked like a toilet roll, though the paper was of tougher texture. Unfurling about nine inches, he held it out at arm's length.

Craning forward, Benson saw a red asterisk somewhere in the middle and a date, 1952, with *born* in brackets after it. Leftwards from this, antecedent to birth, were various entries in different coloured inks, green, black, red. There was the date of his parents' marriage, in 1941. Below this, in a neat column, Hogan had written: *Fall of Dunkirk. Bride wore white crêpe de chine. We stood alone. Blackout.*

"You are going back further still I see," Benson said, with a sense of foreboding. But Hogan had got up, bringing the interview to an end; he had merely wanted to demonstrate his industry. Before leaving he dug out of the briefcase a battered-looking volume, which he handed over with his nearest approach to a smile so far.

"What have you got for me this time?" Benson glanced at the title: *Gems from Emerson.* "Excellent," he said. "Plenty to get the teeth into there." As one of the long-term unemployed Hogan could not afford to pay for these sessions, but he seemed to have access to some obscure store of books; he brought along a selected volume every time. Benson kept a special shelf for them. When Hogan had gone, he added *Gems from Emerson* to such previous offerings as Gene Stratton-Porter's *Moths of the Limberlost*, Macaulay's *Lays of Ancient Rome* and Volume 2 of the Memoirs of Lord Grey of Fallodon. He stood looking at them, arranging and rearranging the titles in his mind, trying to find a clue, discern a pattern. A few minutes of this was enough to make him feel slightly sick.

He drank some whisky as a restorative, made himself a sandwich of brown bread and tinned tuna, then went to sit at his desk for a while – he still continued to spend some part of the day at his desk, though the only result was more anguish of spirit.

Sitting there he tried to find reasons, he murmured over old disasters. Here, or here, some slow poison had been ingested, or some remote detonation was withering him now with its blast. Six years since the break-up of my marriage; three years since that fiasco with Fiona Greenepad; fifty-four years since my father beat me for playing with Lucy Ringer in the garden shed. Her knickers had a floral pattern, little pink roses. The sight of them purchased with pain. Everything has a price-tag, my father was fond of saying. I was nine years old. Warm, exciting, tarry smell . . . Creosote, the shed had just been given a coating of the stuff. Creosote is resistant, proof against time and weather. They poured creosote over the dead to keep the smell down. Was it the beating? Those spans of years, randomly recollected, were all multiples of *three* . . .

But nothing helped. His was a complex affliction; the sense of just how complex was coming near to destroying him. The causes squatted somewhere out of sight; perhaps not in his personal past at all, he sometimes thought, the delayed narcotic, the soundless bomb. Why should this block, this arresting stroke, have been visited on him rather than on another, and when it was too late to change course, too soon to give up? Why me, Clive Benson, a man with an early volume of poetry under his belt, plus a critical biography of Robert Louis Stevenson, well-received, and six novels on historical themes, of which the third had been made into a film by Paramount? I should have been reaping honours, not living drably and penuriously on dwindling royalties, eked out by my literary consultancy and odd jobs of journalism. But I wouldn't care about poverty, he thought, if only I could work again.

Wearying at last, he got up, and then there suddenly came to him the notion of lighting a fire in the grate. This was something he had never done before, partly because the central heating worked after a fashion, mainly because tenants were clearly not expected to do it; the landlady, Mrs Dollinger, had blocked off the fireplace with a square of plywood painted white. But the day was dark and cold and he was despondent. He now saw too that by lighting a fire he would be sending a signal instead of endlessly seeking one; his fire could serve as a cry to the Muse. True,

24

Grenville Street was far from her reputed haunts, his choked mind even farther; but a brave flame might do something.

The idea once conceived, Benson was immediately possessed by it. Rapidly he made his way down two flights of stairs, out the front door, round to the back of the house, where between brick walls the wasted grass awaited the stiffening of spring. Like me, like me. There were some remnants of privet at the far end and an ancient dwarf of an apple tree, bedraggled and full of woe. It was very cold.

In his approach he startled a blackbird, which shot off with accusatory clamour, swallowed instantly by the alerted silence. He began to grub for fallen twigs at the foot of the privet and had soon amassed quite a heap. He tugged at dead boughs on the apple tree and they broke off with sharp cracks. With each sound fed to it, he felt the silence grow more voracious. Amidst the detritus of former tenancies and the infestations of weed he found some mildewed sections of plank and these he set at an angle against the wall and stamped on savagely, splintering them into manageable pieces. He was breathing fast, exerting himself to a dangerous extent, impatient with brute matter, urged on by the trumpeting of his idea.

Intent on the job in hand, he had not heard any opening of a window, but then a voice called down to him, "Votter you up to?" Turning abruptly, looking upwards, he saw Mrs Dollinger leaning out of an attic window. She was regarding him intently, her narrow face framed by the dark-coloured headscarf she wore indoors and out; beyond her, the grey slate of the roof, which had a pallid gleam on it; beyond that, a darkening sky.

In the silence which followed this question – and it was the kind of question he liked least – Benson stood smiling, prey to his obsession, holding a piece of splintered plank. After some moments he made a gesture with this like a weak backhand at tennis. "Good afternoon," he said. "Well, not a very good one, is it?"

"Veather is veather," Mrs Dollinger said austerely. "I am

asking votter you up to in this garden."

"Garden?" He was surprised. "Well," he said after a moment, "what are any of us up to, if it comes to that?"

He knew at once, from her silence and immobility, that this attempt to broaden the issue was not going to succeed. The thing not to do, of course, was tell the truth: she would veto the project instantly. On the other hand he felt that if he delayed much longer he would lose control of the situation altogether. Already the loneliness surrounding them both on this dark wintry afternoon had begun to disturb him. He felt sorry that life had placed her in an attic window, with a headscarf on, implacably interrogating people. We deserve better than this, he wanted to say. We both deserve better than this.

"Votter you up to, lighting a fire?" Mrs Dollinger said.

"Good Lord no. These are natural forms, *objets trouvés*, Mrs Dollinger, different textures of wood. I intend to take them up to my apartment and arrange them."

He turned away from her and crouched and began to forage about, gathering up the spoils: plank first, then apple sticks, then privet twigs. He was hoping that if he took time over this she might withdraw, but no: when he faced round again, stacked with wood from chin to waist, Mrs Dollinger was still there.

"Well, here we go, cheerio." She thinks me mad anyway, he thought; she thinks me an old, untidy lunatic. Besides, she can hardly call me a liar to my face. Balancing his burden with care, valiantly smiling, he began to move off towards the side of the house.

"Don't you go lighting fires," Mrs Dollinger called loudly after him. "We don't allow it."

Benson quickened his steps. In a moment he was round the corner out of her view. Regaining the apartment was awkward, thus encumbered; he left a trail of twigs; he had to unload everything on the landing before he could open his door. By this time he was feeling harassed but no less determined. He locked the door, once he had got the wood inside, in case Mrs Dollinger came to check up.

26

No shortage of paper in the apartment of Clive Benson. Stacks of old *Guardians* and *Observers* lay wilting in corners, in cupboards, at the bottom of his wardrobe, waiting to have items cut out of them and pasted in the current scrapbook. Just what items is the mystic choice of the scrapbook-keeper, through which he expresses his world view, his sense of the human condition. One of the results, or symptoms, of Benson's malaise, was paralysis of the scissor hand – he could no longer see meaning in selection, in salvaging one thing rather than another from the welter of events. The papers had been there a long time.

The square of plywood came away without difficulty. The twigs were damp and would not catch at first; they hissed and smoked and some of the smoke came into the room instead of going up the chimney. On his haunches, eyes smarting, Benson passed hectic moments lighting spills of paper and thrusting them under the hissing pyramid. Then with joy he saw pale tendrils of flame clutch up at the twigs. He laid some of his trusty apple on top; the flames yearned upward to it and clambered, rosier, more nourished-looking, with ambitious throbs and sputterings of violet in their midst. There was a core of fire now; the warmth came out of it.

At this point, with this first warmth, the nature of the proceedings changed dramatically. So far, merely a deeply troubled man struggling to light a forbidden fire. But as he crouched there, wondering whether it was time to put a piece of plank on, he noticed something against the wall, just alongside the fireplace, something black. He shifted over, looked more closely: it was a big shiny beetle, on its back, delicate frail legs raised in a final submission that had not saved it. Benson took the creature gently between finger and thumb, laid it right way up on his palm. Death had been recent; the carapace was glossy still, peacock traces shifted in it with the movements of the flames. Had he brought it in with the sticks? Had it crawled out of some recess, perhaps just now, made its way to the fireplace and so died? But for a man as skilled in messages and meanings as Benson, the stages of the journey were irrelevant: to the place of fire it had come, and fugitive flame colours moved in its cape. Its presence changed everything. No mere wanton blaze, he thought. No desperate signal this, but devotional, *sacrificial* . . .

With movements ordered and measured he took a short length of plank, balanced it level across the edifice of fire, placed the beetle on it dead centre, legs in air as he had found it, as it had offered itself. The plank was half-rotten and resisted for a while, giving off quantities of acrid smoke, some of which came billowing into the room. But then the soft flames licked round it, curled over, enveloped it at last, and Benson, watching intently, saw the beetle surrender its matter in a jet of clear green.

"*I invoke thee, O Muse*," he said aloud, still on his haunches. As he spoke there was a considerable fall of soot, choking the fire and falling out in a flurry on to the tiled surround of the fireplace. The next moment, startling him so that he lost balance and fell over backwards, there came a rush of air before his face, an infernal breath of charred soot and singed feathers, a beat of pinions. Something, a winged presence, was flitting soundlessly in the spaces above. Incredulous, still sprawled there, Benson peered up through the smoky haze: a white owl was flying round and round, high up against the ceiling.

At this moment, startling him rather horribly, there came a sharp knock at the door. "Yes?" he called. "What is it?"

"Votter you up to?"

"I am doing my yoga." He saw his door knob turning as Mrs Dollinger tried to effect an entrance.

"Open this door immediate," she shouted furiously.

"I can't." Benson was sweating. He could feel his heart beating rapidly. The smoke in the room was hurting his throat. "I'm in the lotus position," he called.

"I see smoke come out the chimney."

Benson thought he heard soft sounds of collision above him as if the owl was knocking into things; perhaps all this shouting was panicking the creature. He shuffled on his backside nearer to the door. "I have just been burning a few old *Guardians* and *Observers*," he said quietly, with his mouth close to the woodwork.

Mrs Dollinger remained silent for some moments as if computing this answer. It must seem strange and mad to her that his voice was coming so quietly and from a source so near to the floor. Might she think he meant humans? "Newspapers," he said, sensing the rage of Mrs Dollinger through the thin panelling.

"This I will tell to Dollinger," she said, in a voice loaded with threat. After some moments more of silence he heard her walk away. Relief at this was tempered by anxiety; the idea of Dollinger was intimidating, mainly because Benson had never actually spoken to him or looked into his face. He lived in the basement with Mrs Dollinger, and was rarely seen above ground. Benson had glimpsed him from a distance once, on a Sunday morning, when the Dollingers were returning from Mass, a powerfully-built man in a dark suit. He had close-cut hair and a thick moustache like an old-fashioned wrestler. In fact, that was said to have been his profession.

However, this was not the time to think about Dollinger. There was an owl in his room; a visitant, an omen, but real; it was still there, up against the ceiling, circling in panic silence. He was afraid it would hurt itself. He opened the sash-windows as far as he could, but the owl would not fly low enough to find the opening. His door gave on to the stairwell, two floors above street level: the owl would be in worse case out there. Meanwhile, every sound, every movement he made, terrified it more.

He crept over to the bedroom door, opened it, retreated. The owl got through almost at once into the relative dimness there and found a resting place in the farthest corner, on top of the wardrobe. Benson crouched at the door, peering in. He saw the savage grip of the creature's talons, saw its eyes – frontal, human-looking, like no other bird's – turned unblinkingly towards him. The fire was out now, smothered with soot, and these few minutes with the windows open had been enough to make the room very cold. What was he to do?

Just then he thought he heard Rathbone's door closing: perhaps he had come out for a cigarette. Rathbone was a hypnotist, a good deal of whose business came from people who wanted to stop smoking. They came to him and he spoke to them in his husky, compelling voice, telling them they didn't really want or need cigarettes. However, he was himself a heavy smoker and his addiction put him in a constant dilemma. He couldn't smoke in view of the people he was supposed to be curing; he couldn't smoke in his apartment between clients because the smell would give him away. So quite often he came out to the landing for a feverish cigarette. Rathbone might know what to do about the owl.

Benson opened his door and stepped out. Sure enough, Rathbone was on the landing below, smoking. Advancing down the flight of stairs towards him, Benson said softly, "I've got an owl in my apartment."

Rathbone did not seem surprised to hear this. Benson thought he probably heard all sorts of things anyway, in a profession like this. He watched the hypnotist draw deeply, broodingly, on his cigarette. Rathbone was a dramatic-looking man, tall and gaunt, with black hair and close-set black eyes and a long curving nose. He dressed always in black and had an air of fallen grandeur and gloomy energy about him. He had been struck off the list of licensed hypnotherapists for a sexual misdemeanour which he sometimes hinted at in a veiled, sarcastic manner. He was well versed in symbols and a great admirer of Jung. His ambition was to become a stage hypnotist and make a name for himself and money.

"How would you go about getting it out?" Benson asked.

"Athena's bird," Rathbone said. "A white owl? Interesting. Athena, of course, is the personification of the Anima. I suppose you knew that?"

"Well, yes, I did, as a matter of fact. But at present I am more concerned with—"

"Born straight from Zeus's head. So she is a force within the mind of man, you see. Not woman. Athena is the protectress of heroes, symbolising a positive relationship with the Anima, protecting it against the dark forces of the feminine. It was she who taught men the use of bridle and yoke, which is the representation of an inner female principle enabling man to bridle his passions and yoke the male and female sides of his being in harmony. It was she—"

"Look," Benson said. "All this is fascinating and another time I'd love to hear about it because I do believe that this owl has a meaning for me personally, but Mrs Dollinger might be passing any minute and I have my reasons for not wanting to bump into her just now."

"On the rampage, is she? I thought I heard shouts."

"All I did was light a bit of fire and now she has threatened me with Dollinger."

"That's bad," Rathbone said. "I am told he's a professional wrestler."

"I thought you might be able to give me some practical advice about how to get this owl out of my apartment and back into the freedom of its native habitat."

"No good trying anything in the daylight," Rathbone said without hesitation. "Owls are virtually blind in the daylight. You've got to wait until night. They've got this marvellous night vision. Leave your windows open. Go out and have a drink or two – it's not far off opening time. When you get back you will find the premises vacated."

"I'll give it a try." Benson was already making his way back up the stairs. Rathbone's advice possessed the greatest merit advice can possess, coinciding exactly with his inclination. He need do nothing but have a few drinks and wait for the night to work its magic. He went stealthily back into the apartment, seized his overcoat and left.

4

Four drinks and four pubs later, he was entering the bar of the fifth, when a fat man whose face he knew said hello to him and smiled. These days he tended to avoid people he had known before his block, preferring to talk to strangers, but the man was sitting with two women. Alcohol, sexual deprivation, the feeling the owl had given him that this might be a night of destiny, combined to imbue him now with a spirit of enterprise. He took his drink over and sat down with them.

"How goes it?" the man said, the smile dwindling on his face. Benson knew him now, even remembered his name. It was Morton and he taught in the English Department of the University, where Benson had gone once or twice in happier days to give readings.

"Pauline Rivers," Morton said. "And Alma Corrigan. This is Clive Benson."

"How do you do?" Benson had a confused impression of the two women, one fair and buxom, the other small and dark with prominent cheekbones and bright eyes. "How's life on the campus?" he said looking at Morton.

"Oh, luvverly." The cockney accent was assumed. Suddenly Benson remembered that Morton was given to assuming accents. He remembered too that he had disliked Morton on the occasions he had met him. He caught the dark woman's eye. She looked amused, in a slightly combative way. She was not pretty but her face was vivid, the brows strongly marked, the eyes long and narrow with a glittering quality in them. Her mouth was full, sensuous, drawn with some quality of bitterness. "Nobody knows who's next for the chopper, mate," Morton said, still in his cockney accent. "We're in a state of siege, my friend," he added, in the tones of a BBC announcer.

"That's quite true," the woman called Pauline said,

laughing at Morton's mimicry. "Things really are horrendous with these government cuts. Departments are disappearing overnight. Everybody is terrified of being marginalised."

Benson found it difficult to see her features clearly, as she wore large glasses and her hair fell forward round her face. She had heavy breasts inside a burgundy-coloured jumper. "You don't need to work in the University to be marginalised," he said. "Look at me."

"How's the writing going?" Morton asked. "Clive writes novels," he said to the two women, managing to invest this statement too with a sort of jokiness.

All three now looked at Benson who did not yet feel drunk enough to start talking about his block. He did not want to talk to them about the owl either. "It's not only the University that is in a state of siege, is it?" he said. "I saw a man who couldn't hold out any longer jump off the battlements in Toxteth."

He began to tell them about the suicide, soon losing track of the siege idea, reverting to the simple sequence, the leap, the cry, that carpet-like sidling, the gathering fall, the peculiar crash of impact. As he spoke he grew absorbed again with the shape of it, that crude act of self-extinction became in his stammering mouth a paradigm of human life. "That cry and leap from the source of light, that was *birth*," he said. "And the sound when he fell, when he hit the ground . . . Like this," he said loudly, slapping down a palm, not quite flat on the table top. The blow shook the table and some of Morton's beer slopped out of his glass. "Steady on, laddie," Morton said in a Scottish accent.

Benson fell silent, annoyed and discomfited. The manner of Morton's intervention had made him seem ridiculous, like a bad actor overplaying a part. "Your Scottish accent is lousy," he said, forcing a smile. The puerility of the retort angered him further. Part of his chagrin was due to shame: he had been claiming through his account of this death some importance for himself. He had been showing off too – for the woman opposite, who had not so far spoken.

33

She did speak now, quickly, and Benson sensed it was partly at least to protect him. She said, "It's true in a way, isn't it? You can't walk round Liverpool without feeling you're in a war zone." The voice was slightly metallic, not much inflected, with a modified Northern accent difficult to place. She glanced impatiently away across the crowded bar, then looked back at their faces. "Sometimes you can even see where the lines are drawn," she said. "If you happen to live in Liverpool 8, for example, which I don't, you belong more or less by definition to the poorest and most deprived element in one of the poorest cities in Western Europe. There is a better than fifty-fifty chance you haven't a job. If you happen to be black it's more like eighty-twenty. If you *are* out of a job you haven't much chance of getting one. You can't get out because you have no money and nowhere to go. You can't surrender because they don't take prisoners. That amounts to a state of siege."

She fell silent, glancing aside with the abruptness and impatience that characterised her. Benson liked it. He liked everything about her, the pallor of her skin, the straight dark hair, the narrow eyes with their demonic glitter. He liked the way she had sensed his discomfiture. He liked the way she had said 'happen to' twice in an attempt to give her obviously excited speech an appearance of nonchalant poise.

"I'm really surprised to hear you say that, Alma," Pauline said. "You'll never get a radical movement for change while people are saying, this is Liverpool, look at us, this is a doomed city. Don't you see, that sort of instant mythologising holds the people back. It is complacent and fatalistic at the same time. We produce our own opium without benefit of religion. Very convenient for the ruling class. This isn't a *Liverpool* suicide we're talking about. We should be angry that these things are allowed to happen in Britain in 1988, that people's lives are being wrecked everywhere you look by the unbridled forces of capitalism."

34

She didn't seem angry however; she seemed glad to be in a position to correct someone; her voice had been assured and calm, as if she were conducting a seminar.

"Everything is on the plane of transaction with you, isn't it?" Alma said. "I wasn't meaning to say that Liverpool is a special case."

Her tone was defensive. She had been reproved for rhetoric, caught between feeling and orthodoxy in a way Benson might have found funny if he hadn't felt somehow partly responsible for it. These women were getting cross with each other over a suicide they had never seen. "But Liverpool *is* a special case," he said. "All cases are special. The man who jumped was a special case too. You people always want to lump everything together so you can make a political point out of it. If it wasn't a Liverpool suicide, then it certainly wasn't a Thatcher suicide either. I suppose people jumped off buildings before this government came to power. It may even happen in Cuba sometimes." He saw Pauline gathering herself for another statement of principle. "One thing is certain," he said quickly. "I'll take a different route from now on."

"Think what it would mean," Morton said. "You would have to avoid all high buildings. Then there's rivers and canals, busy roads, railway tracks." He paused for a moment then said emphatically and in a sort of Humphrey Bogart accent, "There is no other route, pal."

Pauline laughed a little at this, in an unwilling and slightly shocked sort of way. Benson wondered vaguely if there were anything between these two. "The suicide rate has risen sharply in all inner city areas over the past ten years," Pauline said, still smiling at Morton. "Since that woman came to power," she added.

"The innah cities," Morton said. "Still, it's a fact though, they're jumping all over the place. That sound you described and demonstrated with so much *brio* just now, bodies colliding with concrete, you hear it everywhere these days. It's the new version of the Mersey Sound."

Benson swallowed some whisky. This was his fifth and

he was beginning to feel it. He looked at Morton's face. What you were supposed to think was that under this jocular façade lay deep reserves of compassion. But the eyes seemed cheerful and malicious under their sandy brows. He was looking at someone or something behind Benson. "No thanks," he said, "there's no point. We are going soon. You've asked us once already."

Turning, Benson saw a flushed man holding a book of tickets. "Want one?" the man said.

"What's it in aid of?"

"Only one prize," the man said. He was drunk and full of joy. "Me giro cheque," he said. "Winning number gets me giro cheque."

"What's that worth?"

"Forty-three pounds seventy."

"And the tickets?"

"Quid apiece."

Benson glanced round the bar. It was crowded. There must have been fifty or sixty people in it. And there were two other bars in the place and a pool-room. With luck – and if he stayed sober enough – he might sell a hundred tickets or so. That would give him a hundred pounds for his forty-three, and someone would get forty-three for the expenditure of one. Nothing illegal in it so long as he cashed his own cheque.

"Kelly is the name," the man said. He smiled widely and held out his hand.

"I'll have one," Benson said, shaking the offered hand. "It's a good cause, isn't it?" He handed the pound over, tucked the ticket into his top pocket and turned back to meet Morton's plump smile. "Private enterprise," he said. "They should approve of that."

"There you see the true spirit of this city," Morton said. "You can't keep them down." He spoke as if he himself possessed this spirit in abundance.

"His wife and kids won't see much of it," Pauline said, with a snap of the lips.

Morton winked at Benson. "Of course," he said, "this is

a very Celtic city."

"There are Celts and Celts." Benson thought of drugged Hogan. This was a better way. He looked at Alma. "Like another drink?" he said. He wondered how old she was. Mid-forties somewhere – getting on for twenty years younger.

"We haven't time," Pauline said. "We've got to go in a few minutes. We are going to a party meeting."

"Conservative Party, is it?" Benson said. "Or do you belong to Dr Owen's rump?" None of them seemed amused by this. "Must be a bottle party then," he said, put out by this priggish silence. "Well, I'm having another."

When he came back from the bar, Alma was alone at the table. "Bill remembered he had to make a phone call," she said.

"And Pauline went with him."

"Oh yes." She smiled slightly, looking down at the inch or so of beer left in her glass.

It was now that Benson made his big mistake. He said awkwardly, "I hope you didn't think I was trying to get some advantage just now, when I was talking about that man jumping off."

She looked up at him. "What advantage?" she said. "I don't know what you mean."

Suddenly, with her eyes on him, he didn't know what he meant either. He said, "The fact is, I took it for a sign. He jumped just as I was passing. Just at that precise moment. It was as if he was waiting for me, waiting till he saw Benson, to plunge out of the light and the silence up there."

"A sign?" She had an air of heightened interest now but it was not of the kind he had thought to arouse. He saw her brows draw together in a slight frown. She was looking at him attentively. "Are you really saying he did it for your benefit?" she said, in a tone of incredulity and anger. "Are you really saying that?"

"Benefit, I'm not sure," Benson said. "In the sense of illuminating—"

"I've never heard anything so monstrously self-regarding in my life. So all the pain and despair he must have felt, all that waste of a life, it was all simply to provide you with a metaphor?"

Her eyes were brighter than ever. He saw fury in them and the beginnings of contempt. Something, some private sense of recognition, rather alarming, began to stir in him. He remembered the curl of the flame, that flare of green, the winged presence in his room. The bird of night had brought him here. *I invoke thee, O Muse.*

"Why should death rob life of a lesson?" he said. "Or even a metaphor, for that matter."

"You don't see it, do you? I'm not talking about death. It's life that you are insulting. You can't insult people with meanings that don't belong to them."

"Any meaning belongs to them that they can be made to bear," Benson said. "Why should it be all right for you to make the man a public symbol, which you just did, and wrong for me to make him a private one?" He saw Morton and Pauline returning from the far end of the bar. He was slightly drunk; he was roused by her contempt; she might be the Muse. The combination broke down his fear of initiatives. "Listen," he said, "I've got an owl in my apartment. Or had. Flying round and round. Would you like to come back with me and see if it's still there? Don't say anything to them."

"It's not usually owls," she said. "Another metaphor?"

"A white owl," he said. "Will you?"

The proposition had not been well-timed. She looked angrier than ever as she got to her feet. She said, "First, I don't believe you, second, I'm going to a party meeting, third, I wouldn't go back with you if you had an albatross in your trousers."

Without looking at him again she moved away to join the others. All three of them were heading for the exit, with Morton bringing up the rear. Benson caught him at the door. "Well, cheerio," he said. "I hope you have a fruitful meeting. Er, Alma . . . is she in the English Department too?"

"No, history," Morton said. He looked for a moment at Benson. "You blew it, didn't you, pal?" With an instinct of kindness that surprised Benson, he said quickly, "I don't think she's attached at the moment."

Benson went back into the bar to wait for the winning number to be drawn. He didn't expect it to be his and it wasn't. Deciding after some internal debate against another drink, he set off walking back to his apartment.

It was just after ten when he returned; he had been away nearly five hours, long enough for a regiment of owls to get away. He felt exhilarated despite the rebuff he had received. A knowledgeable man, Rathbone, he thought. That had really been an excellent idea of his, to wait for the descent of night . . . It was bitterly cold in the living room and he closed the windows at once. Still with his overcoat on he entered the bedroom and switched on the light. He had perhaps five seconds to register the solemn savagery of the owl's regard from its place on top of the wardrobe. Then it launched itself in a gathered rush of panic over his head with a whoosh of air as he stood aghast in the doorway. It flew the length of the room and crashed headlong into the glass partition above the entrance door, deceived by the transparent membrane, the dim spaces beyond. Stunned by the collision, it half fell, half fluttered down, coming to rest on its side at the foot of the door. Benson seized it quickly. Holding it against his breast, he opened the door. On the alert for any sign of the Dollingers he carried the bird downstairs. It revived as he did so, he felt the power of its wings. He tightened his grip, feeling the warmth between his hands, the alien weight, the pulse of alarm.

In the dark garden, where the whole business had begun, he stood for some moments in the bitter cold, holding the owl firmly, fingers pressed against the soft feathers at its throat. Below this softness its heart was beating rapidly but it made no sound. Slowly he relaxed his grip on the wings, slowly he opened his palms to make a launching pad. He raised his arms, offering the bird to the night. Its whiteness was incandescent. For a second it rested motionless on the platform his hands had made for it. Then he felt a prick of talons as it launched away, felt that eerie rush of air, saw the creature rise glimmering into the darkness and disappear.

5

"Accident?" Benson said. "A white owl lodged in my chimney, waiting for my one fire of the year, succumbing to my sacrificial smoke, *just at that moment*? Just as the scarab ignited, just as I was commencing my invocation? Never."

Not for the first time the red-faced, heavily-built man to whom he was talking, instead of replying, opened his mouth wide and bellowed words of encouragement and exhortation to the slight and spindly boys playing rugby. "Come on, Jones!" he shouted. "Come on, Andrews! Get in there and tackle, boy. This is school ground, you know," he said to Benson.

In late afternoon, slightly the worse for drink but still fairly steady, Benson had passed through a gate and found himself standing on the touchline with this discourteous man in sudden, transfiguring storm sunshine that lit the rugby field with vivid green, burnished the bare poplars fringing the far side. Beyond, the clouds were massed, black with rain. The shirts of the players made patterns of colour, now clustering, now thinning, one team blue, the other red.

"Never in this world," Benson said, "Do you know Baudelaire's theory of correspondencies, nature seen as a temple of living pillars? I think there's a lot of truth in it myself."

"No, I don't," the man said. "I don't know anything about Baudelaire. I'm trying to concentrate on this game. This is a trial game for the second fifteen."

"They look very young."

"Well, they are juniors."

"They don't look more than nine or ten," Benson said.

40

In this strange escape of sunshine the shirts and the white shorts had a wild brightness about them. The players were too slight to enact the formal patterns of the game, they fluttered about the field, vivid and weightless, like creatures prompted to swarm by the burst of light, wavering after the ball with high-pitched cries. Tackles brought them down in the space of a stride, like butterflies alighting. A taller boy was acting as referee, one of the seniors presumably. His whistle sounded often and the children grouped and regrouped in obedience to it.

"Oh, for God's sake, Billings!" the man beside Benson shouted in a tone of furious disgust.

Benson was having difficulty now in focussing across the bright field at the wavering players. The pitch kept blurring into abstract patterns of red and blue. "They used to make them dance," he said. "Some of the skippers did. Every morning, weather permitting, they would bring them up on deck in batches and make them dance. One of the ways they kept them alive."

"I'm afraid I don't know what you are talking about. Oh, well-done!"

"Children too," Benson said. "Gladstone was born not very far from where I live. W.E., the Liberal statesman. He was born in Rodney Street in 1809, two years after the last legitimate slave ship sailed out of Liverpool."

"I'm aware of that," the man said. "I teach history."

"You teach these boys history?" Benson blinked at the man wonderingly. It seemed incongruous.

The man had barely looked at him before, but he did so now. "I have a degree in history," he said.

"Ah," Benson said. "Well, I was thinking, you know, when Gladstone was about the age of these lads, slaving from British ports had been illegal then for about ten years or so, but the *implements* of slavery must still have been about. I mean, they wouldn't have disappeared overnight, would they? They were still being sold over the counter in 1807. They went on being sold under the counter for another fifty years or so. They would have lingered on in

41

curio shops, junk shops, scrap metal places. It is quite conceivable that little William Ewart, out with his nurse, pressing his nose against the shop window, would have seen strange metal objects, the purpose of which might have baffled him. What is that, nurse? That is a branding iron, dear, so they would know who the slaves belonged to. And that is a pair of iron handcuffs, and that is a thumb-screw in case they refused to eat or were otherwise recalcitrant. Imagine the effect on an impressionable lad. It is entirely possible that Gladstone's generous sympathy for oppressed races began right here, in the streets of Liverpool.''

"Fanciful, very fanciful. What on earth do you think you are doing, Rogers? I try to give them a balanced view.''

"A balanced view of the slave trade?''

Abruptly, as Benson spoke these words, the clouds descended, cutting out the sun at one stroke, as if it had never been. And with this eclipse it became at once apparent how the sunshine had been abetting the illusion of day. It was suddenly evening, the trees at the far side of the field had taken on some quality of darkness, the boys' shouts and the sounds of the whistle seemed more distant, as if they had faded with the light.

"We tend to think a balanced view is virtuous," Benson said. "Especially when it is applied to our crimes. We are not so keen on it when there are profits to be made. Have your pupils any concept of the ruin and devastation visited on Africa in the course of the eighteenth century, have they any notion of the scale of it?''

"Look," the man said. "I don't intend to stand here arguing. These boys haven't reached the eighteenth century yet, they're doing the Wars of the Roses. I've got to go over and get a closer look at the game before the light is gone. I don't know what you are doing here. You've been drinking.''

"Forty million deaths at a conservative estimate. The Nazis were nothing to it.''

Without replying the man began to walk away from him

42

towards the centre of the darkening field, where the wavering game continued. It seemed to Benson, in the moments
before he turned away, that the cries of the children had
grown wilder, more piercing, as if in regret at the approach
of night.

6

He began to see birds and animals everywhere; he became
increasingly conscious of the encroachments of the brute
creation. He heard the shuddering cries of owls at night, in
the heart of the city. Sometimes he seemed to smell a warm,
rank, feral breath on the air. Once, passing the tall dank
Victorian houses that border Sefton Park, he glanced
through an open gate and saw a fox standing on the gravel
drive not ten yards away; it looked back at him for several
moments before moving off into thickets of laurel. A
woman sitting next to him on the bus, with whom he
discussed the matter, told him that the week before she had
seen not one but two foxes, emerging side by side from a
gutted house in Toxteth. It was on the bus route – she had
seen them from the upper deck of a number five. A council
employee, a road-sweeper with whom Benson fell into
talk, told him he had seen stoats and weasels in quiet streets;
and once, on a grass verge, an adder. Rats too were on the
increase; one day Benson counted four feasting companionably in an alley among ripped black rubbish bags. Later,
when the April weeds were rampant in the enclosure behind
the house, he saw a kestrel swoop down at a sparrow and
narrowly miss, not more than three or four feet from the
house wall.

Predators were coming in then. Benson could picture
them, exploiting the growing areas of waste, breeding in
the choked parks and in the neglected tracts of Liverpool's
dockland, among the miles of ruinous wharves and warehouses, questing through the vales of the suburbs, penetrat-

ing to the inner city where amidst the rubble the small mammals they preyed on would be multiplying too . . .

When he looked at himself in the mirror for signs of kinship he saw a mournful, obsessive animal there, an ageing specimen of *homo bloccatus*, rather handsome, with pale insomniac eyes slanting slightly downward under dishevelled eyebrows, the small triangle of scar tissue showing whitely below the left cheekbone.

By that time he had given up all pretence of working. He continued to compile notes and to offer advice of a professional nature to his Fictioneers. Most of his time was spent walking around the city, waiting for something to happen. He tried to notice things, to involve himself in things, so that he would be ready, so that he would not be taken by surprise. The sense of change was in everything. The lake in the park glimmered with it, the sky was swollen with it, he heard it in the outcries of gulls over the Mersey, in the shouts of the men selling evening papers at street corners. Sometimes a painful, only just bearable tension mounted in him at the thought of this looming, possibly violent transformation. He grew frightened that it might be his own final breakdown that was impending. Once, in the stress of this, he overcame his chronic irresolution and made an attempt to phone Alma Corrigan, whose face he often saw before him. He was in Smithdown Road at the time, slightly drunk. He tried six phone boxes before his resolve failed and found them all vandalised in one way or another, smashed, jammed, wrenched out. When he had recovered from the frustration he was obliged to recognise that this too was a sign.

Often he was still wandering about late at night and in dangerous parts of the city – dangerous for any pedestrian, let alone an ageing man of sedentary occupation. His fear of assault and injury, the knowledge that he would not be so quick or so strong as those that might attack him, that however purposeful he sought to appear he was visibly not securely at home in these streets or anywhere else for that matter – all this engendered a vein of violent fantasy. A fearsome gang of young thugs ringed him round, jeering, preparing to put the boot in, not knowing how adept he was in all branches of the martial arts, not knowing he had studied under oriental masters. They rushed at him in a body, cowardly brutes, ten against one. With marvellous economy of movement he strewed them all over the pavement. *I did not seek this confrontation . . .* Fear, the lonely rhythm of his walking, set up an amazing vindictiveness in him, a capacity for inflicting grievous bodily harm he had not known he possessed. One – two – three – *Tac!* Hammerblow on the bridge of a nose, double kidney-chop. *That'll teach you.* Dextrous, deadly, spin round again and a knee to that bastard's groin, one is kneeling vomiting, another groans and snivels with a broken arm, a third irreparably ruptured, ruined for life. *Thought you had easy game, eh?*

With time, however, this savage sequence grew refined. The sublimation of art came to rescue Benson. He found a phrase full of snarling menace: *banana split.* Now when the gang surrounded him he fixed the ringleader with a cold eye. *I don't think you know with whom you have to deal.* Jeers from the thugs at his meticulous grammar. Level glance, slight smile. *Think again, chump. You've heard, I suppose, of the . . . banana split?* At these words they would cower back, skulk away into the protective colouring of the darkness, leaving him free to pursue his unhurried way.

Thus, in spite of impotence, in the midst of affliction, a belief in the primacy and power of the word still remained to Benson, in fantasy at least.

Words lingered in his mind, snatches of song, things said to him or overheard; he could not decide their exact significance but felt sure they fitted into some close, intricate pattern. Athena, patroness of weaving . . . Then there was the odd remark made one Tuesday afternoon in parting by Carter, senior citizen, archetypal fictioneer. Carter's novel, which was entitled *Can Spring Be Far Behind?*, was running at over 600 pages now, with the central relationship still unresolved. His was the opposite problem to that of poor Hogan, who could not get started.

Carter sat facing him across the desk, grizzled, square-headed, argumentative, in a paisley cravat and a ginger overcoat, which he had declined to take off. Benson was looking in a glazed way through the latest chapter. The silence was lengthening.

Sheila appeared to be musing softly in this flushed and fervent moment between their embraces. Albert urged himself to take the initiative. Knowing her value and her vulnerability, he did not want her to think he was claiming sexual favours in return for doing the plastering job on her ceiling but it was a case of nothing venture nothing win and it was not as if he was breaking new ground as he had been vouchsafed more than kisses on previous visits. To go away with less would be backsliding. He slid his hand along her back under the silk blouse, his fingers coursing and caressing along the warm flesh until they touched the stretched elastic of her unsprung brassière.

Unsprung? Benson looked up vaguely. To *spring* a bras-sière? Was that really the *mot juste*? And there was the rather ludicrous echo, no doubt quite unconscious: to go away with less would be backsliding; so he stayed and slid a hand along her back. Worth mentioning? Probably not. He wondered if Carter ever re-read his work. He said, "Albert is a bit ponderous, isn't he? Cranking himself up to get a hand under her blouse. When you think how often he's been there before." His mind lurched sickeningly over the vast savannah of Carter's novel. "Quite a few times," he said.

"Well," Carter said. "He is a ponderous character. He always ponders everything."

"That is not what I meant," Benson said. "Then there is this habit of alliteration which seems to be growing on you. 'Flushed and fervent', 'coursing and caressing', that type of thing. It's a good occasional device but it shouldn't be over-used or it gives too much appearance of rhetoric. I like 'knowing her value and her vulnerability', because the

46

words describe two distinct strands of feeling in Albert. But, as I say, I should use it sparingly or you'll end by irritating the reader." Benson summoned a smile. "You already risk that by the sheer length of your book," he said.

"I think this chapter takes things forward a bit," Carter said in the accents of Liverpool, which to Benson's ear seemed always to fall somewhere between complaint and aggression.

"Well, it gets Albert down from his ladder. He had been up there quite a long time, hadn't he, plastering Sheila's ceiling? I suppose that is forward motion of a kind. But it is very repetitive, isn't it? I mean, last time he came he fixed the washers on her taps. And it ends up with this sex scene again."

"It is cyclic, yes," Carter said. "But then, so is life."

Silence, after this brief exchange, returned to the room. Benson turned the pages in slow desperation. He felt paralysis threatening him. "That won't do," he said, seizing on a phrase. '*Twin orbs?*'

He paused again, however, working his jaw in the slight, mildly convulsive way habitual to him at difficult moments. He hated to deal a blow in this sensitive literary area, even to Carter, who never admitted faults. "It isn't quite apt," he said at last. "It doesn't do the trick, it doesn't convey anything to the reader. It has an archaic ring to it." A joke might be in order: jolly Carter along a bit, take the sting out of the criticism. "In this day and age," he said, "we can be more direct. This is 1988, we've had eight years of it, we can call a cow a cow." He essayed a puff of laughter. "Not a dairy quadruped, you know."

"Margaret Thatcher is a woman of character," Carter said. "She's got guts. She is making this country great again."

"Tits would be too colloquial, I'll grant you that," Benson said hastily. "What's wrong with breasts?" He had forgotten that Carter was a Tory voter. The last thing he wanted was a political argument. "The word 'twin' is

47

redundant, really, isn't it?" he said. "Everyone knows women have two of them, as indeed do men. I mean, you wouldn't say twin testicles, would you? And as for orbs . . ."

Without looking, he knew the kind of patient obstinacy that would have formed on his client's broad, big-chinned face. Carter never took kindly to criticism. "Redundancy is dangerous, Harold," he continued after a moment. "So is euphemism. One might call them the twin demons that besmirch a person's prose style. You have somehow managed to pack them both into a phrase of two words. We live in a world where language is used to cloak the most appalling realities. You should see some of the things in my scrapbooks. It is our duty as writers not to aid this process."

Benson raised his head and assumed a smiling expression. In the midst of his words he had felt the onset of a familiar pain: that proud use of the collective 'we' – like a thumb pressed on the wound of his dumbness. Below this immediate distress lay a sense of mourning for his ruined world and self so profound that it needed no particular form of words to be released; it was ready to resonate, to gong out in his mind, at the slightest stroke of memory or association. "Not by one jot or tittle," he said.

Carter had not replied and there was no indication on his face that he was about to. Gesture was needed to fill the gap, raise the temperature, inject some *brio* into the conversation. Benson hoisted his shoulders, raised both hands palms upwards and caused them to shake in a small frenzy of remonstrance. "What's wrong with breasts?" he said. "Sheila has got breasts, not orbs, okay? If anatomy is destiny, as Freud said, let's at least try to get it right."

Part of the problem was that in Carter's novel they were never fully exposed, though Albert persevered; they were always encased in some integument, delicate but definite. This constriction must be important to Carter since he had not allowed Sheila to unhook herself as yet. Retreating from the implications of this, he said, "I'll just check the rest of the chapter. Be with you in a minute."

He ran his eye down to the last paragraph. Albert had departed, unsatisfied as always. Sheila was alone in her bedroom. *With the mirrors revealing her breasts she cupped and raised them as he had done, sensing for herself the majesty of their varying contours and gyrations round the central points . . .*

The real question, of course, did not concern anatomy at all. Carter was approaching seventy, a sturdy, practical man, a retired builder, admirer of Thatcherism and the free market economy and the Spirit of the Falklands. That such a man should take to fiction in late career was strange enough but how had it come about that he had gone astray among his own inventions, lost himself in the trackless interior of his own novel, a strangely static world of odd jobs about the house, tea-breaks, unconsummated love and lingerie in blushing disarray, pantie-girdles, cami-knickers, gossamer bra cups, sliding shoulder straps, frictive nylon surfaces? There was deep mystery here, especially since the novel had not begun in that way at all, but as a story of dockland and family life in the Liverpool of the 1950s. Now hero and heroine had gone off the rails somehow; in chapter after chapter dogged Albert was stripping shy Sheila to her undies and then for one reason or another going no further.

Carter had changed too, in a rather worrying way. His prose had got more and more muffled and meandering, increasingly clotted with strange, obsolete poeticisms. Then there were the clothes: the black felt hat, the knee-length, ginger-coloured overcoat with the Edwardian collar trimming in nylon fur. He had been reading literary theory too, it seemed: as his style deteriorated his ability to score points increased.

"I see you've got the phrase 'dizzy orbs' on the next page," Benson remarked, looking up from his reading.

Carter made some reply, rendered indistinct by the fact that he was wiping his nose as he spoke.

"What did you say?" Not for the first time Benson

wondered why Carter kept on coming to see him. Authorial vanity presumably. It was an outing for him too, of course. More to the point, he thought suddenly, why do *I* go on? Hogan due tomorrow, and after him Anthea Best-Cummings in her black leathers, smelling of machine oil from her powerful motorbike, laden with poems full of expletives and references to menstruation. It wasn't the money even when he could get it. *It's because I daren't move.* He noticed that Carter was smiling. "I didn't quite catch that," he said.

"Transferred epithet," Carter said. "Albert felt himself getting dizzy at the sight of them. It's called a transferred epithet."

His smile was triumphant and shy. He was back at school, in the rare position of being able to tell teacher something. Benson felt a sudden rush of affection and a sort of sorrow for Carter, for his heavy shoulders and rough face, the incongruous flamboyance of his clothes, the hopeless ineptness of his prose, above all for his entrapment, in the evening of his days, in these treacherous marshes of fiction. "The sooner it is brought back home to roost the better," he said. "You've been coming to see me for about a year now, haven't you, Harold?"

"Fourteen months."

"And your novel – you had been working on that for some years previously, hadn't you?"

"I commenced it eight years ago. After my wife passed away. I had to do something. I'm well into it now, of course."

"You are, yes. Well, I'll tell you my opinion. I think the book is hanging fire at the moment. Worse than that, it is stagnating. You have got into the marshlands. Now there is one clear and obvious way to take it forward. Albert and Sheila must be precipitated into something. And as far as I can see there are only two choices open: either they must tear themselves apart for ever or they must get much more serious on the sofa." He paused, then said, "Not to put too fine a point on it, these two must finish things or they must

50

fuck."

"They can't, not just at present." Carter spoke in a tone of calm authority.

"Why can't they?"

"Albert respects her too much, for one thing. Besides, he is lacking in confidence. She has been married before and he is afraid of not coming up to scratch. Also, he feels unworthy of her. But he is very good with his hands and he hopes she will be touched by these odd jobs about the house he is doing for her. Like a knight of old, that is his way of serving her. She has been married to this bastard of a husband, she has been badly hurt and feels that she can never trust a man again. She cannot give of herself. What she is doing is protecting herself all the time but Albert doesn't understand this and it makes him feel more unworthy than ever." He brooded for some moments. Then he said, "It is what you might call an impasse."

"But why all the groping on the sofa?"

"I thought you would have tumbled to that," Carter said, with some return of the triumphant look. "It is symbolical. Albert is groping for his identity. This is a quest novel, really. Sheila is questing for her self-respect after this disastrous marriage. She is trying to keep her options open."

"And her legs closed. I see, yes." Benson was dismayed slightly to have been caught out at this symbolic level – one on which he himself habitually moved. "Well, I am looking forward to the next chapter," he said.

It was the signal for departure. Carter began gathering his papers together. "Relationships can be complicated," he said, on what sounded like a confessional note.

"They can, yes." Benson watched Albert and Sheila being shuffled together and stowed away in the bag Carter now used for the purpose. This was capacious and poison green in colour like the grass that grows over bogland. Carter always brought the whole manuscript in case there was dispute or some need to refer back. In the course of time, like some prodigious cuckoo, it had outgrown the briefcase which had been its previous home.

"I'm getting into it now," he said on his way to the door. "I am getting inside the characters."

"You must know Albert pretty well by this time."

It was now that Carter came out with the remark that made him a sort of forerunner, part of Athena's weft, though Benson did not realise this at the time. "Yes indeed," he said, with the pleasurable alertness of an author discussing his work, "but it is Sheila mainly. I am getting close to Sheila, very close. Between you and me," he said, standing on the top step, glancing in the direction of Hardman Street, where double-deckers were passing, "these days sometimes I feel I *am* Sheila."

Lingering there, holding his virulent bag, he seemed disposed to further, deeper confidences, as if his enlargement into the street had dispelled some reticence. Benson, however, felt he had heard enough. "I don't like to seem pressing, Harold, you know that, but you owe me now for three consultations and I—"

At these words purpose and motion returned to Carter. "It's all in hand," he said briskly. "I'll be in touch." With that he was down the steps and away.

Benson went slowly back through the office into his sitting room, where silence awaited him like a deputation. He settled into an armchair and looked around him, allowing the last echoes of Carter's passage to die away. The room was shabby; the walls needed painting and the plaster moulding was chipped and discoloured; but the proportions pleased and soothed him, the high ceiling, the tall sash windows, the arched recesses with the stucco rosettes picked out in white and blue. He had taken down and placed under the bed a large picture of playful kittens and another of Flemish peasants misbehaving at a wedding feast, and this had left the walls bare. A white owl had gone frantic with fear in this bare room and stunned itself . . .

As he sat there he fell into that state of mind familiar to sleepless people, a sort of wondering, half-apprehensive reverie. Not difficult to believe, no. That panic of the bird found the right setting here, amidst these rational proportions. Elegance, restraint, the virtues of the period. Founded on fear strong enough to burst the heart. That fear the black people must have felt, taken from their forest homes, thrust into the open, exposed to the wide sky, the terrible surf. *The terrible surf.* He had read the phrase somewhere and it haunted him. Fear and fever-stench, the stinking hold of the ship, misery so great, so prolonged, that the timbers must have groaned with it, the rigging shrieked. Far-fetched? These elegant houses built in the 1780s, at the height of that fear and fever, heyday of Liverpool's Atlantic trade.

He looked at the things in the room, and experienced again the sensation of shipwreck, as if he had been washed ashore and beached here, amidst other random offerings of the tides, a litter of chairs and sideboard and table and rug, fixed there, immovable, as if half-sunk in sand. Here and there were personal possessions, the few things he had salvaged: a carved and painted chess set bought for a song in Spain; a silver-plated tea-caddy that had belonged to his mother; shelves of books, his own work among them. In pride of place, on the mantelpiece, was the much-treasured, slightly lopsided bowl made by his daughter in some remote school pottery class – she was in her thirties now, married, living in Plymouth; he did not see her very often and he never spoke of his miseries to her because love made him reticent – he confided only in strangers.

Also on view, neatly stacked, were the products of his industry, the notebooks, scrapbooks, the files. The sight of this accumulation depressed him. Since Carter had first dawned on his sight, bearing Albert and Sheila in the shiny black briefcase that had then been their home, he had done absolutely nothing of significance. He had not stood still exactly; there had been movement, but all of it downward: he drank more, slept less, was closer to mania. Other than that, what was there? Occasional lectures; a few articles and reviews ground out with loathing and pain; some readings to literary groups – very numerous these on Merseyside, would-be writers sprouting vigorously amidst the decline of practically everything else. Like apple trees, he thought vaguely – he had read somewhere that dying apple trees have a season of abundant blossoming.

The readings, in particular, had been an ordeal. He had given them up long ago. To recollect them now made him wince and exclaim aloud. He had heard his voice grow ever more hollow and unreal as he read extracts from his work, feelings, landscapes, conversations, remoter than those in dreams. How distant now the excitement that had possessed him. How he craved for that unrest again. He had lived on here in Greville Street, while craving turned to sickness, while the city wasted with him, or so it seemed: with his invincible passion for image, Benson saw his own plight as emblematic of this stricken place, with its traditional occupations eroded or gone, its growing host of unemployed, its boarded shops and decaying buildings, its miles of disused warehouses and docks.

And all the while, perversely, his affection for the beleaguered city grew. He could hardly have found a place that suited him better. He thought it beautiful. He loved the light that lay over it, the sense of luminous distances. He was moved by the endurance of the people, the warmth of the manners, the spirit of desperate comedy that informed everything, perennial optimism in which there was always a knowledge of defeat, joy clashing with distrust to make all occasions seem improvised, all plans provisional. He had been nowhere else where imagination so infused the life of every day – they were all fictioneers in this city. He was drawn to the ramshackle, myth-laden present of the place as he was to its violent and tragic past. He had no thoughts of leaving.

Meanwhile Carter in page after page of spidery writing had pursued his saga of desire, partial undress and postponed consummation among the working folk of Liverpool. He had abandoned realism long ago – Sheila's underwear was expensive and titillating beyond the dreams of whoredom. Compensation, after his wife's death, for all

54

the years of her flannel bloomers? Grief can take strange forms. Is he, through Sheila, keeping his wife alive? Mildred, her name. Idea for a novel there. A character, losing his wife late in life, tries to preserve her in memory by writing the story of their life together. In the process he gets snared between reality and illusion. Is this what she was truly like? What did it really mean, the way she looked that day, the thing she said? Things have to be reinterpreted, disturbing facts emerge . . .

Yes. But in that case, if it were to preserve Mildred, Carter would want his book to go on for ever, or at least until he died himself. Is that why Sheila and Albert can never consummate their love? The true consummation is death. And Sheila's panties, etc., all that frippery and froth, cami-knickery and gorgeous gussetry, simply the plumes and panoply of death, the pastels all one metaphoric sable. Eros and Thanatos inextricably embraced. Idea for a novel there . . .

7

In the watches of the night Albert and Sheila returned to him in strange bemonstered versions, Sir Reginald and Lady Margaret, laughing madly, rode deeper and deeper into the wildwood. His idea for the novel soon lost its élan, sooner even than usual, slipping down into the dark and fetid pit where the botched, unfinished shapes of his imagination stirred and crawled and coupled with the blurred shapes of memory to breed a new race of monsters.

In light, uneasy sleep he saw black people dancing on the deck of a ship to a slow and melancholy African rhythm of drums and tambourines, their forms distorted and rippled as if by waves of heat. They stooped, uncurled themselves, reached up with their arms. The dream was soundless but he saw the fingers on the drums, sensed from the wavering movements of the dancers the insistent pulse of the music.

They were dressed in what he knew to be calico, but the colours were red and blue. They made shifting patterns against the pale glow of the sky.

The lines of dancers parted ceremoniously to show Sheila in a cream-coloured suit, black stockings, high-heeled shoes and a perm exactly like Jennifer Colomb's. She was reclining on a chaise-longue in the pose of Madame Récamier. Albert was there too in the guise of a yokel, in huge poison-green wellingtons and a cap from under which wisps of hair escaped in a sweaty, bucolic fashion. He saw now that they were in a classical portico which was flooded with water – Sheila's chaise-longue was floating. He waded towards Albert and they engaged in a protracted dumb show of mutual courtesies as to who was going to undress Sheila. In the end Benson found himself doing it. The jacket of Sheila's suit now resembled the tunic of a guardsman buttoned right up to the neck but he did not bother to undo it. With an exciting singleness of purpose he directed all his efforts towards her lower half. He lifted up her skirt, revealing the long legs in their black silk stockings. Already, however, as he tugged at the sumptuous knickers – scarlet, trimmed with black lace – he had a sense of something terribly wrong. There is always a price-tag, ancestral voices said, and then they were in a dark, cluttered place and he saw that Sheila did not have a vagina at all but a cock and balls of impressive proportions and when he looked at her face it was big-chinned Carter in a wild, yellow wig, looking triumphant and sly as he did when he felt he had scored a point.

The shock of this discovery, like a change in pressure, sent Benson rising helplessly towards the surface of consciousness through shoals of flickering images. Waking was accompanied by acute anxiety. That triumphant smile of the hermaphrodite, was it telling him something? His prose bedevils my days, by night he poisons my dreams. And he owes me for three sessions.

It was pitch dark in his room. He saw from the luminous dial of his alarm clock that it was twenty past three. He was wide awake now and knew from experience he was unlikely to sleep again. He switched on the bedside lamp, got out of bed and padded through to the living room. Gomer Williams's book on the Liverpool privateers was in its place on the shelf. The passage about dancing was near the beginning. How long since he had read it? A month at least – the dream had been slow to ferment. Benson put on his glasses and after a minute or two found the passage.

When feeding time was over, the slaves were compelled to jump in their chains, to their own music and that of the cat-o'-nine-tails and this, by those in the trade, was euphemistically called 'dancing'. Those with swollen or diseased limbs were not exempted from taking part in this joyous pastime tho' the shackles often pulled the skin off their legs. The songs they sang on these occasions were songs of sorrow and sadness – simple ditties of their own wretched estate and of the dear land and home and friends they were never more to see. During the night they were often heard to make a howling, melancholy noise, caused by their dreaming of their former happiness and liberty, only to find themselves on waking, in the loathsome hold of a slave ship.

No mention of finger drums or tambourines or calico; and nothing in his dream about shackles. How had he got from there to Albert and Sheila? Water must be the connection, he thought, water and cargoes: from ocean to flooded portico, from sailing ship to chaise-longue . . .

He was beginning to feel cold. His scrapbooks were before him, stacked at the side of the bookcase. He picked one out at random and returned to bed with it. By the light of his bedside lamp he read: *A man confessed to strangling his wife and cutting her up with an axe more than twenty years ago after the discovery of a human skull in May, a jury was told yesterday. But the skull dated from 410 A.D.* A picture of the bald, disconsolate strangler, unlucky enough to have a Roman woman's skull in his garden as well as his wife's. A picture of President Carter with a blind smile on his face, surrounded by bulky, unsmiling security men, like an ecstatic lunatic under strong guard. *His vast fortune all but spent, Edward James, the eccentric exile, is putting his collection of surrealist and other art up for auction so that he can continue building his 'Garden of Eden', a mouldering array of fantasy architecture in the Central Mexican jungle.* Picture of white-bearded James with a parrot on his shoulder. *Demoniac forces of violence and evil have been let loose in Britain since the war, the Lord Chancellor, Lord Hailsham, warned last night. The head of England's legal system dismissed the idea that unemployment or poverty have caused the new wave of violence, robbery and rape.*

Loose English that, Benson thought bemusedly. From the head of England's legal system. The senile sage was pictured in legal drag – gown and wig – disagreeably evoking the recent dream. *Sri Lankan army personnel are extracting the eyes of Tamils killed in clashes with troops and sending them to eye banks for export, a Tamil group said yesterday.* No picture of eyeless Tamils. Picture of Deborah Lester-George, a model, at an auction of theatrical ephemera in Shaftesbury with a rubber skeleton that fetched thirty-five pounds. Deborah and the skeleton smiling at each other. She has a hand over his crotch.

What are the roots that cling? Benson asked himself, turning over the pages. Or is it clutch? His depression grew as daylight began to seep into his room. *COPYCAT DEATH OF A SOAP OPERA FAN. FIREMEN SNARE YOUNG CROCODILE IN PARIS SEWERS. MAN SHARES BED WITH GIRL'S CORPSE.*

What could have led him to select these things, cut them out, paste them in, compile these dossiers of absurdity and misery and crime? Somewhere in this sickening welter there must be a thread, a pattern of meaning. He strove to retrace his intentions, the purposes of the man who had wielded the scissors. But it was hopeless. Faces and print in the lamp light, the girl with acid-scarred face, Mrs Thatcher in beaky profile, blindly smiling Carter, corpses and rubble in Beirut – the cumulative effect was silence. Blight of silence lay over faces and words, over all the pages of his industry. And somewhere behind the silence something worse waited . . .

Unable to bear it any longer, Benson scrambled out of

bed and went to make himself some coffee. Then, though it was still early, he decided to do his exercises. These he had taken up since his block, with the idea of fending off death through enhanced bodily vigour until he could somehow get going again. He always observed a strict, obsessive sequence, increasing in violence, feeling his heart labour, watching his effortful face and pale, flailing limbs in the wardrobe mirror.

At ten past nine, with a sense of defences crumbling, he phoned the University History Department and asked to speak to Alma Corrigan. She arrived just as the phone was ringing and sounded breathless. Yes, she remembered who he was. No, she couldn't see him that evening, not even for an hour. Nor tomorrow either. She had too much to do. She was leaving on Wednesday for Oxford for a three-day conference. And when she came back? Well, she would be busy, there were essays to mark, a Ph.D thesis to look at . . .

Benson pressed a hand against his agitated heart. You may be the Muse, he wanted to say. You may be my salvation. How is it you have time for Ph.D students and yet none for me? "Just one question," he said. "Are you trying to put me off? If so, just tell me and I won't bother you again."

There was an appreciable pause, during which he had to control his breathing. Then he heard the slightly metallic voice say, "No, not exactly."

"Well, then. Since I have made my application in due and proper form I think I should be granted an interview."

"Yes," she said. "All right. So long as you don't imagine you're on any kind of short list."

They arranged to meet the following Tuesday, after her return from Oxford, for a lunch-time drink at the Cambridge Arms. But before that meeting could take place Benson had come upon Killer Thompson and heard him singing in the street.

8

It happened late on the evening of that same day. Benson was sitting on a low wall in a side street off School Lane talking to a man whose long matted hair hung about his face. It was around ten. He had been on his way to the Commercial in Ranelagh Street for a final beer and whisky chaser and had got lost in this dark, deserted region of warehouses and back premises of offices and shops. He had found this man sitting on the wall holding a bottle and had embarked upon an exchange of views.

"I'm not saying I have been singled out," he said. "I may even not be the central figure. I may not be getting the full blast of it. Someone else, somewhere else, is probably flooded with revelation and I'm just getting the odd splash. You know what Schopenhauer says, each man is a protagonist in his own drama while playing a supporting role in the drama of others. But how can you tell? At any given moment how do you know which is the principal role and which the supporting one? Or are they *simultaneous*?"

The man took a drink from the bottle he had been holding with both hands against his chest. He sighed heavily. Noises of traffic came from streets not far away but here in this enclave it was dark and quiet. "You are a talker," the man said after a moment or two.

"Ten seconds either way I wouldn't have seen it," Benson said, "I might have heard it but I wouldn't have seen it. So it is just a matter of a few pulse beats. The slaves would sometimes jump overboard but of course they didn't get much of a chance because they were shackled. Then they would sometimes refuse to eat anything, they would starve themselves to death, in spite of floggings and so on, they were so set on it. Then there was what the slavers called fixed melancholy. That seems to have been a great killer. Even when they were in good health they would die one after the other for no apparent reason. It seems that the Ibo were specially prone to this and the food-gathering tribes of what was known then as the Gaboon. I have been reading an account of it by a medical student who shipped on an illegal slaver in 1859. The theory was that negroes, in contrast to the civilised races, so-called, could actually kill themselves by holding their breath."

"That is impossible," the man said. "Do you believe that?" He took another drink, holding the bottle with both hands. Benson saw that his hands were shaking.

"No, I don't." Benson raised his own hands in repudiation of the idea.

"You must be bloody round the bend if you believe that," the man said angrily. "Coming here talking about slaves. You are out of order, mate."

"No, it was shock. Think of it. They were taken from everything they knew. They might have come from a thousand miles in the interior, lived among forest all their lives. They had never seen a ship before, never seen the sea. Think of the shock of it, that terrible surf. No, the point I wanted to make was that they died because of their strength of life somehow. I know it sounds paradoxical. Not like the man who jumped off the building. I could do that. I could jump. You know, one day, just between moments, say it is about three o'clock in the afternoon, bright, blank afternoon, middle of the day more or less, a long way from action or change . . ."

Benson fell silent, unable to explain now, as he had been unable to explain to Alma and the others in the pub, why the elements of that afternoon had so plagued his imagination, the light, that mild, innocuous sky, the white prison of the railing half-dissolved . . . "No one sees much wrong with me," he said after a moment. "Probably didn't see much wrong with him until he jumped. I mean, it is extraordinary. I don't sleep, I'm losing weight, my habits have changed, but nobody—"

"People don't like to say nothing," the man said. "Not to your face. They see it right enough, ho yes."

"What do you mean?" Benson peered sideways but the man was leaning forward and his features were obscured by the thick, matted hair. "Ho yes," he said again, more loudly. "I've been there before, mate."

After a moment or two of courteous waiting, Benson said, "Self-breeding images of sterility and stagnation multiply in my mind. Endless mud flats, halls of mirrors. My own image, my labouring mind externalised, endlessly repeated, to the point of nausea and despair."

"God gave us breath for more than talking," the man said. "You could die in front of their eyes."

"Imagine it, perpetual stimulation, no release. A perpetual tumescence of the imagination. I call it the Albert and Sheila syndrome. That's a private joke but really one is on the edge, on the absolute edge of the abyss. And the abyss—"

"I could do with one myself," the man said. He got down, still holding his bottle, turned away and disappeared down a narrow opening that ran at right angles to the wall.

Minutes passed and he did not return. Benson was obscurely puzzled. He could not fathom the intonation of that last remark. The man had spoken as if they both shared some intimate desire. Simple boredom, probably. A pretext for escape. Suddenly it came to him: could he have thought I said 'piss'?

He was about to proceed on his way when he saw someone move across a piece of open space in front of some lock-up garages opposite where he was sitting. At first he thought this might be the man with the bottle but there was faint lamp light behind him and Benson saw that he was young and that his head was shaved except for a Mohican tuft along the top. He crossed the alley and stood near the wall some yards away. He did not look at Benson, whom instinct urged to move on but who instead stayed where he was and began talking.

"Chap beside me on the wall just disappeared," he said. "Vanished into thin air. Well, we are such stuff as dreams are made on. You learn to live on your own. My wife used to say I was full of self-love. It's not love, I told her, I don't love myself, it is self-absorption. She used to say I couldn't tell the difference between real people and the products of my own fiction. I don't know if you are married?"

"Nah," the youth said. "Why you wanna know?"

"No particular reason. What I mean is, she was accusing me of trying to make people subject to my imagination, to the requirements of a story, instead of seeing them as they really are, with their own needs and so on. It's a very difficult thing to refute, because you can't know, can you? She had some burnish about her the day she came to tell me she was leaving. She looked as if she had got herself ready for an important interview. She wanted to impress me, to be regarded as a good candidate. Even at that moment . . . She had the shine of a lonely decision on her. Like a day-to-day polish or a lustre that people get who are still trying, trying not to go under. I knew someone once, Milne his name was, Alistair Milne, used to play the clarinet, carried it around in a leather case, and the case and the clarinet both had that same lonely shine on them from all the touching and stroking. The polish of loneliness. I think that clarinet was a sexual substitute for Alistair."

"I know what *you* are," the young man said. "You're a fuckin' pooftah." He turned his head and looked across the street. "We've got a fuckin' pooftah here," he shouted.

Benson was dismayed to see three more youths emerge from behind the row of garages. As they crossed through the lamp light he noted the savagery of their hair. The first youth had been waiting for them – perhaps keeping a look out. "Good God, no," he said. He smiled broadly. "You've got me completely wrong." He saw the youths look up and down the street and knew that neither denial nor admission would avail him now.

"You've got me completely wrong, old chap," one of the youths said.

"He's a fuckin' pooftah," the first youth said. "He was just working up to it, talking about doing somethink wiv a clarinet."

63

"Naughty," one of the others said. "That's pooftah lingo for a blow-job."

The four of them were round him now standing close. The face of the one in front was only a few inches away, close enough for Benson to get the smell of his breath. This youth had small, malignant eyes and a very low forehead – the razed hairline lay just above the bulge of the brows. He seemed to be the leader. "You're a dirty old bugger then, aren't you?" he said. "Come on now, what are you? It is people like you what is letting Britain down, not the fans."

Despite something almost playful in the tone of this, Benson knew that they were getting ready to hit him. He knew too that once he was on the ground he would be in danger of serious injury from their boots. The moment so frequently foreseen had arrived. "Just a minute," he said keeping his voice steady with an effort. "You are making a big mistake." The simian face before him seemed to smile slightly as if sensing his fear. In this moment of crisis the resource of fantasy came to Benson, the rehearsed magic of the word. Level glance, slight smile. Still your beating heart. "I suppose you've heard of the Banana Split?" he said.

He saw the smile disappear. "You fuckin' pervert—" Benson lunged sharply against the youth on his right, who was gripping his arm, catching him off balance. The grip relaxed. With a violent movement Benson broke free. He felt a heavy blow in the small of his back. The next moment he was round behind them and into the narrow passage by the wall. The man with the bottle had gone this way. Benson reasoned that there must be an exit and there was: he saw the lights of a street ahead and started running.

He heard no sounds of pursuit but he kept on running, mouth open, lungs labouring, until he was nearly out of the street. Then a sense of dignity slowed him down to a walk. He looked over his shoulder and saw the passage deserted behind him. He came out on to what he recognised as Hanover Street, on the corner opposite Central Station. Here, among traffic and lights and people, he stood still for some moments breathing heavily, open-mouthed still, astonished at this normality, this public indifference to his escape from bodily harm. After a minute or two he crossed in the direction of the station with the idea of making his way home – he was too late for a drink now. As he approached the wide, paved area at the corner of Bold Street, a thin old man in a black top-coat much too large for him moved out of the shadow of the wall. He was crouched slightly, his narrow head cocked and listening. Benson realised that he was about to start singing, he was listening to himself in advance. It was effective, it made you look at him, wait with him, this listening to the silence. Benson stopped and stood on the pavement among a knot of others. His heart was still agitated from his exertions and he felt a dull pain in his back where he had been struck.

The man raised his head. A look of strain and yearning came to his face. Then the words, in a thin, nasal tenor:

"When I survey the wo-o-ondrous cross
On whee-ee-ch the prince of glory died . . ."

It was quite a performance. He moved as he sang, took several paces away from the lamp light, dragging the right foot as if lame, in what looked like a parody of lameness, almost, Benson thought, as if he wished to illustrate the words of the hymn, to show the human soul halt and lame before that wondrous cross he sang of . . . Something in this disturbed him, compelled his attention, tired as he was and shaken still by his encounter with the Mohicans. The age and evident poverty of the singer lent him a powerful appeal. But it was not that only. Benson was reminded suddenly of the beggars of his childhood, dragging through the cobbled streets with songs of pathos and piety, faces tilted up to the windows, on the watch for pennies.

The singer turned, began to limp his few paces back, head raised and shuddering slightly in a palsy of devotion.

"My ree-ee-chest gain I count but loss
And pour contempt on all my pride."

65

As he drew near the lamp again, light from it fell on the left side of his face and with an inexpressible shock of recognition Benson saw high on his cheek the crimson birthmark, still emblazoned there after forty years, still vivid amidst the decay of all else about him, pristine as when he was twenty, the shape of a cloverleaf or trefoil petal, with the centre lobe stunted and marred; and, exactly as if memory had been loosened by this shock, it seemed to Benson that he knew the voice too and the singing style, the nasal tenor, the trailing notes, that doleful quiver of the head; though the last time it had all been to comic effect and to the notes of a badly tuned piano, rising over laughter and the hubbub of shifting feet and scraping chairs . . . Lance-corporal Thompson, 'C' Company, 2nd Battalion Royal Wiltshires, last seen in 1944, in Italy, in the gashed and riven darkness of a May night. Killer Thompson, shape of death in my mind for forty years. Now this shambling hymn-singer.

Benson stood staring, transfixed by this recognition and by the certainty that came flooding with it, that this was what he had been waiting for, walking the streets for – this was where the signs led. For some moments longer he stayed where he was, watching Thompson go through his act. He saw one or two people put coins in the upturned cap on the pavement near the lamp-post. He might have done the same but terror of being recognised held him back. The fear was irrational – he had himself only known Thompson through the birthmark – but it came with all the force of superstition; and when Thompson swung round under the lamp light, presenting the unblemished side of his face, and it seemed for a moment that their eyes met, Benson drew back and after a brief pause of irresolution began to walk away up the slope towards Lime Street.

After a dozen steps he stopped again. The thought of losing Thompson, thus strangely found, was appalling, intolerable, the sum of all losses at that moment, worse than loss of love. Keeping the singer well in sight he walked into the shadow of the shopping arcade at the entrance to the station. From here he could watch Thompson as he made his few crippled steps away from the lamp and back again. The voice came more distantly now but the words were still quite distinct. He had embarked on another hymn:

> "Lead kindly light
> Amidst the encircling gloom
> Lead thou me on."

He specialised, it seemed, in the lugubrious. Benson watched the mouth moving, the cocked head listening. Thompson was listening to himself exactly as he had done in the cellar at Anzio, in Slater's Show, the Beachhead Buddies, singing his lugubrious songs of home and when the bleedin' war is over and the girl next door; exactly as he had listened on that other stage, the one they called the Wadis, to sounds of movement and change, displacements of earth, clink of weaponry against rock, scrape of boots, signs we learned to interpret – and none learned better than he, than Thompson.

Benson looked away for a moment with an instinct of self-protection. To remember so clearly, so immediately, so helplessly, was like a violation of the will. Easier to doubt one's present senses . . . The sight of a birthmark, a puff of devotional breath, and his house had come crashing down – he was amazed to find it so flimsy. Cancelled at a stroke the intervening years, perplexing my brain, marking my face, all the absurdities of my elderly state, this leaf-fall that has drifted silence over me . . .

He had wondered sometimes about the men he had fought with, whether the survivors were alive still, what had become of them; but in the aftermath of war they had no real existence for him, they belonged to the few square miles of the Beachhead, to those few months of stalemate in 1944. The May breakout from Anzio had put an end to that territory for ever, dissolved the borders in blood. Now wheat and vines grew over it all – he had been back once to see it. The Beachhead was not a place at all now, only a region of trauma, and the men who had been there lived only in the fear of boredom of those days, the jokes and rumours, the wet, slithering clay of the gullies, stench from discarded meat cans, the sicklier smell of death, the demented nightingales singing undeterred through it all. They belonged there really, the living and the dead, he too, hiding here in the shadow of the arcade, and Thompson mouthing and limping for pennies: they had both got loose somehow, wandered off into this No-Man's Land of the present.

Thompson belonged in the show, one of Slater's own, one of the Beachhead Buddies. Little, thin-faced man, ferrety and wiry. Ginger hair, blue eyes, angry red mark. He was in the chorus. And he sometimes did solos. Old-fashioned army songs, music hall type of thing. *Take Me Back To Dear Old Blighty*. He did the little man, jaunty, cowardly, shameless. *Call out the Boys of the Old Brigade what made Old England free. Call out me muvver, me sister and me bruvver but for Gawd's sake don't call me.* Piano honking away. Later we had a three-piece band. Subversive or sentimental, the songs he sang, not patriotic, but they liked it – everyone joined in, great roar of voices. You could get five hundred men into one of those cellars. He went on before Walters and me. We would be waiting backstage. Coming on from the dim passage, lights and applause to deafen and blind you and hot with all the cheering men, then a narrow space of silence for Walters and me. Space of the stage exactly known . . .

Thompson had stopped singing. He was crouched over his cap under the lamp light. Counting his money. No, he shovelled it almost without looking into his overcoat pocket. He was getting ready to go. Preparing to follow, Benson thought of tall Walters with the square-cut sideboards and the small moustache that he kept always neat until the day the blood ran over his face and he could do nothing about it. Brown eyes, deep set. Steady, humorous eyes – Walters saw the funny side, while he saw. Straw boater, blazer, white trousers, the Edwardian gent complete, this debonaire suitor when last seen a bundle of mud and blood and torn khaki.

Thompson had started across the pavement towards him. He moved further into the arcade but the other passed the entrance without a glance and went on towards Lime Street, walking very slowly but with no trace of a limp. The overcoat came almost to his ankles. He stopped to investigate the litter bin on the corner. Benson stopped too, watching the other root among cartons and Coca-Cola tins and find nothing. He crossed the road at the traffic lights, turned left down Lime Street then went up the steps into the station forecourt. Benson was in time to see him enter the cafeteria.

He did not follow immediately. He went some way towards the platform entrances, then stopped, momentarily at a loss. With an obscure instinct of flight he glanced up at the departure schedules. From where he was standing he could see Thompson at the counter getting a hamburger and something hot in a plastic cup.

He could hardly have chosen a more public place for his supper. The cafeteria was lit with appalling plenitude by side lamps and overhead neon and it was walled with glass on three sides. Those inside were as open to view as fish in a frondless, floodlit tank. There was only one way in or out. He could hardly lose Thompson here. Nevertheless, he felt insecure, he wanted to be nearer. After hesitating some moments longer he went through the swing doors. Approaching the counter he saw Thompson in a corner with his back to the entrance. He had never been in here before and he was dazed momentarily by the assault of light. It streamed from walls and ceiling, bounced from the orange and yellow plastic of counters, tables, chairs, was reflected in flat gleams from the silver foil that lined the ceiling. Light in here was the visual equivalent of a prolonged scream. He asked for tea. The girl who served him was languid and pallid, etiolated – as if she needed her roots renewing in the dark.

He took his tea to a table near to the door; from here he could see the back of Thompson's head and a section of his

69

overcoat; between them was a woman with luggage and two small clambering children. He took one sip at his tea then put it down quickly; he had caught the smell of burning plastic from it; the hot liquid, acting on the spongy, white material of the container, gave off a smell like burning industrial waste. He had not wanted tea in any case. He was content to wait. So long as he could keep the other man in view he felt at peace.

It was a curious place, all the same, for Thompson to choose. Cheap of course – that would be a consideration; but people were too conspicuous in here; it was not natural for human beings to be so exposed to light, or perhaps merely not natural for Thompson . . .

Far cry from Wadis, he thought. Far cry from that maze of water courses where we squirmed along. There we sought concealment. That was Thompson's habitat – he had strayed by accident into this terrible realm of light. After forty years. After dwelling clay-coloured there in memory for forty years. He would have dwelt there for ever but for this meeting. Watching Thompson's motion-less shoulder in its shabby black, watching the moving forms of people outside, beyond the glass partitions, he intoned to himself a formal description, something he often did in dreams and states of reverie: *Beyond the ridge of Buonriposo, on the Western limits of the Beachhead, lay the upper reaches of the Moletta Stream, a tangled maze of water courses, called Wadis by the British troops from North Africa, because of their resemblance to the dry streambeds there.*

He was rather pleased with this as an impromptu effort but of course they hadn't been dry for most of the time, far from it, and it didn't convey the real truth of the terrain. One might as well say that the stage in the cellar where we all performed under Slater's direction, where Walters was Burlington Bertie and I was Velma the Vamp, was a level projection of such and such an area, raised so many feet above ground level. They were both stages, one where we strutted, the other where we crawled. Acres of the mind. *Yet be assured we have no need to plot these acres of the mind with*

70

tumty-tumty-tumty-tum and monsters such as heroes find . . . But we do, we do have need. Why otherwise have I been led to Thompson after all these years? He fits the description, he is a monster such as heroes find.

Benson saw the black shoulder move, saw the head tilted back slightly, imagined the motion of Thompson's thin throat as he drank. Killer Thompson. The Wadis were a murder ground and you were at home in them, hence that name. Men went off their heads there. You, foot-dragging psalmist, found your apotheosis. You were a great success. You were a famous looter. Rings, watches, wallets, cigarette-cases, lighters, sometimes an officer's binoculars or even a camera sometimes. Sold back at B-echelon or on leave in Naples. And you didn't get a scratch, or maybe later. Not then, not in the Wadis. Slater too – one knew he would never get hurt.

Some of those channels were shallow, hardly more than a scrape in the ground, hardly deep enough to hide a crawling man. Others went down forty feet or so, gorges dug out by the water. Centuries of gouging. And all interconnected, linked by our excavations and theirs into a complex system. The place was death to anyone with no sense of terrain, no sense of direction. Like the one I shot that day, with Thompson looking on. He is there now, in the open, in the sunshine, combing his hair, which is longish, glinting, colour of soiled gold. He is young, about my age. In the open, in full view. He has made a terrible mistake . . .

Thompson got up quite suddenly and moved towards the door. He passed by Benson's table and Benson lowered his head, catching as he did so the other man's smell, a pungent reek of stale sweat and unwashed clothing.

He rose at once and followed. He could not let the other out of his sight until he knew where he lived, where he could be found again. He followed down the steps, back on to Lime Street, round the corner up Mount Pleasant. He kept his eyes fixed on the form before him in the black overcoat several sizes too large, walking very slowly as though tired or sick, bearer somewhere about him of a vital

71

phial, distillation from the past. Certainly nothing to do, he thought, with the man we killed together. He was a dead man before I pulled the trigger, such grotesque misjudgement carried death with it.

Cardinal crime, Slater would have called it. A blunder like that is a crime. Straight, serious brows, very composed face. Second Lieutenant Hugo Slater. Familiarise yourself with the terrain – that was one of his frequent sayings. He applied it to the stage space too, when we were rehearsing. A real slave-driver – he never let up. Not just a question of knowing the landmarks but an intimate sense of relation between your body and the ground, every little bump and hollow, every scrape and hummock. Until you can move about the stage with confidence. That intimate knowledge will make the show a success and it will save your life in the Wadis. Quality of survivors. Thompson had it. And I? I survived too. My cardinal crime killed Walters instead of killing me . . .

At the end of Catherine Street Thompson rooted for some moments in the rubbish bin near the bus stop, again found nothing. Then he crossed the road and began to traverse the wide area of waste ground on the other side. It was very dark here, once the street lamps had been left behind, and uneven under foot. Benson stumbled once or twice among weeded-over rubble left from the demolitions of years before. All over the city these areas of wasteland were growing; whole blocks fell into ruin, became hazardous and insanitary, were pulled down and the wounds left to heal themselves with grass and nettle and willowherb.

In the darkness, in his black coat, Thompson was difficult to see; Benson had to keep close so as not to lose him. They came out onto a narrow street of dilapidated terrace houses and boarded shop fronts. Benson glanced at the names in passing: Genevieve's Hair Styling and Accessories, The Magic Carpet Café, Atkins Family Butcher. Smells of damp and excrement came through the boarded fronts. Monty Carlo's Fish and Chips. That couldn't be a real name

72

surely. Heavily gridded post office on the corner. No lights showed, there were no signs of habitation in any of the houses, above any of the shops. Beyond, as if this devastated street were a first line of defence, rose the bastions of the Railton Housing Estate, towards which Thompson seemed to be heading.

Benson was tired now but he followed doggedly. Thompson passed through a set of bollards then a railed gate. They were in the shadow of the Estate now, in a wide concrete courtyard with buildings on three sides and a row of sheds with metal fronts on the other. In an entry off the courtyard Benson saw a rat running. He felt the crunch of glass under his feet. He followed Thompson through another gate, out into another courtyard identical to the first. Some windows were lit up, not many. Once, from an upper floor, he heard voices and later a baby crying somewhere; but for the most part the buildings were silent and dark.

Thompson went diagonally across the courtyard and entered a narrow lane where the buildings were close together. It was now that Benson almost lost him. Emerging from the lane he was just in time to see Thompson disappearing down the basement steps of a building on the corner.

He stood there some moments longer looking across at the place where Thompson lived, at the drainpipe hanging off the wall, the broken railing, the barricaded windows. Then he turned and began to retrace his steps, taking care to follow the same route. It was after one o'clock when he got back. Though physically exhausted he had no desire to sleep. He drank some whisky but it did nothing to relax him. For a long time he lay awake, restless and in some indefinable way alarmed, as if he had been singled out for something. The signs did not culminate in Thompson, he knew that now. They led beyond. From time to time, like a ritual incantation, the words of his own description came back to him. *Beyond the ridge of Buonriposo, on the Western limits of the Beachhead, lay the upper reaches of the Moletta*

Stream.

They lead beyond, he thought, lying on his back, staring up at the dim ceiling. Beyond is all around us, not just in front. Cautiously, as if the act of recollection might put him in the same danger again, Benson spoke to his frightened, twenty-year-old self: *I, you, Benson, you are crawling on your belly along a crack in the ground, urged on by the cicadas . . .*

PART TWO

Middle Passage

I, you, Benson, you are crawling on your belly along a crack in the ground, urged on by the cicadas. In front of you, some yard or two, crawls Lance-corporal Thompson, you can see the soles of his boots, and his rump, and the back of his helmet. You are looking for a place to put a forward machine-gun post. It seems incredible. You are in fear because this crack in the ground is a shallow one and the enemy positions are close. You know they are close and you think you know where they are but you might be wrong. In this complex delta of the Moletta the lines are hopelessly confused, we are just where the winter offensive left us.

This day is sunny. You are crawling and sweating and afraid and the sound of the cicadas is in your ears. Late April then, not so long before the break-out. In April the weather got warmer. The cicadas seemed to start up at once and all together, like a sudden celebration of something – not peace or an end to fear and boredom. But it was a cry of life. It laid a pulsing swathe of sound over the ruins of war and winter, the devastated landscape of the Wadis. That shrilling intensified with the heat as if in some way a response to pain.

That must mean there was shrub. Yes, the ground in that sector was not churned up so much. Good cover then. Walters behind you . . . No, not that day. By that day you had been doing your act for a month, more than a month. Burlington Bertie and Velma the Vamp. No, you are with Thompson. This was the first day of heat. This was the first day of real heat. This was the day you came upon the German and shot him.

He was there, inexplicably in the open, in the sunshine. He had taken off his helmet, He was combing his hair. In some way quite beyond determining he had mistaken

77

matters, misunderstood the terrain. Cardinal crime. Otherwise what was he doing there, alone, dreaming, unprotected, the Spandau before him, its barrel pointing towards the ground? The sun had brought him out. Some hope, relaxed caution, prospect of change after the misery of winter, the weeks of stalemate, the murderous closeness of the lines? That long constraint of the trenches, the random deaths, the oppression of fear. Then the rain stops, the clouds roll away, the sun shines down. Like an unwary insect. No, human.

"He's yours," Thompson whispers courteously, keeping his head down. "Shoot the fucker."

You can't shoot him yet. Why not? Is it because he seems to be putting on a performance, not merely enjoying the sunshine but somehow, though he doesn't know we are there, *signalling* his enjoyment? He is handsome with his fair hair and prominent chin. He puts the comb away. He yawns and pats his mouth. He stretches his arms and arches his back. Alone there, with no audience that he knew of, he was acting. Like a child. You glance from him to ferrety Thompson, whose eyes under whiteish lashes are fixed, staring with ferocious intent. Go on, he says. Shoot the fucker. Thompson despises you. The cicadas are loud. The German doesn't know that Thompson and you are watching him but he behaves as if he had an audience. That is strange, metaphysical. So he is performing for death. What else? So he is not in the wrong place at all. You can smell the sweat and clay of both Thompson and yourself. For fuck's sake get on with it. He must have heard the sound of the bolt because at the last moment he raised his head. You squeezed the trigger, smack in the temple, twenty yards. His legs jerked up, he fell backwards. As he went over he made one single loud squawking sound like a hen. Ugly sound, oddly contemptuous. It was exactly as though he had booed himself off stage.

That is the way the show ends, not with a whimper but a squawk. You have killed him over again a good many times since. Not so much out of guilt. He was there to be shot just as you were there to shoot him. Why else were you crawling about with a gun? No, because he, Thompson, compelled you, with his rage and contempt. Shoot the fucker. In some sense you have been in servitude to Thompson ever since. To this noisome street singer, bin-scavenger. Thompson noted the place so he could return in the dark, pick over the body. Star looter Thompson, he brought the helmet back. That was another day. That was the day Slater spoke to you about his idea for putting on a show. He spoke about it that same night, back at B-echelon, after we had been relieved.

Well after midnight when we got back. We were exhausted. Can you spare me a few minutes, Benson? Why did he choose you? There was a full moon that night. We stood talking near the water in the shadow of a bombed house. Dirty-smelling haze over the water from the smoke canisters we used to protect our shipping. Through this the sea had a smooth, oily gleam on it. Slater's face haggard, handsome in its severe way, very regular, level brows, straight mouth. His mouth sharp in the corners. His eyes were light – pale blue or grey. Alive and eager that night because of his idea. "I want to get a concert party together," he said.

The gods had favoured Second-Lieutenant Slater. You knew that, little as you knew of the world, little as you knew of him. Not so much visible signs of privilege or wealth, but it was there in his voice and looks. Most of us there were reduced to common paste, mere blobs of humanity, even the officers. But there was a distinction about Slater, as if he knew himself to be special. "I want to get a sort of concert party together," he said. "Using people from the unit."

As he spoke there was a swift flash of gun-fire from somewhere further along the coast, then a whole series of flashes, one after the other. In that second of silence the sky was lit up and Slater's face caught some light from the glow. He was smiling slightly. He began to say something else, but then the crashes of the guns came, drowning his voice.

That was the same day. Earlier that day, early in the morning, Thompson came back with the German helmet. Looter Thompson had to come back with something. He carried it up-ended, like a begging bowl . . .

"You don't look well." Rathbone took a feverish drag at his cigarette. "That woman," he said, apparently in reference to his last client. "Very unfortunate for you," he said, "getting on the wrong side of Dollinger. Has he made his move yet?"

"No."

"Well, he takes his time over things, Dollinger does. He keeps his seasons and his rages. He moves in a mysterious way. Dollinger was a wrestler, you know."

"So they say."

"The story goes that he was forced to retire from the ring after killing a man. Have you seen her?"

"Yes, once or twice. She just gives me a look, you know. Dragon."

"Don't malign the dragon. It's a very complex symbol, terrible but necessary, something you could hardly say about Mrs Dollinger. Only he who conquers the dragon can become a hero. Jung goes so far as to say that the dragon is a mother image."

"Really?"

"Of course it can be anything. I've been thinking about that fire of yours, that started all the trouble. The difficulty is to know whether to take the positive or the negative side of it. If you take the positive side it looks very good indeed because the owl is Athena's bird and she is the principle by which a man can combine power and wisdom. She is the embodiment of harmony, enabling us to see the pattern and the meaning of life. And of course the beetle, which rolls its eggs along in a ball of its own dung, is an age-old symbol of creation. From that angle, as I say, it looks very good, especially for someone in your line of business. But of course the owl is the death harbinger too. Balance and order can become inflexible and sterile. This aspect of Athena's nature is reflected in her shield, which bore Medusa's head, and in later fairy tales where the birds symbolically associated with her had the power to turn men to stone. As for the beetle . . . have you read Kafka's *Metamorphosis*?"

"Yes."

"Well, there you have the negative symbolism of the beetle. Industry and the brittle shell – the façade adopted for work – have completely taken over. Take someone like yourself, a writer. Suppose for the sake of argument you are drying up. As your creative impulse gets more and more crusted over, you spend less time actually writing and more and more time researching, making notes, keeping records of one sort or another. Now the culmination of that process—"

"Excuse me," Benson said. "All this is fascinating stuff but I've got a client due to arrive in a couple of minutes."

"I hope you're telling them all about my show?"

"I am, yes."

"They can have a free ticket," Rathbone said. "Money is not the object. I want a good audience. You won't forget the date?"

"No."

He was not likely to forget the date: Rathbone was making his debut as a stage hypnotist on May 22, the day of the break-out from Anzio.

He duly told Hogan, the client referred to, about Rathbone's show, not of course mentioning the coincidence of the date. Rather to his surprise Hogan said he would like a ticket. Benson entered his name on the list and told him the address. Rathbone was having his show in an obscure church-hall off Lodge Lane – he had not succeeded in getting a proper theatre.

"It should be interesting," Benson said.

Hogan made no reply to this and a silence developed which Benson for some time lacked energy to break. He felt exhausted this morning, after a night of uneasy memories and broken dreams; and Hogan's face, which misery had made stiff and immobile, seemed, in a rather nightmarish way, like a projection of his own psychic disorder. The other's props and attributes too gave him this morning the same disturbing sense of emanating from himself, from some dark, unacknowledged recess of his own being: the navy suit, the neat maroon tie, the shiny briefcase with gilt clasps, the expanding scent of sweetness from the plastered hair, were like secret vices of his own.

"Well," he said at last, with a sense of enormous effort, "how is your novel coming along?"

"I've been getting on with the research," Hogan said.

With a continued sense of unwilling involvement, Benson watched the other open his briefcase, saw him extract the roll of paper, saw him unfurl it, hold it out, saw words and asterisks and arrows in red and green and blue. There was more of it now – the unfurled part was eighteen inches long at least. Hogan sat holding it up to view.

"But you are going farther and farther back into the past." With feelings of dismay Benson peered at the strip of paper. "Last time you had stopped at your parents' wedding," he said. "I thought that was pushing it a bit for an autobiographical novel. Now I see references to Zeppelins and your grandfather's emigration from Donegal." There were ominous arrows pointing even further back. "Death of Queen Victoria," he read. "Potato Famine." Hogan had slipped into the nineteenth century.

Benson took a deep breath. "Michael," he said, "this can't go on. What will happen, how will you keep it all in your scheme? You can't go on adding things to the roll. It will be impossibly long." He paused a moment, casting around for arguments. "What happens when it gets too long for your arms?" he said.

He looked across the desk. Hogan's blue eyes were dilated, enormous. He was disappearing, swooning into the past; he was in the grip of an infinite regression. Benson felt he should throw him a lifeline, try to tow him back. But

82

it wasn't that altogether, it wasn't a surrender. Hogan's face registered so little, that was the trouble. Faces vary in their power to register sorrows and below the pallor and rigidity of depression Hogan's seemed to lack all notation.

"You must come back to yourself," Benson said gently. "This was to have been a novel based on your own life, perhaps not completely, but in general outline based on your early life, experiences of childhood and so on and in particular the love affair of the adolescent boy with an older woman, Mrs Rand, then his return to childhood sweetheart, Mirabel, whom he marries. That was about it, wasn't it?"

Hogan nodded.

"Then why all this about Zeppelins and the Potato Famine?" But, even as he asked this, Benson knew the answer. Life had broken the idyll for Hogan. The promise of the plot had not been fulfilled. Experience of passion with Mrs Rand, return to virginal sweetheart Mirabel, happy ever after. But he had lost his job and failed to find another and Mirabel had walked out on him, taking the children. Now with his arrows and his coloured inks he was trying to find a place in the past for the blame to lodge. Am I not doing the same? Benson thought. He had been lying awake half the night trying to do the same. What was there to be found now, at this stage, in that murderous labyrinth of the Wadis, but some clue to the crusted silence of the present? Empty bellies in Ireland, Thompson crawling with the German helmet up-ended like a begging bowl . . . Brothers, he thought, looking at Hogan's rigid face.

"If only you could find a beginning," he said. "A few words are enough to begin a story. 'Her eyes were shining', for example, or 'A gin and tonic, please'. Even one word is enough – 'Dawn', say, or 'Mosquitoes'. An expletive will often do the trick, 'Fuck it!' for example. Then you are launched."

He enlarged on this, time passed. Hogan had stood up to go, was extracting from his briefcase the volume he had brought to give Benson, when the door bell rang. It was

Anthea Best-Cummings, in such haste to read her latest poem that she barely paused to acknowledge Hogan's presence.

"It's called 'Flying to Byzantium'," she said, tossing back her hair. "With apologies to William Butler." The accent was extraordinary, the invincible, throat-articulated modulations of the upper class conflicting violently with Anthea's efforts to sound like a prole.

"Go ahead." Benson noticed with some surprise that Hogan had seated himself once again and folded his arms with every appearance of interest.

"It's quite short." As always, Anthea passed from haste to hesitation when it came to the actual moment of reading. She had come on her motorbike, he saw – she was dressed in her studded black leathers. These gave her a squat appearance, belied by her face, which was thin and under-nourished-looking, with spots here and there. She wore her usual tense, sulky expression. Not for the first time Benson wondered what Anthea's parents must make of it all. She had fled them and the green belt of Surrey where they lived, fled ponies and promising young men and a job in an art gallery run by one of daddy's friends, fled the lush lands of the South for this decaying city. What did they make of her in the wilds of Birkenhead, where she had chosen to live? Life is more real here, she had once said to him. Standing there, frowning over her piece of paper, she seemed to him now a living battleground of nature and nurture. Training, precept, exhortation had clashed with Anthea's yearning for urban slums and heavy rock and black leather and poetry and pot. But there had been no victory; the unhappy, defensive face proclaimed that.

"It needs reworking here and there." She glanced at Hogan, who gave her a sudden smile of encouragement.

"Well, we are listening," Benson said.

"Here goes then:

"Borne on the wings of a dick-trip
Through icon haze and star burst,

84

Uterine splendours of purple and gold,
Sperm shower,
To that city of coiners and theologians
Where my cunt
Conquers the cross."

Anthea looked up. A flush had crept into her face. "It needs one or two things doing to it," she said.

"Hm." Benson was silent a moment. Then he said cautiously, "That's an effective ending, with the repeated hard 'c' and those strong monosyllables. But haven't you made a mistake in the first line? You seem to have transposed the syllables. Shouldn't it be triptych?"

"Good God!" Anthea cried, running a hand through her long and rather greasy hair. "You've missed the whole point. It's *meant* to be written like that."

Suddenly, most unexpectedly, Hogan leaned forward and began to speak. "As I see it," he said, "this is a play on words. The poem is about a trip, right? A trip is a journey but it is also an experience. Now the experience in this poem is to do with female orgasm. So it is a dick-trip, right? But a triptych has wings and they could carry you off into a different sort of experience. As I see it, this is a very complicated pun."

Benson felt his mouth inclined to fall open. In all his dealings with Hogan, he had never heard him say more than half a dozen words together. Now his face had lost some of that terrible stiffness. His eyes had a light in them.

"That's it exactly," Anthea said excitedly. Again she ran a hand through her hair. In suddenly lowered tones she said, "You have understood my poem completely."

"It's a very good poem," Hogan said. "As I see it, it is also a feminist poem."

Anthea looked at him like the first woman looking at the first man. It was a look that pierced through Hogan's despicably bourgeois appearance and went straight to the core. "Are you a writer too?" she said.

"I am working on a novel," Hogan said.

"What is it about?"

"Well, it is partly autobiographical. It's about childhood and adolescence in Liverpool. When the hero is eighteen he meets this older woman at a dance. She is from the South and she – you are from the South too, aren't you?"

"Yes." Anthea was ashamed of it. "Surrey," she said.

"Surrey," Hogan said lingeringly. "Anyway, they, you know, have an affair."

"You two carry on," Benson said. "I'm going to make some tea. Oh, Michael," he added, turning at the door, "You might remember to tell Anthea about Rathbone's show."

From any distance away this great deathtrap vanished, the torn and devastated earth seemed to heal its own gashes, all the gullies and channels of the labyrinth closed together, smoothed themselves over. From the road that went north to Carroceto it looked like a dead level plain. Nothing was visible of their lines or ours, the water-courses, the crumbling dykes, the corpses cluttering the streams, rotting in the soft earth of the banksides and the brambled ditches. There was nothing, absolutely nothing, to indicate that in the fighting of that winter whole regiments had been swallowed up here. If you had fought in them, seen people die in them, looking across those innocuous-seeming levels brought a terrible sense of unreality and despair, as if some last vital shred of meaning had been taken away. Enough to make one distrust for ever all appearances of peace. Perhaps it was that, echoing childhood fears of the still surface, scum on a deep pond, motionless leaves or grasses, which gives me now as I enter old age such a taste for signs and emblems – meanings that lurk below the placid surface. Once through that calm screen you are in the jungle. Archetypal Jungle, must tell Rathbone that one . . . I wasn't much more than a child, at least from present perspectives – twenty years old, I was twenty that April. Those few months my only experience of battle. It was like being a child again. Childhood games of stalking and hiding, make-believe of terror, not much different from the real thing.

He lay on his back staring up through the darkness, wide-eyed and sleepless, the silence of these memories constricting his heart. There was the smell that lay over everything; no healing perspectives could cloak that. Not death only: a compound odour, wet clay, excrement, decay. Smell always plays the traitor. Like a pall over the place. The docks of Liverpool stank of the slave traffic, the shambles-odour mixed with smells of tar and rum. It came from the holds and decks of the ships. The stench of it would have been wafted on a sea breeze to the nostrils of the wigged merchants and their rouged wives on the steps of their fine houses. On warm days through open windows into their stuffed parlours. Easier to avert the eye than block the nose. Much easier for me at least with my famous sense of smell. Hearing too first-rate still and my eyes, until recently . . . Some, of course, who neither see nor smell anything untoward, they could wade through shit and come out smelling of lavender. The inimitable Doctor Dobson, for instance. Writing in 1772 he found Liverpool the most salubrious of places. Slave-trade at its height, worst urban slums in Europe . . .

Perhaps not so surprising. The ships went forth with goods not offensive to the smell – Lancashire cottons, trinkets, small arms. And when they got back months later to Salt House or Queen's Dock they were stuffed with the aromas of the New World, sugar, coffee, tobacco. The cargoes they carried in between, on the Middle Passage, the long haul from Africa to the plantations of Jamaica and Carolina, these printed stronger odours. No scrubbing or hosing could get rid of it. Ship after ship, year after year. How many? Seventy years of it. Perhaps two million men, women and children carried in those Liverpool ships. The smell of misery ingrained in the timbers . . . Steam of blood and soaked khaki, between two rows the medic walks down, looking right and left, not pausing long. Walters a

87

bundle of bloody rags left alone there in the gully, his face dark with blood and the boot polish we had put on for the patrol. He lies still, legs drawn up, as if he is ashamed to have lost half his insides, ashamed to be dying . . .

Benson lay tense, taking shallow breaths, tracing repeatedly in the darkness familiar, darker shapes, the lines of the wardrobe, owl's launching pad; the folds and drapes of the curtain; the marble horse on the table below the window – this he knew well as he had often held it in his hands, and so was not sure now, in the obscurity of his room, whether he was seeing or merely remembering the lines of its body, jags of its mane. We charge things with reality by giving our attention to them. One of the great seductions of literary creation, godlike to confer reality. *What I miss, what I lack.* Truth is the glory of reality, Simone Weil said. *I don't understand that,* he whispered in the darkness. *That is the religious view.* My father might have understood it. He was after all a man of God. But reality for my father was something not to be transcended but corrected. He corrected my realities with the rod. Squawk of the killed soldier, Walters dying for my mistake, the man clambering over the white railings in that freakish weather, miseries of the slave-trade, a baby crying in the night in the condemned estate where Thompson lives, the peculations of financiers, prominent in my scrapbooks, insatiable greed of men who live in mansions, who have millions, these are realities to me. What could unify and transcend them, spread over them this glorious paste of truth?

The horse was real, he had touched it. Sheila's body was real too, though he hadn't. As real as Alma Corrigan's, more real in a sense as he had not so far permitted himself to think in that way about Alma, not charged her body with reality, so to speak, though her face came often to his mind, the slightly bitter mouth, the brilliant eyes, contempt in them for what she saw as his self-indulgence. He felt the stirring of excitement. *I invoke thee, O Muse.*

The Wadis were real for ever, though long since drained and bulldozed into vineyards. I all but left my bones there,

I, you, Benson's bones, the bones of Voluptuous Velma, the Beachhead Vamp. Slater asked me to be the woman. You have such small bones, Benson, the reason I ask. Little Benson, he called me.

They liked it, one great roar when we came on stage, our act was twenty years out of date even then, but they liked it, that duet we did and the dance, I sang falsetto, hurt the throat. Parody of Edwardian flirtation and then the bit of stripping at the end, down to my bra and pants. The CO stopped that. I can see myself in the red silk dress or the black blouse with mother-of-pearl buttons, black stockings, garters. I shaved my legs. High-heeled shoes. Blaspheming companionably there with Walters, waiting to go on, listening to Killer Thompson's dirges. *When this bleeding war is over, no more soldiering for me.* He always struck a mournful note. Hymns now. I wore make-up, wig, all padded out. They ransacked the wrecked houses of Anzio and Nettuno to get costumes for us.

Anzio, Nettuno, Carroceto, Campo Leone . . . He drifted back into sleep on this litany of names and woke groaning and fearful in the first light of morning with shreds of names and nicknames fluttering still in his mind. Stonk Corner, Gordon's Ridge, Smelly Farm. *Beyond the ridge of Buonriposo lay the Wadis of the Upper Moletta Stream . . .*

Buonriposo, good repose. The irony of some of those names. Isola Bella, Campo di Carne. He lay on his back while the light strengthened slowly and the fear that had come with waking grew less. That geography of the war varied strangely in intensity. Features that had gone unregarded would assume terrible importance. A ruined farm house, a few yards of embankment. An hour later, after the deaths, they might as well have been on the moon. Significant only because they were fought over. We gave them our attention, charged them with reality. Perhaps it was this that made me want to write, a wish to make the places constant, rebut this indecent fluctuation. No, childhood formed my intentions without my knowing it, seeing my

89

composition on the wall with a gold star from the teacher, my parents and others stopping to look, my father with something to be proud of at last. That is when I started to want to make the names constant and splendid.

Not many gold stars lately. My sixty-three-year-old body under the sheets in this room not my own. The same that danced and strutted in its red dress and the silver lamé shoes with ankle straps, smooth, shaved legs in sheer stockings. *Every little movement tells a tale.* That was the best one we did, our best number. Thompson came back from a killing trip one morning with the stain of orgasm showing through his trousers . . .

He raised his head, looked carefully at the shape of his wardrobe, followed with his eyes the complex folds of the curtains. Ritual inspection was a habit he had formed in terror-ridden childhood and never lost; he had used it all his life like a sort of meditation, to ward off evil; he had used it in the Wadis, striving to print on his mind the configuration of the ground in the most intimate detail possible. *Familiarise yourself with the terrain.* Slater meant the stage as well. We were frightened there too, he thought. There on the stage. Frightened of displeasing Lieutenant Slater, who had put on the show. Frightened of getting the steps and movements wrong somehow, spoiling things, disappointing the audience. What an audience that was. Acting, moving about on the stage, every movement buoyed on sound. They knew the song by heart. The words flickered through his mind again in their precise, imperishable order.

> 'Every little movement has a meaning of its own,
> Every little movement tells a tale.
> At the back, round *here*, there's a kind of
> wibble-wobble
> And she glides like *this* . . .'

With every inflection there was a movement to make, a place on the stage for me to be. Walters too, aping the Edwardian Johnnie, doing the sort of comic, randy, strutting dance that Slater had taught him, rather stiff, leaning forward slightly, sticking out his bum, leering, winking, raising his straw boater. A parody of course, because I wasn't a woman, everybody knew that, though I was indistinguishable from one. In a sense it didn't matter. Objective gender description was hardly the point. On stage, made-up, padded-out, wiggling and gliding, schooled by Slater, I was a woman. I was a symbolical woman for the thousands of men there, a woman in the eyes that watched me and the throats and mouths that applauded. And punctuating the dance that great breath of applause, the rising ooh when the skirt lifted, derisive, savage, and the baying roar for Walters, whose movements, as Salter had designed them, made every man in the audience an accomplice.

This same body, he thought with wonder. The same that danced. The same that crawled through the maze of watercourses. Lying now so quiet and apprehensive, prey to recollection. He tensed his body, curled and flexed his fingers. The things these hands have done . . .

"Would you be interested in a free ticket to a stage show that is being put on by a friend of mine, a hypnotist?"

"Yes, yes," Jennifer Colomb said. "Give me one, no two. Perhaps father might like to come." She was fidgety, impatient as always to hear his verdict on her latest pages.

"Well now," he said, looking down at the neat page. Jennifer always typed her work immaculately.

Lady Margaret sat her chestnut yearling like the true horsewoman she was, her posture erect and supple. "So now," she said, "I trust your conscience is at rest."

Despite the teasing intention of her words, they came a thought hastily, a thought breathlessly. She had mused much upon this man in her maidenly reveries, aware of his power and domination, the steely will that lay behind his gentle manner. In his words there was sometimes the insinuation of some special relationship between them. Did she want that? Could she handle fire without getting burned? There was something dark in him, a hint of brutality in

the curl of his lip, something restless, permanently unsatisfied,
which in her woman's way she could surmise but never understand.
How different from the gentle Sir Denis, to whom she was
affianced, who was away now on a tour of the family estates in
Dulwich. Denis, with his guileless blue eyes, his love of country
pursuits, coursing and rackets and partridge pie. Denis, whom she
knew so well. As different, she thought, seeking to find the words
that would do justice to her thought, yes, as different as the hawk
from the dove.

She fell into a dream as they rode ever deeper into the wildwood,
their horses treading softly on the leafy carpet. The trees closed
around them. Gradually, without her noticing it, they had left the
lords and ladies of their retinue far behind. She was startled,
almost, to hear Sir Reginald's deep voice at her side. "The trees
grow close here," he said. "Shall we play a trick on them? It
would be good sport to conceal ourselves somewhere about these
thickets and give them the slip. What think you?"

Veteran of many a desperate throw, he was gambling on her
youthful spirit of adventure. Madcap Maggie, she had been called
in her nursery days – not so far behind, as she was barely eighteen
summers. All the same, she hesitated. Despite the jesting tone
there had been that in his voice that might inspire caution in a maid.
Something was here that needed to be brought out in the open.
"La, Sir," she said. "I don't think that would be a very good
idea."

"Well," he said, "it's coming on." There was not much,
by this time, that could really be said about *Treacherous
Dreams*. It went on its way, followed a certain obscure logic
of its own. Strictures would merely wound the author.
Sooner or later whatever it was that needed to be brought
out in the open would perhaps flash forth, but there seemed
no reason to suppose it would be very soon.

"Do you really think so?"

"I do, yes."

"But do you think I'm getting the feel of the period?"

"What period is it?" Benson said unguardedly.

"What period? Do you mean to say that you have been
reading my novel all this time and you still don't know

what period it is?"

"Well, of course," Benson said hastily, "there is a flavour of the Regency in it. Sir Reginald is a Byronic character, isn't he?"

She had flushed, he saw, and seemed close to tears. "It is eighteenth-century," she said. "I have tried so hard to get the true accent of the time." She paused, clutched her handbag, tried to smile. "Of course," she said, "I know how busy you are."

How is it, I wonder, he thought, that all of them, without exception, manage to say something in the course of these sessions that goes straight to my heart? In a lifetime of self abnegation this novel was her only autonomy. "No," he said, "not busy, just terribly stupid. It's not really much excuse but I am a bit preoccupied these days. You go on with your book, Jennifer. Try to get the feelings right. Period detail can always be tidied up afterwards."

Later, sleepless, pages strewn around him, he tried to come to his own terms with the accents of the period:

Some wet and blowing weather having occasioned the port holes to be shut and the grating to be covered, fluxes and fevers among the negroes ensued. While they were in this situation, my profession requiring it, I frequently went down among them, till at length their apartments became so extremely hot as to be only sufferable for a very short time. But the excessive heat was not the only thing that rendered their situation intolerable. The deck, that is the floor of their rooms, was so covered with the blood and mucus which had proceeded from them in consequence of their flux that it resembled a slaughterhouse. It is not in the power of the human imagination to picture to itself a situation more dreadful or disgusting. Numbers of the slaves had fainted, they were carried upon deck, where several of them died, and the rest were, with difficulty, restored.

The Grand Pillage is executed by the King's soldiers, from three hundred to six thousand at a time, who attack and set fire to a Village and seize the Inhabitants as they can. In the Lesser

93

Pillage, parties lie in wait about the Village and take off all they can surprise which is also done by Individuals who do not belong to the King but are private Robbers.

Sestro, december the 29th 1724. No trade to day tho' many Traders came on board, they informed us that the People are gone to War within Land and will bring prisoners enough in two or three Days in Hopes of which we stay.

The 30th. No Trade yet; but our Traders came on board to Day and informed us the People had burned four Towns of their Enemies and indeed we have seen great smoke all morning a good Way up the Country so that tomorrow we expect Slaves.

On leaving the Gulf of Guinea, that part of the ocean must be traversed, so fatal to navigators, where long calms detain the ships under a sky charged with electric clouds, pouring down by turns torrents of rain and of fire. This sea of thunder, being a focus of mortal diseases, is avoided as much as possible, both in approaching the coasts of Africa and those of America.

The slave ship Louisa *on her fourth voyage, having sold 326 negroes at Jamaica for the sum of £19,315, 13s, 6d, the profit (after adding interest on account sales, £1051, 19s, 7d, and deducting £1234, 2s, 8d for disbursments & commissions etc.) amounted to £19,133, 10s, 5d, which was apportioned among the owners as follows: —Thomas Leyland £9566, 15s, 2½d; R. Bullin £4783, 7s, 7¼d; Thomas Molyneux £4783, 7s, 7¼d.*

No gold finders can endure so much noisome slavery as they do who carry negroes; for those have some respite and satisfaction, but we endure twice the misery; and yet by their mortality our voyages are ruined, and we pine and fret ourselves to death, to think we should undergo so much misery, and take so much pains to so little purpose.

> *I own I am shocked at the purchase of slaves,*
> *And fear those who buy them and sell them are knaves;*
> *What I hear of their hardships, their tortures and groans*
> *Is almost enough to draw pity from stones.*
> *I pity them greatly, but I must be mum,*
> *For how could we do without sugar and rum?*

Speculum oris; This instrument is known among surgeons, having been invented to assist them in wrenching open the mouth as in the case of a locked jaw; but it is used in this trade. On asking the seller of the instruments on what occasion it was used there, he replied that the slaves were frequently so sulky as to shut their mouth against all sustenance, and this with a determination to die; and that it was necessary their mouths should be forced open to throw in nutriment, that they who had purchased them might incur no loss.

The degrees of the soil, the purity of the waters, the mildness of the air, the antiseptic effluvia of pitch and tar, the acid exhalations from the sea, the pregnant brisk gales of wind and the daily visitations of the tides render Liverpool one of the healthiest places in the kingdom.

"I mean it," he said. "I think it is coming along quite splendidly." It was a relief to be able for once to be totally sincere. Elroy Palmer was his most promising client. He was also the only black person that had come to him in the whole history of his consultancy business. For an unemployed young black to come here at all meant breaking through quite a number of barriers; it argued determination and a strong sense of literary vocation. Benson had hopes of Elroy. He sat opposite now, across the desk, in a fringed black leather jacket, dreadlocks surmounted by the long red rasta hat, gold hoop dangling from his left ear. His expression was watchful and at the same time curiously heedless. He said nothing in reply to Benson's comment, merely nodded slowly in full agreement. There was a certainty about Elroy which was impressive. Benson looked down again at the passage he had just been reading:

Zircon bring down the spacecraft with its black and silver official markings, careful like setting down an egg, dead centre of the landing stage marked out on the Ministry roof. The last thing he wants is his mission getting screwed up in the traffic regulations on

Gareg, this the most viciously bureaucratic of planets, traffic offenders classed with violent psychopaths on Gareg, Park Pretty the eleventh commandment. Zircon knows he has been watched coming in. Typical, that area marked out by the white lines. No reason why you shouldn't land outside it, plenty of space. But that is Gareg all over. This whole planet gone mad through too much regulation. He sent to put this right.

He taxies carefully over and park his craft in the space for visitors, park exactly equidistant between the lines. He switch off his engine, opens his nearside door and gets out. Then he lean back in again for the black briefcase with the big gold crest which have in it his official letters of credit. Afterwards he shut and lock the door and walks at the regulation pace, you got to walk one speed on this planet, towards the entrance to the Ministry complex, this huge, each office is exactly the same, same size, same shape, square of course, it occupies the whole of this twenty-storey building in the heart of downtown Zandor.

"There is still this business of the third person singular," Benson said. "It would be better to leave the 's' off altogether than to have it sometimes and not others. Since the book is written in the present tense, this is an issue of some importance. But I wouldn't worry until you have got the whole thing together. A little careful editing—"

"I don' worry," Elroy said. "He's going in there, look around, decide what he got to do."

He always spoke of his hero Zircon as if he were an independent being and it was this certainty about the responses of the character to the exigencies of the situation, that most heartened Benson with a belief in the ultimate success of Elroy's story.

"I think," he said after a moment, "that there is too much dwelling on the series of actions Zircon performs on arriving on the Ministry roof. I mean, switching off the engine, opening doors, getting out, shutting the door, locking it, getting his briefcase. Anyone does that who parks a spacecraft, don't they? In general, things like that are only worth dwelling on if they are important in some way."

"Jarrold watching every move he makes," Elroy said.

"So it is important to say everything he does."

Benson thought for a moment. He was reading the book in bits and pieces with intervals between; in that way one lost something of the continuity. "Maybe you are right," he said.

Jarrold was the demented hermaphrodite ruler of Gareg, who had imposed his mad passion for order, symmetry and rectilinear form on the unfortunate planet, reducing it to a sort of gigantic geometrical theorem. Curves of any sort were forbidden; there were no arches, no tapering lines; hats were square and even shoes were fashioned in right angles. There was a vast bureaucracy endlessly engaged in monitoring infringements, which were punished with ferocity by Jarrold's eunuch guards. An army of slave labourers was currently employed under conditions of great hardship and brutality in straightening the roads. However, there was a revolutionary group in Zandor, whose secret signal was the sign of the circle. Jarrold was now threatening to secede from the Galactic League and cut off access to the valuable mineral deposits on Gareg. Zircon, a sort of super interplanetary diplomat and hit-man, had been sent to negotiate with Jarrold and make contact with the rebels.

"It's looking good anyway," Benson said. "Tell me one thing. Is Zircon going to kill Jarrold?"

Elroy considered a moment, looking at his long bony fingers and their array of copper rings. He looked up at last and fixed Benson with a sombre stare. "He might have to," he said.

"So I may have unleashed upon the world a concussed, demonic owl that will become a man-eater in due course. I may have disturbed the whole ecological balance. Who knows? We never see the whole shape of things."

The floodlit cathedral rose above them into the night sky. On this razed plateau, with the huddle of mean streets beyond, it was like an outpost of some extinct race of titans. Below, where the slope levelled out a little, they could see

97

the lights of the Chinese restaurants and food stores on Lower Duke Street. Beyond that, a sense of space and luminous distance, the constant glow of the city, one of its greatest beauties to Benson.

Dolores uttered a groaning sigh.

"Yes, I know what you mean," Benson said. "It's like this cathedral. Liverpool was dying when it was built. Or even earlier, when they were expanding, building the new docks to accommodate the slave clippers, the writing was on the wall. Look at the Mersey Tunnel, longest underwater tunnel in the world when it was built. Look at me, for instance. Because of a basic complaisance of demeanour, no one suspects anything is wrong with me. I am slowly dying and no one suspects it. Yes, I'm talking about death, ceasing upon the midnight. I can't talk to people who know me. If there's a relationship I feel inhibited. I can't talk to my Fictioneers, they come to discuss their work. I have to talk to somebody. I saw an old mate of mine the other night, singing in the street. Hymns. Thompson by name. Comrade in arms. He was a killer. Still is, I suppose. The leopard doesn't change his spots, does he? Did you say something? Less scope for it now, of course. We were at Anzio together."

Dolores made a sudden movement with his left arm and Benson saw that he was starting the process of lighting a cigarette. Across the road, through the wire mesh fence that closed off the building side, he thought he saw a figure moving slowly against the faint glow of the sky. "People still camping out there," he said. "No fires tonight. You are too young to have been in the war, aren't you? Been in your own war by the look of it. This man I am talking about was always on his own. That way he didn't have to share. If you could get to the body before anyone else, you could get a wallet, a watch – amulets, chains, things people wear for luck. Wedding rings. An officer particularly – he might have something like a gold-plated cigarette-case, hip flask, anything. It was surprising, you know, what people took with them. Thompson amassed quite a collection, he was noted for it. It wasn't only the Germans, he combed through shelled-out villas for things that had been overlooked. I saw him once with a gold and onyx cigarette lighter. He had a set of ivory monkeys, hear no evil, see no evil, speak no evil. He had a beautiful rosewood cigarette box. He could have set up a shop with what he got."

Benson paused. Dolores was silent beside him. It was true that Thompson had been more interested in keeping things than selling them. His was a pure love of loot; they were trophies. And of course they were a pretext for the killing. He wanted to tell Dolores about the dark patch of ecstasy on Thompson's trousers, but it was a violation of people to tell them things like that.

"He has a birthmark on his left cheek," he said. "That's how I knew him. I once heard him telling somebody how you can suck a ring off a finger."

He fell silent again, thinking of this. A driver in a Signals Regiment, the man was – Thompson's only friend. Scottish name. McIvor, McInlay? The only one he talked to. He drove the officers around, picked up things. Thompson's friendship wouldn't be an unmixed blessing . . . Perhaps this is what I ought to be writing about, he thought suddenly, instead of ransacking the past for horrors, crushing my mind with the slave-trade. Horrors enough here.

"I've got ideas," he said, "but there's no pressure to express them. My situation is opposite to that of King Midas's barber. Perhaps you know the story? I read it when I was a child, in a book called *Tales from Olympus*, which had beautiful coloured plates. Midas was foolish enough to get on the wrong side of Apollo by voting against him in a music composition. To show what he thought of him as a critic Apollo gave him ass's ears instead of his human ones. Midas was extremely ashamed of having these great hairy ears standing up at the sides of his head. He wore a turban indoors and out and never told anyone about it. But the one person he couldn't keep it from was his barber – you'll stop me if you've heard this, won't you? The barber was astounded when he unwound the turban and saw that the king had ass's ears. There was a picture of it in my book, the king sitting there in the chair and the barber all goggle-eyed. He didn't dare to tell anyone because Midas threatened him with instant death if he did. He didn't dare tell his wife or anybody. After a while the secret began to get too big for him. He had to tell somebody, he couldn't contain it, he was bursting with this enormity of the king's ears. He couldn't sleep. So one day he went out into the countryside and he told it to the reeds along a river bank. 'Midas has ass's ears,' he whispered. After that he felt a whole lot better. But the reeds picked it up. Every time the wind blew through them they whispered it, *Midas has ass's ears, Midas has ass's ears*. The reeds told everybody in the end.

"The reason this story stuck in my mind was the picture, first of all, and then that marvellous sibilance. *Midas has ass's ears*. It is human speech and at the same time it is the language of the reeds when the wind shakes them. The most perfect example of assonance in the English language, if you'll forgive the pun, and it was right there in my book. But lately I've come to see the story in a different light. I see it now as the perfect illustration of the literary impulse. All literature begins with the pressure of a secret, some unique perception that needs urgently to be expressed."

Benson was silent for some moments looking down towards the lights of the city. "I used to feel that urgency myself at one time," he said. "People talk about writer's block as if it were some humorous occasional impediment or recurrent hazard of the trade or just a sort of swank term for laziness or a headache or a hangover. This takes no account of the violence in the word, the choked arrest. *Block*. It's a violent affliction. I have become sensitised to it. I see it in the eyes of children, I see it on the faces of people walking about this city, mothers pushing prams, mad old ladies, men in business suits with briefcases. Block is the great psychic disease of our time. It atrophies those parts that other diseases cannot reach. It isn't a joke at all. It is nausea and dread, it is the foretaste of dissolution. When I listen to myself it's like the silence of a battlefield after the cries have died away, before the birds start singing again. Of course, I've been thinking a lot about the last war lately."

In the silence that followed he was startled to hear the distinct clicking of teeth. He saw Dolores make a sudden rearing motion of the head. The voice, when it came, was hoarse and deep. It uttered a single syllable.

"Did you say something?" Benson was astounded. For some moments he still could not believe that the other had actually spoken. "What?" he said. "I didn't catch it."

"Gold. He turned things to gold." Dolores was still looking rigidly before him, in the direction he always looked, towards the glow in the sky above the river.

"Do you mean Thompson?"

"Couldn't get his teeth into it."

"Midas, you mean? Yes, that was another story about him, that everything he touched turned into gold. He was a miser and he was given a wish and he wished that everything he touched would turn to gold. He couldn't eat anything because it turned to gold before he could sink his molars into it. Is that what you mean?"

He waited anxiously as the moments passed. He heard the click of teeth again. Then a series of strange, harsh exhalations. Dolores was laughing.

It was chilly in the room. Benson took off his pyjamas and put on the pair of red boxer shorts that he always used for his exercises. He looked at himself in the glass front of the wardrobe. Need some sunshine, you do. His skin was white. Over his chest and shins it was glazed and shiny-looking. The lines of collar-bone and rib-cage were clearly traceable. Some sunshine and a bit more weight and you'd look better. Not sleeping enough makes you thin. Unless it is some wasting disease. Not bad though, on the whole. No senile blotches, no purpurea. Musculature firm enough.

Beneath this façade of imperishable man a frantic deterioration going on. Losing collagen at a furious rate, brain cells dying, tissue degenerating, marrow drying out. It'll happen quite soon, he thought. I shall wake up to find myself an old man.

He began to do his reaching exercises, up, down, up, down. Limbering up. Then the one for stretching the waist muscles, turning the body from side to side, arms outstretched, hand following round, left – one – two, right – one – two. His limbs were reluctant. *When feeding time was over the slaves were compelled to jump in their chains.* I am chained in my skeleton, Benson thought. My collar-bone a halter, my shin-bones shackles . . .

As he proceeded his body warmed, his heart quickened, he began to breath more deeply, think more calmly. Eyes always on his turning, stretching, genuflecting body, he thought again about the war days, that distant life at the Beachhead. Why had he been led to Thompson? It must mean something, if he could disentangle the threads. Precisely what, though, was the difficulty. Like trying to keep my plasticene separated out in its pristine colours. Those strips of primary colour in their chaste tissue wrappings, every time I got a new set I vowed in my first delight to keep them pure and apart forever. It worked so long as you only used one colour. You could make a red elephant or a blue monkey. But then you might want to make Dopey the Dwarf, for example; and he would have to have a red nose and blue blobs for eyes and perhaps a green or yellow cap. The heat from your hands while you tried to make a good Dopey would start to get the colours clogged together. The penalty for ambition was always the same: you ended with one amorphous lump, in which could still be seen the swirls and veins of original colour, forever lost.

That happened over and over again, he thought. It was possible as a child both to know it would happen and to promise not to let it. And now? The faith much less. Those few months of the war branded on me. Some things not possible to see or think about, even after so many years, except through the prisms of that time; and yet the colours run together.

Veins of colour in the lump: dead, bloated sheep, song of the nightingales, the beetle races we used to have back at B-echelon. Walters's face. Brown eyes, very clear and steady, short-lashed, so they seemed prominent, black hair, a mouth slightly pouting, giving him an expression of protest, not petulant though – humorous rather. Your happiness to be with him. Even there, when the world was the range of a grenade, the field of fire not much more than the length of this bedroom. Moist, crumbling sides of the banks held together by wet blankets to stop them falling in on us. The horizon the top of the next scrub-covered ditch. Even there.

In April the weather got warmer. The cicadas seemed to start up all at once. They shrilled louder with the heat, as if in pain.

He paused, breathing deeply, *in* – one – two – three, *out* – one – two – three. He had suddenly remembered the torture of spiders, witnessed in remote childhood, when boys too fearsome to challenge, armed with magnifying glasses, subjected them to slow combustion by intensified sunlight. Slowly those tortured creatures smoked into ash. In silence. But if they had been able to make any sound at all, he thought, it would have been like that, a shrilling that got louder with the heat . . . Birdsong too, by that time the valleys of the Moletta were showing fresh green. Thrushes, some kind of pipit. Tentative, desultory song, more like the birds of home. But the nightingale was the bird of the Wadi country. It sang in the light and the dark, through all the fighting, in a bubbling melody that had no register for violence, an incessant, demented chorus. Hateful in the end. The bubbling voice of wounds. The sense of something beautiful betrayed and made mad.

He was on his back now, arms outstretched, grasping his weights. Forty years on, still trying to keep death at bay, still with lumps of metal in my hands. He brought his arms up slowly till the weights touched, lowered them again.

103

Up, one – two – three, *down*, one – two – three. He heard his regular, small grunts of exertion, felt his body brace to take the weight. The frogs too made a great din. After the rain there was a big population of them in the marsh up the gully. When they heard someone coming they stopped croaking. They were silent the night Walters died . . . Another time, another time, before that, it was still very wet, I, you, Benson, you are crawling along a gully, Walters is just behind you, he always was behind, you were the one who knew the ropes, knew the ground, your only talent. Thompson had it too. You are quite close to the platoon lines, looking for a place for a latrine. You see them first, blue-grey bundles caught in the brambles in the bankside. They had been picked over – usual flabby litter of papers, photographs around them. Litter lying in litter. Drained, waxen faces, eyes and mouths open. Their teeth looked sharp. We crawled over, checked for watches, rings, but there was nothing. Everybody stole from everybody, from the dead, from the disabled. On your own side too – wounded men were lucky to get to the field hospital still wearing a wrist-watch.

It was another day, before that, before the Show started, early in the morning, misty morning, when Thompson came crawling back with the German helmet up-ended like a begging bowl. He always had to bring something back. Deep Panzer helmet. Alone – Thompson was always on his own. Most people teamed up with someone, like Walters and me, but not Thompson. Nearest thing he had to a mate was the Signals driver. They used to play darts and drink together when we were out of the line. Scottish name. The mist was dangerous, it had rifts in it, difficult to judge the ground. And your own body always denser than you think. But Thompson knew all that, none better. He gave the helmet to Crocker.

Crocker's face streaked with blood. He daren't raise his head. He has to crouch down there to wash the blood out of his hair. The Welshman is sitting in the mud on the floor of the trench, huddled up against the wet clay wall, his head and face and body are up against the wall of the trench. Evans. Nobody can make him move. Eyes wide open, looking at the trench wall. Something went wrong with him during the night. After many similar nights. Now nobody knows what to do with him. The Sergeant put his arm round Evans's shoulders and talked to him but it didn't make any difference. He is sitting in his own shit. In the fear we knew you could clasp yourself for comfort, you could keep the heart in your breast. But Evans has gone beyond this, his body has loosened away from him. All he can do is keep close to the wall. Crocker, gross, fat-faced Crocker, middle-aged joker, takes the helmet from him, from Thompson. Give us that a minute. Flat Midlands accent. He was a builder's labourer in civilian life. He takes the helmet and puts it on. Self-appointed clown. From under the helmet his face looks alien. Loose jowls – trench life has taken the flesh off. *Jawohl*, this face says, thin lips. He crouches to make a Nazi salute. No one thinks it is funny. *Rausch rausch*. All the German he knows. He starts to creep up on poor, jellied Evans. Crocker winks at whoever will catch his eye. When he gets close enough he prods Evans with his rifle in the small of the back. *Rausch, rausch, schweinhund*. Bursting with laughter. Evans jerks like a stranded fish and his eyes are all whites. Crocker laughs and chuckles, looks around for applause. Brute. Then he gets a thoughtful look like the moment you realise the baby has peed in your lap . . .

Benson released the weights, moved his hands down to his sides and began his breathing exercises, five seconds in, five seconds hold it, five seconds out, remembering with pleasure undimmed by the years that deepening thought-fulness on Crocker's face, and then the exact sequence of his actions. He takes the helmet off, looks closely into it, throws it down. He raises his hands to his head, sandy-coloured hair. Full of fucking dust, he says. He has dust from the helmet thick in the roots of his hair. Thick dust. Too thick for dust. He scrabbles at his hair, can't get rid of the clogging stuff. He looks at his fingers, sniffs at his

105

fingers. Everyone is watching Crocker now, he has his audience at last. Everyone but Evans. It is blood. He has got the roots of his hair full of dried blood.

Breathing exercises over, he rose to his feet. He always rounded his exercises off with some running on the spot. Up-down, up-down. Three hundred times. Raising the knees higher for the last fifty, trying to keep on breathing through the nose. Crocker's face danced before him, up-down, up-down, watered blood running over the forehead into his eyes. Water was short, we were due for relief that night, that was the same night Slater spoke to me about his idea of putting on a show. Crocker had to use a billycan of drinking water to wash the blood-dust out of his hair. He couldn't put his head up over the trench – he had to do it crouching. The German's blood, reliquefied, ran down Crocker's face in a pink stream, making a cursing clown of him. Poor brute Crocker, he was killed in the break-out.

How much of this is truly remembered? he wondered. How much embroidered, how much invented? Does it matter? Memories have to be aided by invention or they could not be formulated at all. He watched his body in the red shorts, making these motions, jogging up and down. These panting breaths, this labouring memory. Servitude.

What happened next? Baxter started pontificating. Cavernous face, never smiled. Good light baritone, very good for an untrained voice. He was in the show for a while. Ballads. *Last Rose of Summer. Martha, Lovely Rose of the Wildwood.* Clean chap. Brushed his teeth every morning. Hair wet-combed. Off stage he was always laying the law down. He knew all about the intentions of the high command. He had a sidekick, forgotten his name, freckled, small, little round spectacles. I must name him, so I do – Popeye. These two, Baxter and Popeye, made up the Bren-gun unit. They always spoke in turn, Baxter leading. Something like this:

"That is not last night's blood. Never in this world. Hasn't had time to dry out since last night. Stands to reason."

106

"Hasn't had time to dry out and powder up, couldn't of humanly fucking done it, course not."

"It would of still been wet. Another thing. It's been raining, ain't it? It's been raining on and off since we come here. Am I right or am I wrong?"

"Sunny Italy."

"Well then. If that helmet had been standing wrong side up the rain would of kept the blood wet. If not, the blood would of run out before it got a chance to dry. Am I right or am I wrong?"

"You fucking cunt." That is Crocker.

"Right, mate."

"Well then. What I'm coming to is he must of fallen with his face in it, then bled in it, see what I mean? That way the rain wouldn't of been able to get in."

"He must of bled for a good long time then. You need a fair bit of blood to make that much powder. You'd need a fucking pint."

"More than that, mate. Nearer two."

Baxter wasn't in the Show for long. A limited number of appearances. In April, before it stopped raining, he got a leg blown off.

"Aren't you *sorry* for Albert?"

"He has to work out his destiny," Carter said.

"Well, I must tell you that I am. Apart from anything else, he must have a monumental balls-ache by this time." The language of literary debate between Carter and himself was degenerating, Benson was obliged to admit. After waiting some moments for the other to reply he said, "Well, let me read this to you as an illustration of what I mean. Sometimes, you know, hearing your work read aloud gives you a fresh perspective on it."

Carter nodded warily, as if he had recognised a gambit or seen a trap opening. He was less offended by criticism now than at the beginning, having apparently decided to view these sessions as contests which he could win if he could

107

manage to justify what he had written; his talent for this type of polemic was growing steadily as the quality of his prose deteriorated.

"It's on the same page, no, next page, wait a minute, here it is." Benson paused and looked at Carter, who this morning, in deference to the warmer weather, was wearing a sports jacket with a vivid pattern of yellow and green checks. "Albert has just removed Sheila's blouse and skirt. He is looking down at her. She is in her bra and panties, suspender belt, stockings. She is saying, please no, Albert. But of course words like that just bounce off Albert by this time. He is about to strip the rest of her things off. Do you remember the bit I mean?"

Carter's eye had a fugitive gleam at the recounting of these details but Benson thought he looked a bit bemused too – small wonder, with so many closely similar scenes scattered through these latter wastes of his book.

"Page 703." Benson thought suddenly of the reply made by Mephistopheles to Faust's question concerning the location of Hell: *Why, this is Hell, nor am I out of it*. In Hell times and distances were cancelled out. He had come in a finger-breadth, in a whisper, from his labouring fictions of the night, clay smell, rot smell, Crocker's streaked face, to this maze of words, the square-faced, obstinate fictioneer before him. As if I took a wrong turning in the Wadis, slithered down and found Carter squatting in the deeps, armed with his deadly green bag. "Albert was reaching out to remove her briefs," he read aloud. "Suddenly he stopped in his tracks. He was brought to a standstill, dazed, dazzled and completely taken aback by the magnitude of her whole ensemble."

He regarded Carter for some moments in silence. Then he said, "That is very imprecise, Harold. A new note is creeping in. What you seem to be doing is somehow simultaneously blurring and inflating things, so we are not really clear what Albert is after. Are we to understand something transcendent? The Promised Land? The gate to the rose garden? The flight of the soul? Are you saying there is something more to it than just getting between Sheila's legs? I don't mean he doesn't respect her and so on," he added hastily. "I know he does."

Carter settled back in his chair. "It is a variety of the quest novel," he said. "Wayne Booth, in his *Rhetoric of Fiction*—"

"I know the book you mean. Tell me, these odd jobs Albert is always doing for her, tightening up the washers on her taps, for example, polyfillering her cracks, plastering her sitting-room recess and so on, I've been meaning to ask you whether that is a system of sexual symbols, based on the notion of Freudian transference, whereby you set out to satirise the fact that we live in a ruttish age?"

Long before reaching the end of this sentence he was deeply sorry he had begun it. In his haste to forestall a disquisition on Wayne Booth he had said the first thing that came to his head. Carter was looking at him in surprise and some indignation. This is one below the belt, he seemed to be saying. "Albert is good with his hands," he said after some moments of pause.

"But he isn't terribly, is he? Not when it comes to Sheila anyway."

"That is the whole point." To his dismay Benson saw that Carter had made a recovery. His face was wearing again that sly, triumphant look of the small boy about to catch the teacher out. "You've missed the whole point," he said.

"Well?"

"Albert's ability at odd jobs, his dexterity as you may say with his tools, is meant to be a contrast with his uncertainty and clumsiness about feelings and relationships with the opposite sex. This is a statement about man the tool-wielding animal losing touch with his own tool, as you might say."

Carter folded his arms with the look of a man who knows he has made a palpable hit. Suddenly Benson knew that he could not go on any longer with Carter. Not money, not habit, not his intermittent compassion nor his fearful passivity could make him endure these absurd discussions any longer. Without some sort of jolt Carter would die before he finished his novel, thus condemning Albert and Sheila to an eternity of unfulfilled desire, a sort of endlessly repeated reaching for the briefs. He could not have it on his conscience.

"Harold," he said, "I think you will have to stop coming to see me."

Carter's look of triumph vanished at a stroke. "But why?" he said, and the hurt in the question and the dismay on the rough face brought a feeling of tightness to Benson's throat. Carter depended on these visits, he knew that. "I can't go on," he said. "Let me tell you a story. It's about a patient in a lunatic asylum. He was totally apathetic, he seemed to be indifferent to everything, just passed his days in a sort of stony silence. They tried to interest him in things, construction kits, model aeroplanes, weaving, painting pictures. Nothing worked. Then one day the doctor suggested that he might try to write something. He brightened up at this. 'Yes,' he said, 'as a matter of fact I've always wanted to write a novel.' 'But that is marvellous,' the doctor said, and they provided him with everything he needed, paper, pens, a quiet room with a view over the grounds. After a while the doctor asked him how he was getting on. 'I'm getting on very well,' he said. 'I shall need some more paper.' The doctor was delighted. They had given him quite a lot of paper to begin with. Now they gave him a whole lot more. 'What is your novel called?' the doctor asked him one day. 'It's called *Riding through the Desert*,' he said. 'That is a very good title,' the doctor said. 'How far have you got with it?' 'I am at page 420,' the man said. 'Surely it must be nearly finished by now?' 'No,' the man said, 'I'm barely half way through. I'm going to need some more paper.' So they gave him a few hundred sheets more. Finally the man came to the doctor with his manuscript. It was over 800 pages by this time. 'I've finished it,' he said. 'I'm really pleased to hear that,' the doctor said. 'May I read it?' The man said yes, he could read it if he wanted and so the doctor took it home with him and after supper he settled down with eager curiosity to read it. He saw that the first page consisted of *clippety-clop, clippety-clop* repeated over and over again, and as he read on he found that every page was exactly the same, covered with *clippety-clop, clippety-clop*. Then, on the very last page, right at the end, there was a change. The last two words of the novel were, *whoah there!*

He glanced at Carter, on whose face there was no expression at all. "The ride was over, you see," he said. "The man knew exactly how long it would take to ride across the desert. He had a strong sense of form, of the dynamic of his narrative – and that includes, it must include, the sense of an ending. Now if you want to go on writing clippety-clop for the rest of your days, Harold, I can't stop you, and it may even be what you need, but I don't feel I can assist in it any longer. I'd like you to think this over very carefully."

There was a long silence. It was clear from Carter's face that he was hurt and offended. He began to put Sheila and Albert slowly back into his green bag. He stood up to go. At the door, however, he rallied. Some flicker of controversy, the final desire to score a point, returned to his face. "It doesn't add up," he said. "If he was riding across the desert, the hoofbeats would be muffled. There wouldn't be any clippety-clop."

At this moment, possibly the last in their professional relationship, Benson felt more sympathy for Carter than he perhaps had ever felt. Prose-mangler, Thatcher-lover, tormentor of his own creatures, it nevertheless had to be admitted that he had spirit. Benson smiled at him with genuine affection. "That is true," he said. "There's a fault in verisimilitude there and you have put your finger on it. But the man was mad, don't forget."

"But why Banana Split?"

"I don't know, really. Probably some sinister resonance from my childhood. It has a snarling menace about it, don't

111

you think? I carried it around with me, like a sort of verbal talisman or magic formula to keep off evil, or in this case grievous bodily harm."

I'm talking too much, he thought. He was nervous. Alma's face was only three feet away in the quietness of this noontime pub. There are faces that disappoint on a second encounter but hers was not one of them, not for him. The glitter of the eyes, the tenderness and bitterness of the mouth, the abrupt, impatient movements, were enhanced rather, making his memory of them seem poor. He wanted her to like him.

"Well," she said after a moment, "it doesn't seem to have worked on this occasion."

"Oh, I don't know. I thought at first it had been a failure, just another example of the mildewed Logos. As if I needed examples of that. I know more about loss of word power than almost anybody." He paused on the brink. Mustn't start boring her with my block. "No," he continued, "when I thought about it afterwards I realised that it had worked, in a way. They were about to start on me when I said it. They must have thought, you know, that I was making some filthy proposition. They were outraged, they were shocked that someone about to be bashed would have the invincible lechery to suggest an evil perversion."

Alma smiled. It was the first time he had seen her do this and the effect on him was considerable. That drawn look of the mouth in repose gave the smile when it came a look of elemental joy about it.

"So," she said, "in the first shock—"

"They relaxed their grip, just enough for me to break away." He said nothing about the undignified sprint down the alley. There were limits to confidence after all. "Like another drink?" he said.

"My turn."

When she came back from the bar the smile was there no longer. "It's no wonder," she said as she sat down, "that you've got these disaffected young people, when you think of the damage to the social fabric of this country that woman

112

and her junta of yes-men have done in two terms of office."

"Disaffected young people?" It seemed an odd way of describing the youths that had ringed him round the other evening, whether they'd had the proper chances in life or not. "If you were one of my fictioneers," he said, "I would take you to task for a phrase like that."

"Who are they?"

"Some people I help with their writing."

"Well I'm not, thank God. There's too much fiction in the world already, just look at the newspapers. What's wrong with it, anyway?"

"It does what language shouldn't do. It is tendentious. It tries to make those thugs look better for the sake of making the government look worse. You can't really think that a readiness to batter unoffending strangers half to death has been brought about by two terms of Tory rule?"

"I'm quite ready to batter the Home Secretary half to death, or the Minister for Health and Social Security, and they're both complete strangers to me. Of course they're not unoffending. I suppose you're right, one must be even-handed. I'd be willing to admit that those thugs in the Cabinet are no more than disaffected middle-aged or elderly persons, victims of narrow education, moral under-nourishment and a deprived imagination, or perhaps I mean depraved. That satisfy you?"

The smile was there again but it was different now, tauter, combative – it was the mouth that gave instant register to changes of feeling on this face, the brightness of the eyes was unchanging. Accident of physiognomy, the eyes, he thought. Some capacity for holding more light than was normal . . .

"You take a reasonable line, don't you?" she said. "I've got you down for an Alliance voter."

It was as close as she probably ever allowed herself to come to a sneer. Benson felt his blood quicken. She was waiting with something of the air of a prosecution lawyer but he would not let himself be cross-examined for his political views – or lack of them. Attempting to explain oneself gave up too much ground, it was bad tactics – he would need tactics, he suddenly saw, if he wanted to keep on with Alma. He would have to contest the space. Doctrinaire, foe to metaphor, impatient of the delicate middle ground of doubt on which all fiction depends – what kind of muse was this?

He leaned towards her with a contrite expression. "It's not only that, I'm afraid," he said. "I'm fond of opera too."

He saw the belligerence leave her face. Quite suddenly she laughed. "Yes," she said, "you have a penchant for owls too, haven't you?"

"I don't aspire to albatrosses." Should he tell her about his sacrificial fire, his invocation? No, better she should feel her body desired than her spirit – and perhaps that was the truth of it anyway. "There was one, you know," he said.

"Was there?" She looked away for some moments, glancing through the window at the street outside. The bar door was open and sunlight from this warm May morning fell in a broad shaft half across their table. "All the same," she said, "there is a generation growing up in the rubble of the inner cities that has known nothing but Thatcherism. Think of what it has done to them. Now we are in for another four years of it. People don't know, they don't know what has been done to Liverpool. I'd like to bring people up in bus-loads from the Home Counties and take them around Toxteth on a guided tour, show them the realities of this property-owning democracy of ours."

"Yes," he said, "it is appalling what has been allowed to happen here."

"*Allowed to happen?* They have brought it about, it's the direct result of Conservative policies."

Benson felt oppressed: she allowed no space for difference, vagueness. It was assent she wanted, instant, total. At the same time the words seemed to come to her unexamined, too easily.

"Well," he said, "I am older than you and more cynical, I suppose. What is happening here seems to me to be because no one has cared enough, no one with the means of change

114

has been capable of caring enough, none of the parties. When you look at the sum of folly and misery in Liverpool and on this planet as a whole, when you see how far things have gone, people who put the blame on a particular system seem like solemn lunatics to me, whether they do it at Westminster or at City Hall – or here in the Cambridge Arms, for that matter. This place is rotting from the heart while people argue about priorities."

"Where is that?"

"What?"

"This heart you are talking about?"

"I was thinking of Toxteth, of inner-city decay generally."

"I don't know how it is," she said after a moment, "but some things seem to come from you too easily, as if the words were more important than the thing you are describing. I get the same feeling I had before about you, as if the whole thing is there just to provide a metaphor. Toxteth isn't the heart of Liverpool. It's just a ghetto."

Benson took a swallow of his beer. It was what he had been mentally accusing her of some minutes before. "All right," he said, waving his glass as if to give her the platform.

"The North of England is full of ghettoes. You don't need walls, people are kept there by poverty and illness. Do you know what the life expectation is in places like that, compared to the national average? The incidence of chronic illness caused by sub-standard housing, the figures for mental disturbance, break-down, suicide? They've been trying to suppress the medical reports for years on one pretext or another. Not that it would matter if they shouted them from the roof tops. There's nothing left to shock in the conscience of this country or that gang would never have been voted back in again."

Her voice had softened as she spoke, her whole manner grown less combative. It was with the vehemence of what she was saying, he realised suddenly, something that happened to him quite often. The last shreds of his resentment at her dogmatism were dissolved. He said, "In the sense you mean, the heart of this city is where the heart of a city always is, where the capital is managed. That goes on pumping away whatever happens in Liverpool 8. But that heart is ramiform – you can't locate it."

"Ramiform, that's a good word." With a sort of awed fascination he saw her mouth draw down into a taut line, the whole face harden into an expression of passionate violence. "If you could locate it, we would have torn it out long ago," she said.

"Metaphor is an instrument of truth too," he said slowly. "A good one is worth a lot of doctrine. It was with a metaphor that you defended me, that evening when we met."

"How did I defend you?"

"You remember, I was talking about the man I had seen jump from the top of a tower block. I was making it into a story, which I shouldn't have done. I got a bit excited and I spilled some of Morton's beer. He said something that made me feel a fool."

"Oh, that." She made the sudden movement of the head he liked so much, impatient, defiant, proud – he could not quite have said which. "Ben Morton is a lightweight character."

A certain silence followed upon this, one of those pauses that lengthen when no appropriate response is found. Benson looked at the broad shaft of sunlight streaming in through the open door. It lay across their table, shone on the brass handrail of the bar, on the head of the landlord as he leaned over his paper, gleamed on the bottles suspended behind him, upended, like vessels in some complicated life-support system. Did she mean she would have taken anyone's part against Morton? And he himself, how did she rate him as a contender? On her scales he would probably weigh in as a bantam; useless at any weight as he didn't really believe in fighting. She did, it seemed; but fighting, actual warfare, was practically the only area of experience, apart from male orgasm, that she couldn't make equal claim to. She wouldn't be interested in heroics. But it was not heroics that he now suddenly and urgently wanted to talk to her about.

"I saw a man in the street the other night," he said, not quite looking at her. "That same night, the night of the Banana Split. Someone I was in the war with. I was in the last war, you know."

"Which one was that? Chad, the Lebanon, Afghanistan, the Persian Gulf?"

"I'm talking about the Second World War," he said steadily. "That was the last war for me. I only saw action for a few months of 1944. I was in the Anzio landing, the fighting of that winter to establish the Beachhead, then the break-out on May 22. I was wounded during the break-out and spent the next three weeks in hospital in Naples. By the time I was fit again we had taken Rome and I stayed behind there in an office job. That was the end of the fighting for me."

"Is that how you got the scar on your face?"

"Yes. I got a bigger piece in my thigh. I was lucky not to lose a leg like poor Baxter."

"Who was he?"

"One of the others. He was always laying the law down. Most of the wounds were from shrapnel, you know. Grenades, mortars. Both sides used air-burst shells. And mines of course."

Alma was silent for a moment, then she said, "Did you say May 22? That's the day I was born, the night rather. May 22, 1944."

"During the night?" He looked at her in wonder: her birth cries might have coincided with his wounds; two voices, one blended sound. "That is extraordinary," he said.

"Perhaps it is." The remarkable smile lit up her face again. "One or two other people might have been born that night too, you know."

"He was singing," Benson said. "Singing in the street. Begging. It seemed strange because he used to sing in this

117

show some of us were in, run by a man called Slater, Second-Lieutenant Slater. We put on a show during those months of the stalemate, while they were building up for the attack. There were a lot of men there and almost no women. People were bored, a lot of the time. The show was a great success. Slater made it a success."

"What did you do in it?"

"I was one half of a double act. Song and dance. The other half was a man called Walters."

He paused on the name. Now he had come to it he was afraid he wouldn't be able to control his voice. There were other risks too: he knew that if she mocked him or became sarcastic he would get up and leave and that would be that.

"In conditions like that," he said, "you form strong links with people, either of liking or disliking. Conditions of fighting, I mean. It was very difficult ground and the positions were always shifting – not very much but enough to make things uncertain. Walters and I always went out together. We were a double act at the front too. We were what you would call inseparable. He was very funny, you know, quick to see a joke. He was a good mimic too – he could take people off, other people in the platoon, various officers. It was an extraordinary friendship in some ways. We came from quite dissimilar backgrounds. His parents were working people. He had left school at fifteen and gone to work in a bank – he was a bank clerk in civilian life. I had grown up in a Norfolk vicarage, been to boarding school and so on. But it didn't matter."

He paused for a moment or two, then he said, "I suppose I loved Walters."

He stopped again and waited, looking not at her but at the table between them, their almost empty glasses. If this was tedious or in some way distasteful she could make an excuse to leave, she could change the subject. But she did neither. Glancing up he saw that her eyes were fixed on him, not discernibly sympathetic, but intent. "I wouldn't have expressed it like that at the time," he said. "Free use of that word is the licence of age. It was a very possessive feeling. I was an only child, you know, and I had never had a close friend. I was jealous if he seemed to be getting on well with other people. I wanted to keep him with me. I had one strong advantage, which was a very highly developed sense of direction and the kind of visual memory that makes a print on the mind of landmarks, details of ground. I had sharp senses too, hearing, smell. Still have, as a matter of fact, though my eyes are going now. In the Wadis – that was what we called this part of the front – that sort of thing was very important. It was a kind of labyrinth, you see. I used to line things up, a barn with the door hanging off, a heap of rubble of a particular shape, a shattered tree stump. Even down in the stream beds, thirty feet below ground . . . No features look exactly alike if you look hard at them, and I did. I always knew where I was. Nearly always. I navigated by a system of signs, pointers – almost like a private language of symbols. I find myself doing the same thing now when I am walking around."

He drank the rest of his beer. "Not much of an accomplishment," he said, "but it was useful there. Like another drink?"

"No thanks. I'll have to be leaving in a few minutes. Do go on."

"You're sure I'm not boring you?"

"I'd let you know if you were."

He nodded. The question had been merely a reflex of politeness; he was intent in his story now. "Thompson had it too," he said. "That's the man I saw the other night. He used it differently. I just wanted to survive. Some people, quite a few actually, were without it completely. Walters was one of them. On his own he was liable to go astray, and that could be fatal. He followed me – I always went in front. He trusted me completely. One night we had gone out to recover some ammunition. We were short of Browning ammunition and there was a stack of it in a position we had recently abandoned, a forward observation post, as they were called. It was up a gully near a bridge. The ground near the bridge was marshy. After the rain there was a

119

population of frogs there. They kept up a chorus of croaking, quite loud, but they always fell silent if there was anyone about. There were three of us, me, Walters and a corporal, a man named Peters. He was in charge really but I led the way. I always went first. We had blacked our faces and hands but there was a moon, we knew we could be seen. We came round a bend and saw the arch of the bridge perhaps twenty-five yards away, quite clear in the moonlight. The frogs were absolutely silent. I stopped – I was afraid to go on. The others stopped behind me. As soon as we stopped we heard a rattle of bolts in front of us and a shout and the Spandaus opened up. They had been waiting until we got as near as possible. I could see the traces of the bullets going by me and I could see the flames from the barrels of the guns. By some miracle none of us was hit. There was a channel, a sort of shallow ditch going off the stream bed, and we got into it in time and started crawling back. We had to make a number of detours – we didn't dare show ourselves above ground. We got into a narrow gully about eight or ten feet deep. I knew we were going in the right direction for our platoon position but I didn't recognise this gully. At least, I wasn't absolutely sure. Moonlight is deceptive and there had been no time to take bearings. This was an area we had mined ourselves but there were tracks through it, all of which I thought I knew. We had an argument. Peters said this wasn't the right track, we should make a wider detour so as to be sure of it. He was frightened. We all were. I saw that Walters was listening to Peters. I said I was certain it was the right track and I started off down it. Walters followed me and then Peters. After I had taken about twenty steps everything went up in a sheet of flame. I felt a tremendous punch on the back of my neck. I was thrown forward onto my hands and knees. For a while I couldn't see or hear anything. Then I heard moaning sounds. I turned round and I saw Walters lying with his knees drawn up. It was he who was making the noises. I tried to lift him. Then I saw that the middle part of his body had been blown away. I took his head in my hands and he

120

stopped moaning. Then, after a few seconds, he made a single sound which I can't describe and I knew he had died. Peters led the way back, inch by inch, prodding the ground with his bayonet. He wouldn't speak to me. He never spoke to me after that.''

Just another story, he thought, trying to shift some impediment in his throat. I'm always telling stories of one sort or of another. "Walters's body wasn't recovered," he said. "The unit that relieved us poured creosote over the corpses to keep down the smell. Of course, I didn't need Thompson to help me remember all this. In a way I've never stopped thinking about it. But I thought, you know, he might help me to find direction somehow. In my life now, I mean. If I could line him up, the way I used to line things up in the Wadis.''

"It was the kind of mistake anyone might have made," Alma said after a long moment.

But he knew this was merely an impulse of sympathy – it could not be what she really felt. "No," he said, "I was jealous, I thought it was my only power, the only thing that kept him with me. I still think so. I tried to make the ground conform to my conception. It was an early example of my propensity for metaphor." On an impulse, to forestall any further kindness on her part, he said quickly, "A man I know called Rathbone is putting on a sort of show next Saturday evening. I've got two tickets. I don't know if you'd like to go. Oh, but it's May 22, that's your birthday, isn't it?"

"What sort of show?"

"It's a hypnotism show. It is this man's début as a stage hypnotist.''

"It's being my birthday doesn't matter." She made the abrupt movement of the head with which she seemed to accompany all apparent concessions. "I don't make much of birthdays." She glanced at her watch and stood up. "I've got to go," she said. "I've got a meeting at two. What did this Thompson say? Did he know you?"

Benson had got up too. He hesitated briefly, then he said,

"I didn't speak to him. I followed him to where he lives but I didn't speak to him. I don't seem able to take initiatives these days."

"You took one with me," she said. "Where does he live?"

"On the Railton Estate."

"But those blocks are condemned."

"There are people living in them all the same," he said. "Do you mean that you'll come on Saturday?"

I could have asked her out to dinner, he thought. Something like that. Why this wretched hypnotism show? But he had promised Rathbone.

Alma paused, considering. She was quite small, he noticed for the first time, now that they were standing close together. He was not a tall man but he was taller than she by some inches. He took, in this confused moment of hope, a rapid inventory: the vivid, small-boned face, the straight shoulders, the breasts below the thin jumper not large but definite, and obviously unconfined.

"Yes, if you like," she said. "But I wish you would go and see this Thompson first."

All the same it was Zircon the assassin that finally decided him. Elroy Palmer came to see him next day, bearing a key passage. Zircon had now penetrated into the inner sanctum of Jarrold, demented hermaphrodite ruler of Gareg, a planet stultified by too much order, where only straight lines were allowed and wheels had to be enclosed in square casing. Jarrold had just signed his own death warrant by refusing to accept Zircon's authority as imperial envoy.

Zircon laugh with a laughter inside himself. This the Assassin laugh. He is trained to do this laughter. Not a muscle of his face is moved. Out of your own mouth, Jarrold. At the same time he laughs he feels eloquent disgust for this obscene person stood there in woman's clothes, red robe with lace trimming, big blond wig all in square waves. Silver baton of power cradled in his soft white arms. Jarrold, your time has come. Not because he dress as a woman, people can dress how they like. But he is an obscene tyrant.

122

*Zircon works the blade down from its pouch in his armpit. No
scanning device known on Gareg can detect this knife. His eyes
flicker to Bender on the right. Bender going to take care of the
guards. In his palm now. This knife will fly at speed of light,
aimed by the impulses of Zircon's brain. He is trained for this
work. He perform again that inside laughter as he seeks out with
his eyes the target vein on Jarrold's neck. That laughter part of the
killing, works up power for the knife. Now good-bye, Jarrold.
The days are accomplished. Now this knife restore the world of
forms, flow of life comes with his death blood.*

Benson considered this for some moments. There were
the usual vagaries of grammar and syntax but this was
Elroy's language and it worked effectively in subverting an
over-regulated planet. He wasn't sure about eloquent disgust and suspected that Elroy had put the adjective in
because he liked the sound of it, which was something he
did quite often – it added a certain mysterious charm to his
work. And he wasn't convinced that Zircon could have got
an audience with Jarrold without being subjected to a body
search. All the same . . .

"Elroy," he said, "this has power. Making the maniac for
geometrical form himself soft and indeterminate is a
masterstroke. I congratulate you."

Elroy looked back at him seriously and nodded but did
not speak.

"He does actually kill Jarrold, I suppose?" The death was
not yet described and Benson had the fear still that Zircon
would get blocked with his own murderous mirth, trapped
for ever in a soundless paroxysm, eyeing the tyrant's
jugular in that room of square-faced sycophants.

"He dies in the next paragraph." As always Elroy spoke
as if the decision had been made elsewhere.

"I'm delighted to hear it. There is one point that occurs to
me. Don't you think it would be better if the weapon that
puts an end to Jarrold were curved somehow? A
boomerang, say, made out of the same undetectable metal,
or a scimitar or a razor-sharp disc? The symbolic shape of
liberation, see what I mean?"

"They talked a lot about it on Vekrona before Zircon set off," Elroy said. Vekrona was the ruling planet of the Confederation. "They understood it had to be the right symbol. They know about symbols on Vekrona. Zircon can kill in any way, he is a trained man. But Jarrold sentenced to die by his own excesses. He is killed by what he loves too much."

"Killed by what he loves too much," Benson repeated slowly. He looked at Elroy with a sort of wonder and Elroy looked back with the placid watchfulness which was all his own. Everything about him was the same: dreadlocks, earring, voluminous red hat; the full, slightly everted mouth was set in the same firm mould; the eyes in their boney sockets were heedless, really, of anything he might say, but without insolence. Benson looked down again at the last words of the paragraph: *flow of life comes with his death blood*. The sign was there. It was not simple but it was there.

He had, almost from the beginning, looked for certain kinds of indications in the productions of his Fictioneers. Relations with them might vary but were always intimate, with something of the intimacy of the confessional; he had thought it possible that threads of vital communication might creep into the texture of what they wrote, pointers, something that might show the way forward.

On the whole he had been disappointed in this. Poor Hogan was burrowing backwards all the time and looked like ending up as some more primitive form of life altogether. Anthea's poems had a certain shock value but they certainly didn't prompt anything in him. It was true that Albert and Sheila had affected him in various ways, but none of them constructive. In any case these two seemed trapped in an endless cycle now – the only imminent prospect in *Can Spring Be Far Behind?* was a broken spring in Sheila's sofa. As for Madcap Maggie and the saturnine Sir Reginald, they were riding ever deeper into the wildwood, side by side, oaks and anachronisms thickening around them. Not much hope of daylight there.

124

Zircon was a different matter entirely. Zircon redeemed them all. Here was a man in the remote future, bubbling with lethal laughter, about to act, to break out, to restore the world.

"Elroy," he said, "I've just decided something. Several things in fact. One of them is that I am going to give up my consultancy business, I'm going to disband my Fictioneers. Clive Benson's name comes down from the door. But I'll go on with you if you're willing. I'll give you any help I can." He smiled at the serious Elroy. "I would regard it as an honour," he said.

PART THREE

Reunions

1

Benson had felt sure he would be there, in the same place, going through the same motions, four paces forward, four paces back, dragging one leg, singing his lugubrious hymns. Armed with a bottle of Scotch he had made his way there at the same time of evening, hoping to contrive a meeting somehow – it would look more natural than going knocking on his door.

But Thompson was nowhere to be seen in the vicinity of Central Station, nor was he in the pedestrian precincts around Church Street, where street musicians sometimes performed. He wasn't down at the Pier Head either, flaunting his crippledom and his crimson mark by the waters of the Mersey. He wasn't in any of the places where Benson thought of looking for him. It was after eleven when he gave up the search. He knew he couldn't go home that night without finding Thompson, speaking to him.

He caught a bus to the end of Catherine Street, then followed the exact route Thompson had taken, entering the darkness of the waste ground, feeling under his feet the crunch of broken masonry from old demolitions. The route was printed on his mind in every detail, the exact sequence of ruinous shop fronts in the silent street, commercial dreams long dead. Beyond this there was open ground again, site of more recent demolitions, enclosed on three sides by the blank walls of houses still partially standing. All had been silent and deserted here on the night he had followed Thompson; but now a fire of ripped-up planks was burning in one corner and there were three men and a woman sitting round it on the ground, looking like a picket, he thought – but there was nothing here to guard or defend. Two thin black dogs lay close together against a wall; he could see their sleeping muzzles in the firelight.

He had paused in the shadow of the wall on the corner farthest from the fire. He would have to pass close by it to reach the way through, a narrow passage between the crumbling, half-demolished houses. Normally he might have felt an impulse to join these people, talk to them. Now he wanted only Thompson. He saw one of the men raise a bottle and drink. There was a leap of flame and the woman's face was lit up by it, ravaged and loose-mouthed.

The fire leapt again and there was a smell of burning tar. In the light of the flames he could see the vegetation of the waste ground, grass sharp with spring, blueish unopened flower-balls of thistles, clumps of dock, the whole expanse clotted with scraps of rag and paper and a wind-drifted refuse of plastic. In the reddish, deceiving light of the fire this litter looked like a crop, like flowers. Across from him, beyond the leap of the flames, the street continued, met another at right angles. He saw people pass, blurred slightly by ripples of heat from the fire, a tall, shambling negro, a woman in an apron, further figures beyond, hard to make out. They seemed to Benson to be moving very slowly as if dazed or stricken in some way. All the life was in or near the fire, with the voices and faces round it, the leaping energy of the flames themselves. He was starting towards it when he saw Thompson, unmistakable in his cap and outsize overcoat, move slowly through the heat blur, pass without looking at anyone between the fire and the wall. Benson saw the birthmark like a shadow on his face, saw the movement of his shadow on the wall behind. Then he had disappeared down the opening between the houses.

Benson followed at once. He felt no surprise. The woman spoke to him as he passed and one of the men laughed but he paid no attention. Thompson was not in sight when he emerged but he knew the way. He went through the sets of bollards, the railed gates, across the crunching courtyards of the estate. No baby cried tonight but there were lighted windows and he heard quarrelling voices from an upper floor.

No light showed from Thompson's windows. Benson went down the steps without a pause – delay would create suspicion, it must not seem to Thompson that he had been tracked down, but seen and recognised just now in the street. However, at the foot of the steps he stood still for some moments in the darkness, gathering himself together. His heart had quickened. The bottle of Scotch in his coat pocket, his only credential, swung heavily against his side. Debris of some kind, indistinguishable in the dimness, had gathered round the doorstep and along the narrow entry. There was no bell or knocker – he used his knuckles against the peeling wood. Through cracked panels of frosted glass in the upper part of the door he saw a dim light appear inside, saw a shadowy form approach down the passage. For some fumbling moments Thompson loomed against the glass. Then the door was opened and he stood there, still in cap and overcoat, two steps above.

The light was behind him so that his face was in shadow still; there was nothing to be seen of the birthmark but a greater darkness there on the left cheek. Benson's face was in the light, naked, upturned: and Thompson, it was immediately clear, didn't know him.

"Yeh?" he said. Then after a moment, when Benson didn't answer, "What you want, mate?" The voice was chesty, clogged somehow; and in it there was already a rising tone of suspicion or belligerence, tone of the wretched, who have much to fear.

"You don't recognise me," Benson said. "Do you remember someone called Benson? We were together in the war."

There was a smell from inside, a fetid compound of odours not immediately identifiable. Benson heard or thought he heard a brief phrase of birdsong. "Benson," he repeated, smiling. The lonely announcement of identity, here on the step, was painful to him. This was it then, the shape the years had pressed out.

"Benson? No Benson here, mate. It's the bloke was here before you want to see." He was beginning to close the door.

"No, no, I am Benson. You're Thompson, aren't you? C-Company, Second Royal Wiltshires. We were in the same platoon. We were at Anzio together." He brought the bottle out of his pocket and held it up. "I thought we might have a drink on it," he said. "You know, old times."

"Anzio," Thompson said. His eye was on the bottle. "How'd you know where to find me?"

"I saw you just now. Outside in the street. I recognised you."

Thompson looked at him for some moments in silence. He did not ask how he had been recognised. From somewhere above them came a sudden blare of music as if a radio had been turned up. "Them blacks," Thompson said. "That's a bleeding lifetime ago. There *was* a Benson. Digger, they called him."

Bleeding deathtime ago, Benson thought, veteran word-smith, standing there on the step, holding up his bottle. He had never to his knowledge been called Digger. "You've got a good memory," he said.

"Some things you remember." Thompson opened the door wider and stepped back. "Always digging, you was. You better come in. You go first, I got to see to the door. Mind the bird." He was fumbling with a block of wood nailed against the door to act as a bolt. "People round here is thieves," he said.

In the narrow lobby there was a wire cage on the floor with a goldfinch in it. Unsteady light was coming from an open door beyond this. Benson walked past the cage into a small bare room where an oil lamp inside a globe of milk-coloured glass gave tremulous light. There was an ancient, cylindrical paraffin stove which had just been lit – he could smell the heating metal and see the coil of blue flame through the blistered celluloid panel. Near the wall stood a wooden hutch with a big grey-blue rabbit in it, pressing an inquisitive nose against the wire mesh. Not much else: bare boards of the floor, two upturned boxes, one with a tin kettle and white china mug on it, a slashed, half-gutted black sofa, listing on one side where the casters had come off, a heap of bedding in one corner. Thompson's abode. Everywhere on the walls were the mottled stains of damp, fluent bruises on the original pale green of the paint. The floor was gritty with plaster dust, he could feel the slight crunch of it under his feet. Glancing up he saw a flaking delta of fissures in the ceiling. There were long vertical gashes on the walls too, from which the plaster had leaked. Behind him came the slow shuffle of Thompson's step.

"I got to find a place to put that bird," Thompson said, in his laborious, impeded voice. "They like to be higher. Keep your coat on till it warms up. It takes a bit of time to get warm in here, that's one of the drawbacks."

"That's a fine rabbit," Benson said.

"That's Brenda."

In response to their combined regard, Brenda flattened her handsomely fringed ears and stared back with pensive eyes through the mesh of her cage. She wrinkled her nostrils delicately, as if investigating Benson's aura. A smell of pissy sawdust came from her hutch.

"Pedigree chinchilla," Thompson said. "I know where I could get twenty-five quid for that rabbit. Now. Tonight. Cash. Trouble is I only got one article here that a peson could drink out of. I been travelling light."

"I can drink from the bottle." He had placed this on one of the upturned boxes and busied himself now unscrewing the top, pouring some out into the chipped white mug. When he turned round again he had the brief impression that a stranger had entered the room and was sitting on the sofa; then he realised that it was Thompson without his cap. The other man's face was fully revealed in the lamp light; and on it, with total certainty, Benson saw the print of death.

Perception is a leaping thing and the gatherings of the leap are always obscure. It seemed now to Benson that he had heard death in that palsied singing, that he had sensed it while he followed Thompson's slow steps back here to his lair, that the knowledge had informed the memories of

133

these recent days and nights. It was in confirmation, not in any doubt, that he registered the sunken, colourless eyes under the fair brows, the narrow mouth, the drained pallor of the skin, the incongruous splash of colour on the cheek. Thompson's small, neat skull was more evident, clearer in shape now that the hair was so sparse – his scalp showed through dead white. The eyes that looked at Benson were bemused and fierce, eyes of an animal unable to understand its own ruin.

Nothing was sure on this face except the imminence of its dissolution; this larger truth swamped the piecemeal operation of memory, made even familiar features questionable, even the birthmark; but Benson remembered suddenly now the delicacy of skin that Thompson had possessed and the undefended eyes with their short lashes – he had suffered in the hot sunshine of that May, before the offensive.

"Well, cheers, mate," Thompson said. "It's a small world."

"Cheers." It seemed at that moment a very large one that could contain them both. He did not know what to say to Thompson. It was hot in the room now but the other still kept on his coat. Benson slipped off his own coat and laid it folded on the dusty floor beside the box on which he was sitting. The smell was intensifying with the heat, a compound reek of damp-soft plaster, sodden sawdust from the rabbit's cage, acrid odours from the bedding and from the folds of Thompson's person. With a curiosity intense but strangely limited, physical, he watched the brief convulsion of the other's throat as he drank. That death on his face gave him dominance, made all his actions momentous: it was with a sense of breaking free that Benson raised the bottle. "Happy landings," he said.

"Them was the days." Thompson took another drink. His mouth made a thin smile and his head shuddered slightly. "Them was the days all right. Smoke?" He had taken out a tin in which were some hand-rolled cigarettes.

"No thanks. I don't smoke very often." He was pretty sure Thompson's cigarettes had been made up from butt-

134

ends gathered in the street.

"Them was the frigging days all right," Thompson said. "How did you know I was here?"

He saw that Thompson was peering closely at him through the smoke of the cigarette. In the silence he could hear the goldfinch moving in its cage outside. "I didn't," he said. "I told you, I passed you just now in the street, I recognised you by—"

"An accident, that's what you're saying. You knew me by this." He touched his cheek for a second. Without speaking he held out his mug for more whisky. He was drinking fast. "You live round here then?" He said.

"Greville Street."

"Where's that?"

"Off Hardman Street, not far from the Philharmonic."

"That's bleeding miles away. What you doing down here?"

"Just walking."

"Just walking," Thompson repeated slowly. "It's midnight, you got a full bottle of whisky in your pocket, you see me in the street and you know me by this." Again he raised a hand to his cheek. "That's what you're saying."

"That's right."

Thompson's mouth stretched in a brief smile, exposing yellow, strong-looking teeth. "Funny how things come together," he said. "You can go for years, nothing happens. You wasn't sent, I suppose?"

"What do you mean?"

"Nah, 'course not." Thompson was silent for a moment. Then he said in a different tone, "Digger Benson, that was it. You was always digging. Still at it, ain't you?"

"I was never called Digger, you know – I meant to tell you." Benson had begun to feel uneasy. The drink was effecting a change in Thompson's manner but the nature of the change seemed caused by something else; it was as if Thompson thought they shared some knowledge that was not from the past, not from the war. "No," he said, "I think you're mixing me up with someone else. Of course, it's a long time ago now. No, I was Velma." He met Thompson's strange stare, lingering, confused and fierce. "Velma, the Beachhead Vamp," he said. "You must remember that. I did a song and dance act with a man called Walters. He was Burlington Bertie. *Every Little Movement Tells a Tale* – that was the song we did. Don't you remember?"

"Course I bloody remember."

There was a snarl in this, a quarrelsome note – he had not liked being contradicted over the nickname. Benson remained silent for some moments. He thought of leaving. It would be a relief to get out into the open, escape from the squalor of the place, the fetid smells, the look of death on Thompson's face. But he could not leave with nothing, could not return home with nothing . . . "Slater's Show," he said.

"You a friend of his?"

Benson looked back in silence, at a loss how to answer. A musical rasp came from the hutch against the wall: Brenda had put her forelegs up against the taut mesh. "I haven't seen him since those days," he said. "He came to see me in the hospital after I was wounded."

Thompson nodded slowly. The whisky had brought traces of colour to his cheeks. "If it was my own place," he said, "I could have a few ideas about it. If I could get a bit of capital together, know what I mean?" He looked round the small room with its mess of plaster on the floor, the cracked and crumbling ceiling, the mottled bruises of damp, the gashed walls. "Bit of a sweep-out," he said. "Coat of paint. Works wonders. Bit of nice pinewood furniture. I could make this place into a home from home. You get sick of moving around. Besides, there is the animals. I got to get the animals together. I got a prize-winning hamster being looked after for me in Leeds. I got two budgies in Hudders-field. I can do without the electric and the gas, that's no problem. But I got to have some capital."

He was silent for a while and the wheeze of his breath was audible in the room. "No bleeding choice, anyway," he said at last.

"Why? Have the services been cut off?"

"Cut off? Jesus Christ. They never been on, not while I been here. I'm not talking about the *services*, for Chrissake, I'm talking about the metalwork, the pipes." He held out the mug for more whisky. The bottle was half-empty now and Thompson had accounted for the greater part of it. The effects showed in his thicker speech, in the greater openness of his contempt, oddly at variance with the vagueness, the bafflement, that would now and again come to his face. Benson remembered it now, this contempt. It had survived the ruin of the years. Contempt had kept Thompson solitary in the Wadis, not only the desire for loot.

"What pipes?" he said.

"Jesus Christ. They broke in here, didn't they? They knocked the boards out and come in through the window. Broad daylight. They took everything, all the metal. There was a bit of lead piping through there, they took it." He nodded in the direction of a door near Brenda's hutch. "They took the taps, they took out the water pipes for the copper. They took the wiring out the walls." He looked round the room slowly, in pallid and furious outrage. "They stripped the place," he said. "I don't know what this country is coming to. You would think there would be such a thing as neighbours, fucking solidarity in a place like this, people living here ain't got much, but no, all the empty flats in this block been done. They would take the bread out of your mouth. I come back here to find the place stripped. An old man like me. How old are you?"

"Sixty-three."

"I'm sixty-eight. You come back to find not one bit of metal in the place."

Thompson's eyes had lost focus now but his face still wore that expression of angry bafflement as he looked round his devastated room. "Neat job," he said. "They didn't do no unnecessary damage. They didn't touch me rabbit or me bird. But that's not the bleeding point, is it? I got to get a kettle of water from upstairs if I want to brew up." He paused, then said with sudden rage, "A hundred quid, he wouldn't feel it. They owe us the money. I'm going soon as I feel a bit better. Haven't been feeling well lately, everything I do makes me breathe heavy. It's no bloody good sending people with whisky."

"What do you mean?"

"We done our bit, that's what I bloody mean."

You did more, Benson thought, remembering the solitary expeditions, the trophies, the stain of ecstasy on the battledress trousers. "Nobody sent me," he said slowly. They are the same, he had to remind himself, that distant killer and this dying man in whom the drink seemed to have intensified some mania.

"Business good, is it?"

It took Benson some moments to realise that this was Thompson's way of asking him about his life. "Yes," he said, "I suppose so." One could hardly complain of poverty or neglect to a man living like a rat in a hole.

"What line are you in?"

"I'm a writer, a novelist – historical fiction mainly. Haven't done much lately as a matter of fact. Bit of a block, you know."

"Block?" Thompson said. "Novelist?"

"Yes, but as I say, lately—"

"Done pretty well for yourself, have you?" There was doubt in this. At some point Thompson had registered the well-worn sports jacket, vaguely oatmeal in colour, the far from pristine cotton trousers, the scuffed suede shoes.

"Not particularly." Benson shrugged. "I've never made much money."

"I know what you mean, mate."

It was the note to start him, like a tuning-fork. In wheezing tones, with frequent pauses, he began to relate his career. This was a confused story and difficult to follow because Thompson himself did not seem sure of the order of events. There were quarrels and divisions in it, wanderings, blows of fortune. No talk of wife or children. He had stayed on in Germany after the war, worked in a club in the

138

Allied Zone, a period of affluence this. After that he had gone back to the army, fought in Malaya. There had been a period as an assistant in a shoe-shop in Peterborough, various jobs in hotel kitchens, a woman named Bella who had let him down badly, God help her if he met up with her again, a rifle-range on the Pleasure Beach at Blackpool, lengthening periods of unemployment, a confused story of a pet-shop, someone who had done him out of five hundred pounds. "God help him," Thompson said, "if I meet up with him again. Now I don't even get the full fucking pension," he said. "I missed out on me stamps."

Benson nodded. These wavering lines had ended here – Thompson was back underground again. The talents he had shown in the Wadis had been no use outside. Serving drinks, carrying people's luggage in the livery of some seaside hotel, easing with his shoe-horn the passage of the soft foot into the stiff new shoe, singing with crippled gait on the corner of Bold Street – all these were assumed roles somehow, like the shifts and disguises of persons sought – or feared – in dreams. His career had been a masquerade, rendered spurious by those few months of his authentic existence, when duty had coincided with talent and pleasure with reward.

"I haven't been feeling so good lately," he said. "Do you remember them cats?"

"What cats?"

"There in the Wadis. Place was full of blind cats, the owls blinded them. You could hear them crying. I used to feel sorry for them."

"No," Benson said, "I don't remember the cats. There were dead sheep everywhere, I remember that." Both sides had used sheep as mine detectors. "And the nightingales," he said. "Singing through it all."

"They was claiming their territory." Thompson got up and replenished his mug with movements that were fumbling and unsteady. His hands were small, blunt-fingered, the backs of them covered with purplish blotches.

"Do you remember the beetle races?" Benson said. His

eyes were smarting, he had to narrow them constantly to keep Thompson in focus. "You remember," he said. "Back at B-echelon. They used to chalk out a circle and put the beetles in the middle. The winner was the one that got to the chalk line first. Crocker had a champion, used to make twenty pounds on a race, then one day this Canadian trod on it accidentally on purpose, you know, and there was a fight—"

"Crocker?"

"You remember Crocker, don't you? Remember that day he got blood in his hair? It was in that German helmet you brought back."

"There *was* a Crocker," Thompson said.

"He was killed in May, in the break-out."

"I don't remember bringing back no helmet. What would I want with a Kraut helmet?"

"Do you remember that one we shot? Well, I shot him. You know, that one we just came upon. He had got the lie of the land wrong somehow. He was sitting up there, right in the open. It was sunny, a sunny day."

He looked across at Thompson and saw nothing, no faintest shadow of recollection in the pale, dazed eyes. "He was combing his hair," he said. In an effort to stimulate Thompson's memory he raised a hand and made combing motions. "He had forgotten there was a war on. He had forgotten where he was. He didn't know anything till he heard the click of the bolt. We watched him, we were together, you and me. You told me to shoot him. I got him in the head. He had forgotten what his part was, he was being somebody else. It was a different kind of performance, different from the one we were putting on." He knew this was the wrong language, wrong for Thompson; but he had no other – these were the elements that had lived on in his mind for forty years. "He made a sound like a hen," he said. "Do you mean to say you don't remember?"

He looked at Thompson incredulously. Was he pretending? Narrowing his eyes for better focus, he scanned the other's face, as if the secret of this amazing forgetfulness

140

might lie there, in that deathly pallor from which even the flush of drink had faded now, in the flaring trefoil of the birthmark, the narrow, bloodless mouth, the eyes almost colourless, like shallow water below dull sky. The face of a bleached ferret, tenacious, undistinguished; but it had the fascination, for Benson, of a mystery of survival – as if he had unearthed, in some obscure recess, an object of childhood terror or delight, seen now with sadness, with wonder at the creature he himself had been, that had survived.

"It *was* you that brought back the helmet," he said. "You always came back with something. It doesn't matter, it was all a long time ago." There was no point in staying longer; he and Thompson had nothing to say to each other; they had been through a terrible time together but it might as well have been a summer stroll.

"There *was* a Benson," Thompson said suddenly. Something slightly gloating or salacious had come into his face. "I remember you," he said. "You was the one dressed up as a tart. Did you like putting them things on? You liked it, didn't you? They said you should of been a tart."

"Who said that?" He watched Thompson help himself to more whisky with the fumbling, parodic deliberateness of the very drunk. "It was just an act," he said. "That was our act. It was part of the show. Walters dressed up in a straw boater and blazer and white flannels but that didn't make him the man who broke the bank at Monte Carlo."

"Thass different," Thompson said. "Thass not a tart, is it? Well, live and let live, I always say. Walters, yeh, I remember *him*. Silly bugger. You sang that song. Walters copped it there."

"He was blown up," Benson said. "Trod on a mine."

"Silly bugger. Mines and mortars, it was them what did the damage there." His mouth had fallen a little open and Benson saw the slow movement of his tongue. "I always remembered that silly bugger," he said.

"What do you mean?" Benson said sharply. "Why do you call him that?"

"Course I remember." Without any warning at all, Thompson raised his head and began to sing in his thin, nasal tenor:

"Every little movement has a meaning of its own,
Every little movement tells a tale . . ."

Benson watched the mouth move as it went through the chorus. He was aware of a feeling almost of sacrilege, hearing Thompson sing this song which had belonged to Walters and himself. This merged into a sense of the terrible strangeness of the white face before him with its crimson blemish, rapt in its singing. This same mouth had closed softly round a dead finger, the tongue licking and salivating, loosening the rigor mortis with warm spit, sucking with the patience of a lover, working to elicit the throb of the sliding ring. And the ring in his mouth still, the treasure on his palate, he would come crawling back . . . Benson was possessed with wonder at this sucking love of Thompson's, in the dark night of the Wadis, alert all the time for sounds that might mean danger, a gathering or a silence. It was impossible to believe almost; yet it had happened – this mouth had done those things.

"He turned the lights down low
And she looked at him like so
Every little movement tells a tale."

Thompson ceased. His eyes drooped. The exertion of the singing had increased the asthmatic wheeze of his breath. Benson understood now why he had paused so between the lines of his hymn, thought he knew too, with sudden pity, why Thompson should choose to go for his supper into that appalling brightness of the station cafeteria. He heard the other mutter something indistinguishable.

"What?" he said.

"Over the water," Thompson said. "Just over the water."

"What did you mean just now? What was so stupid about Walters?"

142

"He could of stayed behind, couldn't he?"

Contempt was back in the slurred voice; it was contempt that had kept Walters preserved in his memory all these years and Benson was suddenly grateful for it. "Stayed behind?" he said. "Who told you that?"

"He could of had a transfer. Before the break-out. But the silly bugger wouldn't go."

"But nobody was transferred," Benson said. "Nobody stayed behind." He was bewildered. "Except Slater," he added.

"We didn't have no bleeding choice, did we? Mackintosh heard them talking, that was my mate. He picked things up from driving the officers round."

"But he never told me . . ." Benson said. "He never said anything – you must be mistaken. Who signed the papers?"

Thompson's eyes almost closed, jerked open again with a look of startled suspicion. "They better not try it again," he said. Looking all the while at Benson he reached across his body with the right hand, slipped it inside his coat, tugged a little. The hand came out holding a shortish, broad-bladed knife with the hilt on one side only, like a bayonet. The blade was clean, oiled-looking, with a dull lustre on it.

"Is that the same—?"

"Kept it all these years." Thompson's voice was mumbling, awed. He turned the knife slightly in his mottled paw and light flexed along it. His head drooped, reared up again. He said, "They better not fucking try."

In that evil-smelling room, hazy now with smoke, in the faintly lapping light, the fabulous gleam of Thompson's knife confused Benson's eyes. Looking beyond it, he caught Brenda's gaze fixed on him, her eyes softly shining, like glass.

"British-made," Thompson said virtuously. "None of this wog muck. In them days it meant something. In them days you could be proud to be British." With fumbling movements he restored the knife to its place on his person. Then abruptly, as though the successful achievement of this had released him, his head fell back against the sofa, his

143

mouth opened and a loud sonorous sound, half-sigh, half-snore, broke from him.

Benson remained seated on his box, looking with amazement at the white, open-mouthed face before him, lost in sleep. His back was aching, he felt nausea from the whisky and the bad air; but he could not bring himself to leave yet, as if even now, even in face of the other's insensibility, he might find some further clue, something that could seem like evidence for the amazing thing he had just been told. Because of course they had all hoped in a way to stay behind, especially when the show had turned out such a success, hoped that it would be transferred to Naples and all of them along with it, a groundless hope but quite irrepressible, kept alive by whispers and rumours. In the event only Slater himself had gone, with the rank of acting Captain, Officer i/c Entertainments.

Sitting there, listening to Thompson's painful breathing, the occasional musical rasps caused by insomniac Brenda, faint crepitations from the heated metal of the stove, he tried to recall the night Slater had spoken to him about his idea for the show. They had been relieved, after how long he could not remember, but the feeling was always the same, hasty exchanges between the platoon commanders, stumbling away in the dark, single file, through the slippery gullies. They had talked near the harbour, in among the wrecked houses. There was a moon but the moonlight was hazy because of the smoke generators round the Beachhead perimeter, they made hissing sounds like escaping gas. Supply ships out at anchor in the bay, visible intermittently through this milky haze of moonlight and smoke. The smoke was filthy, he suddenly remembered, the carbonised oil of it got into your hair, throat, nostrils . . . *Have you got a few minutes, Benson? Yes, sir.* Confident accent, voice of our rulers. Sure, despite the courtesy, of full claim on your time. His face in the moonlight narrow and handsome, fatigue smoothed away by the eagerness of his idea. He was, let's see, three or four years older than me. *I want to get a sort of concert party together.*

144

Just as he spoke there was a flash of gunfire from further along the coast, then a whole series, soundless, like glimmers of summer lightning rapid and sustained. His face caught some light from it. *The men are bored.* He was still saying this when the thunder of the guns came. Yes, that was the order of things, first the flashes, barely time for half a dozen words, then the crash of the barrage. Thuds of the explosions out in the German lines like the strokes of a padded hammer. This was only March still, but we had started the softening-up process, bombardment of the German positions. That went on until the break-out.

Lieutenant Slater smiled through it, waiting to resume. When it died away he repeated that the men were bored, professional entertainers rarely came to the Beachhead, what did the men get but a few old films always breaking down? There was a need for it. Yes, sir. They would put on their own show, just the members of the unit – to begin with anyway. He was going to see the Company Commander about it next day. *I wonder if you'd care to come along? Yes, sir.* Concealed order really. He had thought it all out. Better to go with one of the men, it looked more representative. I suppose I felt flattered. He didn't ask me to be in it at first.

No objection in any case, none that I remember. The Company Commander probably thought we were mad. Burroughs, his name. Major Burroughs. *Next step is advertising.* Notices to the NCOs in charge of billets. Anyone who thought he had any talent could attend for an audition – Slater did the auditions. Your only talent is wanking, the Sergeant told Crocker. But even Crocker found a place on the show, he helped with the lights. Assistant Stage-Manager, he called himself – wanting, like all of us, a title, a claim to indispensability, with that hope we all shared, Al Jolson, Baxter the baritone, the man who was such a marvellous whistler – he only lasted two or three performances, whistled a few tunes, did some bird imitations – the Comic Teuton, the Cockney Comedian, name of Fox, I think, Walters, me. All of us. And only Slater was held back. Not to be wondered at. We were just the performers. We strutted on that stage below the rubble of Anzio, as we sweated in the Wadis, for the benefit of our overseers. But not Walters – not if Thompson could be believed. If this thing he had been told were really true, Walters had acted for himself, he had died in his own person, even though in travesty, face blacked, making those terrible noises.

Not you either, he thought, looking at Thompson's oblivious face, listening to the harsh breath. You toiled to no one's enrichment but your own, sought to please no one but yourself. You had the licence to kill and pilfer, all you needed. That's why you were so alone. Mackintosh, the driver's name. How could stray words, overheard so long ago, retailed in drunkenness by someone else, whose mind was going, how could such words be believed? Only Thompson's contempt gave them any credence. He would have told me, he thought. If he had been offered something like that he would have told me. Like that day, the stream bed deepened, we were down a few feet, four feet, five feet below the surface. Walters just behind me. Usual relief at being below ground, usual fear of ambush – there were zealots like Thompson on their side too. What were we doing, why were we there? Something to do with getting water. Dangerous if so, because the containers were awkward to carry, hard to stop them clanking – you never went for water in the night. The banksides were overhung with bramble and there were bees in the white bramble flowers. April? The ditch got deeper. It veered away, followed a course of its own, those watercourses never went for long in the direction you wanted to go. So there was unknown space widening above us as we went deeper. We found a sort of recess, a place where the bank had fallen away, making a narrow chamber, just big enough for the two of us. We crawled in there and stayed for a bit, close together, talking in whispers. Down here, twenty feet below ground, with that fearsome, unknown space above us, we felt safe for a while. For a while only – like the brief, excited immunity of childhood hiding places before the fear of your

146

own existence drives you back to what you know. Walters took his helmet off. His face was pale, exhausted, with sweat coming down at the temples. He whispered to me. *We-are-getting-the-whiphand-over-the-Jerries.* Mouthing the words elaborately, imitating one of the officers who actually did say things like that. Righty-Ho, we called him. Bodies close together, we talked in whispers about our homes and the days before the war and what we were going to do if we got through it. *He would have told me . . .*

He looked in disbelief at the sleeping man on the sofa. Thompson's head was thrown back, exposing the thin tendons of his throat with the adam's apple pricking out the skin like a thorn. Some merciful shift in position had eased that difficult breathing; he was silent now. The eyes were not closed completely; light from the lamp elicited a faint gleam from between the lids. This, and the silenced breath, made his look of death complete.

Benson stood up, cautiously flexed his cramped limbs. His head felt heavy and his eyes were sore. He looked at his watch: it was half past two in the morning. There was no point in rousing Thompson now, asking him more. His temper was uncertain, he would be fogged with drink and sleep. In any case, he couldn't take any more of Thompson tonight – or ever, probably.

He looked round the room, at the cracked ceiling, the gashed walls, the barricaded windows, the poor debris of boxes and bedding. Ears flattened, Brenda slept at last in her cage. It was difficult to believe they were in a populous city of an advanced nation: it was like some ruinous outpost. Others too, he thought, remembering the quarrelling voices, the baby's cry. Thompson was below ground still, sleeping the exhausted sleep of someone returned from patrol, from a night sortie, as he might have slept after returning with the German helmet that misty morning when Crocker got the blood in his hair. But there were no spoils now; he had his knife to guard a gutted room.

The lamp had begun to flicker and Benson had a moment of confusion, thinking of the leaping fire he had seen while he was lingering on the waste ground. He ought to put the lamp out, the stove too. But Thompson might be cold. He stepped round the sofa, went over to the pile of bedding, picked up by the edge a tattered blanket. Fastidiousness, a reluctance to touch the material any more than necessary, caused him to tug at the blanket sharply, thus disturbing the pile. Half-folded between the wall and the stained pillow he saw a magazine with a face on the cover. Obeying an impulse of curiosity he picked it up and laid it flat on the quilt Thompson used as a matress. It was the *Observer* Colour Supplement and the face was that of Salvador Dali. In the dying bursts of light Benson looked for some moments at the protuberant eyes and waxed moustache of the charlatan Spaniard. Then Thompson stirred and caught his breath with a harsh, choked sound and Benson turned back towards him hastily, guiltily. Gently, with a sudden feeling of tenderness, he laid the blanket over Thompson. He found the small wheel at the side of the stove and turned it to the off-position. He blew down the glass to put out the lamp, then groped his way down the passage, catching the goldfinch's cage with his foot, hearing the bird flutter in the darkness.

The night outside was completely silent. Thinking of nothing much, concerned only to put one foot in front of another, Benson made his way back through the courtyards of the Estate, through the deserted streets beyond.

2

When he arrived home he was exhausted. He lay down on the bed without bothering to undress and fell asleep immediately. In tangled dreams he came upon a mild-faced sheep trapped in thick mud, attended a police ball where policemen in uniform played twanging tunes on their teeth. Through these strange vibrant sounds he heard a woman's voice raised in loud bursts of weeping and he was searching for the voice through the rooms of an abandoned, collapsing house. He could not discover where the sound was coming from, it was everywhere around him. Then he understood that the house itself was uttering these bursts of lamentation, like salvoes – he could see the sparks of the weeping showering through the sky. Like splinters, like shrapnel . . . He opened his eyes on broad daylight, remembering unwillingly Thompson's bleached face, Brenda's soft, inquisitive gaze.

He was briefly surprised to discover that he still had his coat and shoes on. I'm going to pieces, he thought. His head ached and he was generally aware of being dirty, dishevelled, degenerate. He made strong coffee and drank it as hot as he could and felt almost at once considerably better, ready to negotiate the shower: a certain alertness was needed for this, as he had discovered from experience, the vagaries of the antiquated immersion heater making some nimbleness of footwork necessary if one wasn't to be scalded or chilled.

He stayed a long time under the finally regulated jet, eyes closed, letting the hot water deluge his head and face, run over his motionless body. Under this healing stream he began to think again about the night before. Some of Thompson's remarks had been distinctly odd. He seemed almost to expect me. No, not that exactly, but he didn't seem surprised. Suspicious, as if I had designs on him, until he got too drunk to care. He didn't believe it was an accident, my being there. Was it just because I had come prepared with the whisky? *No bloody good sending people with whisky*. Of course, Thompson is a bit mad now – always was perhaps, maybe that's why he flourished so in circumstances of madness.

Drying himself, putting on clean clothes, making yet more coffee, he continued to go over these puzzling aspects of Thompson's behaviour. Then there was the magazine. The *Observer* Supplement was hardly the sort of reading matter one would readily associate with Thompson. Verisimilitude, yes, a valid point, but we have to remember that the man was mad . . . There had been nothing else, no other books or papers. He would hardly have bought it. Probably picked it up in some litter bin in the course of his scavenging, brought it home to read. It had been tucked away there against the wall as if with an intention of concealment.

What remained of the morning he spent on his researches. He had been trying from the available figures to establish the extent of the Atlantic slave-trade in the eighteenth century as carried on by all nations, but comprehensive figures were extremely difficult to assemble. Fage's estimate of seven million shipped to the New World during the century seemed low to him: in the desire to avoid exaggeration too much allowance had been made for the interruption of the traffic by European wars and the upheaval caused by the American Revolution. Benson could not believe the trade had suffered to that extent; it was too lucrative. Perhaps an average of a hundred thousand slaves a year, with the English of course supplying at least half, probably more. Say sixty thousand. Liverpool would have had the lion's share, certainly in the latter half of the century – in 1800, which seemed an average sort of year, it appeared that Liverpool had sent one hundred and twenty vessels to the African coast as against London's ten and Bristol's three.

A virtual monopoly. The only reliable figures he had were for the decade 1783–93. In that period Liverpool had delivered a total of 303,737 slaves to the West Indies, which of course didn't include those who had died on the way, say three in ten. Getting on for half a million. Then there were the deaths inflicted in the process of capture, the deaths through tribal conflict incited by the traders, the lingering deaths caused by misery, imported diseases, the destruction of the economic bases of life. Beyond calculation. The familiar sensation of bafflement and wonder came to him, the suffocating sense of the enormity of it. This was just Liverpool, just ten years.

Among all those who had practised it, the seamen, the

skippers, the merchants, he had not so far found a single questioning voice. Protest there had been, but not among those in receipt of the profits. The trade was sanctioned by law; for the men in the ships and the counting houses that had been enough. Even men of conscience . . . The words of the Reverend John Newton, ordained after many years a slaver, came to him now with a peculiar chill: *In all the years I was engaged in the slave trade I never once questioned its lawfulness.*

He couldn't have been talking about legality – he knew perfectly well it was legal. No, he meant permissible, justifiable, he was using the word in its contemporary meaning – one of the great achievements of that appalling age to frame a word that could so nicely blend the notions of the legal and the permissible. *Lawful.* Perhaps that blending itself due to the moral contortions of the slave trade. We live with it still, he thought. It was Eichmann's defence . . .

He tried to dwell on the known and familiar objects around him, find solace, healing virtue, as he had done in frightened childhood, by tracing lines and patterns, the folds of a curtain, the threadbare roses on the chintz of his chair; but their talismanic power failed him now, they gave nothing back, not even the chess set, not even the treasured bowl . . . *We would do it again*, he whispered in the silence of the room. *I know we would do it again.* This had been no mere aberration, it had gone on too long. Worst of all, impossible to resist, attacking him now with the usual horror, was the knowledge that it had never really stopped . . .

With an instinct of self-protection, he took pencil and paper, began to make some calculations. By that year then, by the close of the century, Liverpool had engrossed more than ninety per cent of the English trade, which must mean close on half of total European black cargoes, say three-sevenths. The average price of a plantation slave at the time was around fifty pounds. That meant that the gross income of the Liverpool merchants in an average year would be somewhere around one and a half million pounds.

He closed his eyes, rested his head against the back of the

151

armchair, trying to get some notion of the meaning of this sum. Doctor Johnson told Boswell that a man could manage to exist on six pounds a year and live comfortably on thirty. Swift's Stella lived almost luxuriously on an income of a hundred pounds a year: the price of two slaves in prime condition.

These statistics could only be blunted with the help of a large whisky. Then, fighting off a sick reluctance, he ate a poached egg on toast and two soft, forgotten apples.

Afterwards he set off for the public library in William Brown Street. Horror merely fed his obsession. He wanted to look up some details concerning the slave ship *Zong*, subject of a celebrated appeal case in 1782. He found the book he wanted, *Black Cargoes* by Mannix and Cowley, but there was not much there about the legal process, merely an outline of the main events, with most of which he was already familiar.

The *Zong*, sailing out of Liverpool with Luke Collingwood as master, had left Sao Thomè on September 6, 1781, with 440 slaves and a crew of 17. The Middle Passage had been difficult – they were delayed by bad weather, mortality among the negroes was very high. On November 29, with land in the West Indies already sighted, the captain called his officers together. There were only 200 gallons of fresh water left in the tanks, not enough to last out the voyage. If the remaining slaves died of thirst or illness the loss would fall on the owners of the vessel, but if they were thrown into the sea they could be regarded as legal jettison, covered by insurance. Following this conference, 132 slaves were thrown overboard in three batches. Back in England the owners claimed £30 insurance money for each of the jettisoned slaves. The underwriters refused to pay. The owners duly appealed. The appeal was heard at the Court of Exchequer, presided over by Lord Mansfield. After admitting that the law was with the owners, Lord Mansfield said, "A higher law applies to this very shocking case", and he found for the underwriters – the first case in which an English court ruled that a cargo of slaves could not be treated simply as merchandise.

Dangerous precedent, Benson thought. The owners must have been very alarmed. Puzzled too, probably: what kind of higher law could this be, that said a cargo was not a cargo? That damned crank Mansfield, he imagined them saying, standing together on the Custom House steps, he ought to stick to his own business. Does he think he is a bishop? Now, of course, they were saying more or less the same thing about the bishops . . .

On the way out he found himself passing the door to the Reading Room. Without any particular sense of decision he entered, went up to the counter and asked for back copies of the *Observer* Colour Supplement. He had not thought to look at the date on Thompson's magazine. All he could remember was the face on the cover, the manic showman's pop eyes and waxed moustache.

"Perhaps it was about a Dali retrospective," he said to the not much interested assistant. He was embarrassed at being so vague. "Fairly recent," he said. But when he eventually found the issue he wanted he saw that it was nearly three months old. Either Thompson had fished it out of some bin not often emptied or he had been carting it around with him for weeks.

In that case, he thought, sitting alone at the long table with the magazine before him, in the latter case he must have brought it with him, perhaps from Leeds where he left his hamster or Huddersfield where he deposited his budgies.

He began leafing through the advertisements. Could Thompson's interest have been aroused by the offer of a bathrobe in white or navy blue, mailed within two weeks of receipt of your cheque, a Vauxhall Cavalier, a holiday with the Club Méditerrané, membership of the Wine Club? It seemed unlikely. There were some Dali paintings reproduced in the middle section – the skin of a hand neatly draped over a rail, pyramids on a beautifully shadowed desert, telephones, floating eyeballs, all immaculate, distinct to the point of hallucination. Accompanying the pictures was a piece about the artist's career and his protracted dying. Perhaps it was simply this then, he thought without conviction – for reasons best known to himself Killer Thompson had become interested in Dali, in this world of illusory images alien to the true experience of sight, a clarity falser than shadow.

On almost the last page there was an article entitled 'A Room of Your Own', one of a series in which wealthy or famous people, or people in the news for some reason, were pictured in their home surroundings. It was a double-page feature, with a photograph on one side of a woman in a white gown and gold bracelets, with a face vaguely familiar, standing smiling in a room full of opulent clutter. He read the name under the picture: Sylvia West. He thought he remembered her now: she had played English-rose-type heroines in some swashbuckling English films of the fifties. He was about to turn over the page when he noticed a small picture on the opposite side, a heavy-set, grey-haired man in a tweed suit standing on a terrace against a background of grey stone. The print underneath said: *Merchant Banker Hugo Slater on the terrace of Brampton Manor, his Cheshire home.*

Slater was not such a rare name of course, but Hugo Slater – that cut the field down a bit. This man on the terrace looked about the right height and the general cast of his features were not dissimilar, though the face was heavier now and the form thicker-set. His Cheshire home. What had Thompson said? *Over the water.* I thought he meant the river Jordan.

He looked at the picture of the woman again. She had kept her stage name. It was not a dress she was wearing, he noticed now, but white silk pyjamas, loose-fitting and full-sleeved. She looked strangely like one of the features of the room rather than its occupant, a life-sized, smiling simulacrum standing amidst mirrors, clocks and china dogs. Stray phrases caught his attention. *In the arcane language of the antique world . . . Sylvia West also collects Derby ware . . . I come here and listen to Verdi. . .*

154

He began to read with more attention, hoping to find some confirmation that this Slater was the one he had known. *Like the rest of the house, the room shows style and discrimination. The handsome eighteenth-century bureau is in walnut. In the arcane language of the antique world the bureau bookcase has a broken pediment. 'Positively riddled with secret drawers, darling,' Sylvia says with the same radiant smile that used to look down at us from the screen in the days when heroines were virginal and heroes were brave and strong and offered marriage. She laughs. 'They are so secret that I don't know where half of them are myself.'*

The side chairs are walnut too. Sylvia likes walnut because it ages so beautifully and has such superb colours in it. On the middle shelf, alongside a set of Roman oil lamps in terracotta, there is an antique Syrian glass scent bottle her husband, financier Hugo Slater, brought back from a business trip. A devoted collector himself, he generally picks up a little something for her too on his travels. Sylvia also collects Derby ware. 'I love things, objects,' she says. 'I love clutter, I guess, so long as it is elegant clutter. It is my great dream to restore the concept of the boudoir. Such a pity it has gone out of fashion, don't you think? A room where a woman can have her pretty things about her and be alone and private and yet still receive her intimates or her lover or whatever.' She glances as she speaks at the huge divan with its design of peacock plumes and peacocks.

Benson looked up from this with relief. It was written in the kind of arch and knowing style he found repulsive. There was nothing more about Hugo Slater in any case, only some further stuff about how Sylvia liked to go to her boudoir, close her curtains, listen to Verdi and forget the world for a while. Well, we know what you mean, Sylvia.

He emerged on to William Brown Street to find that the edges of the cloud had lifted. Sunshine was striking across the city with a visionary radiance under this dark canopy, gilding the neo-classical porticoes of the Walker Art Gallery, bringing splendour to the dishevelled starlings on the curving gutter of the Rotonda and the stiff foliation of the Corinthian capitals below. He crossed the street, passed

155

through the long shadow of the Iron Duke on his ninety-foot pedestal, traversed the cobbled forecourt of St George's Hall, glancing with customary amazement at the long colonnaded sweep of its façade. Worthy of ancient Athens, as Queen Victoria once remarked. The broad terrace at the back of it was deserted and he stood for some time here looking down the gardens towards Pier Head. The twin towers of the Liver Building, surmounted by their fabulous birds, looked pale, ethereal almost, in the luminous air above the river. Beyond them the sky had a faint reddish tinge, like the stain of some distant, stealthy conflagration. The civic dignitaries on the descending terraces were all looking that way too, Liverpool's famous men, the bronze skirts of their frockcoats melting in this sudden sunshine. Slater on his terrace too, member of the landed gentry . . .

It must be the same man, his mind insisted: Slater of Anzio, Slater of the Beachhead Buddies. There was the name, the picture in the article; most compelling of all was the fact that Thompson had kept it all this time. He tried to recall the conversation of the night before but it had been so disjointed, Thompson had wandered so much, it was difficult now to get any sense of the sequence of things. *A hundred quid, he wouldn't feel it . . . I got to get the animals together . . . silly bugger, he could of gone to Naples . . . you a friend of his?* Did he think Slater had sent me? Or was I somehow just a sign, a portent for Thompson, part of his struggle to make the world intelligible, preserve the contempt which seemed all now that kept him alive? *Silly bugger, I always remember that silly bugger . . .*

He began to walk back towards Lime Street, then turned off at random, not much noticing where he was going. Among blank streets, a no-man's-land between thoroughfares, a drunk held out a hand to him. The man's face was covered with contusions of some kind, dark, mulberry-coloured bruises. He had a surprisingly hard grip – Benson had to use force to get his hand away. Immediately afterwards he passed a little girl with her mother and the little girl smiled at him, a gap-toothed, confiding smile. Though hardly noticing his surroundings, he registered these incidents with an extraordinary vividness as he did the changing sky, in which clouds were breaking and thinning to show broad rifts of blue.

Weariness brought him finally to a pause. He found himself in Aigburth, near the entrance to Otterspool Park. He went through the park gates and sat down on the first bench he came to. Before him, on the other side of the path, there was a chestnut tree in full flower, the great cones of blossom standing erect among the thick leaves. From somewhere in the depths of the foliage a warbler was singing, the same repeated cadence, sweet, deliberate, somehow intensely secret. There were not many people about. On another bench further along an elderly, unkempt woman was sorting through the contents of a canvas bag. After a few minutes a young man in a tracksuit came running past. Of course it was a weekday. Today must be Friday, he thought. Tomorrow was the 22nd of May, day of Rathbone's show, anniversary of the break-out. Alma's birthday too—he would be seeing her. Thompson had put it out of his mind.

He got up and began to walk further into the park, between the steep banks that rose on either side, thick with shrubbery, shot through with sunlight as the sky continued to clear. Nettles and bluebells grew among the azaleas and the ash trees were in first feather; great clumps of rhododendron flowered dark red among the dense green of their leaves. This is a kind of gully too, he thought, remembering that distant spring, the last few days before the attack. It was only when not fighting that you could have any idea of what you might be fighting for and that, as he remembered it now, was the recovery of a certain kind of sensation that had been lost. We had all, he thought, brought ourselves or been brought to the belief that the expense was somehow necessary. What we were purchasing, the nature of the transaction, we didn't really know, but we thought we knew it sometimes in the spring of that year, in the valleys back behind the lines, the soft air blowing up from the south, new wheat, flowering fruit trees, somebody singing somewhere. Song of home – all our hope in it, however trite the words. Not like the slave songs; they knew they would never see their homes again. *The songs they sang on those occasions were songs of sorrow and sadness, simple ditties of their own wretched estate* . . . Cruel too, that spring weather, any blade of grass could remind you of the men who had not stayed alive to see it. And relief and guilt at being alive yourself. If Walters could have lain in the open like some of them, a death among others, scattered like husks, then it might have seemed, it might have come to seem, that his death was fruitful somehow. From husks to seeds, merely a change of metaphor. But not that death, alone there in the gully, soaked in the creosote they had to throw over him. Irrational, of course . . . If he did stay back, could it have been for me, could it have been for my sake?

At the end of the path there was a paved area with a boarded-up pavilion in the middle; beyond this a short field rose steeply. Benson climbed, reached the crest of the slope, saw the river below him, a wide, pale glitter with the plumed chimneys of Birkenhead to the north and the line of the Welsh hills in the far distance. Over the water was Cheshire. He didn't mean the Jordan, he meant this. Hugo Slater, merchant banker. On the terrace of his Cheshire home. A devoted collector himself . . . A devoted collector and producer of entertainments, certainly, in those days of the Beachhead. That enthusiasm, that dedication, could it all have been simply a desire to get out of the fighting, save his skin? Impossible to believe: he could not have feigned so well.

He began to walk across the level ground towards the water. The grass had been cut here recently; long swathes of it lay across the field; withered now, but the sun brought out again the sweetish smell of its perishing. He went down steps to the paved promenade, crossed to the rail and stood there, looking first across the bright, idle expanse of water, then below him to where in the shadow of the wall the river

158

reverted to its true nature, mud-coloured and sullen, lapping slowly against the stone steps.

Slater did everything, he thought, watching the skirmishing of gulls over a paler patch of water spreading from the bank, effluent of some kind, sewage probably. He gave all the time he had, all the time he wasn't at the front, auditioning, rehearsing. Not only that. He inspired people, no other word for it. The show was Slater's creation. Any talent, he would find it, even if they didn't come forward. He found that cross-eyed man who had been in an operatic society – he sang bits from Gilbert and Sullivan, still does for all I know. He found the Cockney comedian who was killed on the same night as Crocker. He found Walters and me. He knew what he wanted – he wouldn't take just anybody. The man who did the impression of Al Jolson, he wouldn't take him. Little man, throwing himself about, mouth open wide, *Swanee, how I love yah.* I'm afraid it's just not good enough. Al Jolson was the only thing he could do. He said he'd done it in pubs before the war. Disappeared one night, wandered off, no one ever saw him again. Then there was the one who did the German officer. How Slater found him I don't know. He was brilliant but it was all Slater's idea, turning the German propaganda into a comic sketch like that. And he found the man to do it, he was an officer in the London Irish. The joke was to use stuff from their leaflets and the radio broadcasts they put out. He would come on in the uniform of a German officer, strutting around, monocle. 'Hello, boys.' A sort of comic-Teuton accent, very slow and laborious. 'Have you heard about Private Fox? He went out on pat-rol and stepped on a shoe-mine. Nasty things, shoe-mines . . .' Just then someone would let off a detonating cap like the sound in a toy gun but louder and that would be a shoe-mine and he would have his foot blown off. He would hobble off stage and come back on a crutch, still talking in that same ingratiating way. 'Have you heard about Private Jones? He got in the way of a piece of shrap-nel. Nasty stuff, shrapnel. He was only half a man after that, get what I mean,

159

boys?' Another loud bang and he clutches at his balls. In the end, after various kinds of damage, he is still moving around the stage on his crutch, one arm in a sling, bandage round his head but he's still got the monocle in. Still the same slow delivery. 'Remember the hell of Dun-kirk? Think of the terrible hours when the German broom swept your fellow soldiers off the Con-ti-nent. How many brave Tommies kicked the buck-et. Take my advice, boys – *get out while you are all in one piece.*'

That was the punch-line. Surprising how popular that sketch was. They would laugh to see this maiming process night after night. Slater knew – somehow, from somewhere – that a certain kind of subversiveness can improve morale, make for unity as well as laughter. The man who did it was very good but it was Slater who directed him, went through every move, every intonation, rehearsed it over and over until the timing was right.

He did the same with us, with Walters and me. He chose the song, he drilled us in every movement. That stage was as big as the Beachhead to me at first. Slater took us across it. He taught us how to move about. He chalked the stage into sections for us, nine sections. He made us learn them. *Move down left two steps . . . Cross to up right.* We were scared of displeasing him, scared of making a mistake. It was Slater that taught me the rule of six feet: never come closer than six feet except for love or battle. Only for a fight or a fuck. Interpreting those terms broadly, Benson. Yes, sir. Don't bother about the 'sir' down here. Just concentrate on getting it right, okay? We would have done anything for him.

The first time we did it I was scared but I knew from the start it was going all right. We moved about the stage in the movements we had rehearsed. We were borne along, taken through the steps, lifted and sustained by the music and the words and that great breath of excited interest, varying with our movements but never ceasing, falling as I turned towards it, rising as I turned away and the dress lifted in that swirl of movement. At the end we went forward hand in

hand to bow – first to finish the chorus, then take the bow.
We stood facing them with the piano thumping away.

> "When alone no words they utter
> but their hearts begin to flutter
> and every little movement tells a tale."

Then we ran off, Velma first, blowing a kiss, then Bertie
in that randy, loping style he had developed, bum sticking
out, straw hat raised at a jaunty angle. Crescendo of cheers,
wolf howls, whistles. In the passage behind the stage we
paused to listen. We were exhilarated by our success, by the
applause. We faced each other smiling. We were standing
close together in the narrow passage, listening to the sounds
we had left behind, feeling relief after the tension of nerves.
His face was moist under the greasepaint. Impossible now
to remember which of us moved first.

A cargo boat with a rusty hull and a name in Cyrillic
letters passed slowly downstream with three figures standing side by side at the stern rail. Benson began to walk along
beside the water in the direction of the city. The back-ache
which had troubled him the night before had returned; his
feet felt hot and swollen inside his shoes. At intervals along
the promenade there were small square shelters facing
towards the water. The sun was low now, it laid a gleaming
band across the river. Most of the shelters were empty but
one or two had a solitary man in them, sitting with face
raised to the warmth.

Quite impossible now, he thought. He could remember
how they had faced each other in the passage, listening to
the hubbub they had left behind; and he could remember
that they had smiled at each other broadly, in congratula-
tion. Walters had spoken first. "Well, we did it," he said and
whether he moved first or I did I can't be sure but we
lurched forward into an embrace, a bear-hug, in immediate, delighted celebration of success and I felt his body
against mine, like my own body, yet mine realised at that
moment as intensely different, smaller, lighter, lissom in
the flimsy material of the dress. We held each other and let

161

each other go and we were still standing close together but not touching. I felt that something in me had changed and I saw that the quality of his smile was different, it had become mixed with a kind of half-painful, speculative expression, apprehensive almost, though his eyes still looked directly into mine . . .

As he walked along he wanted to keep this face before him, hold it in his mind longer, but it was replaced almost at once by others: the drawn, exhausted face in the underground chamber where they had crouched together in that charmed immunity of childhood and Walters had mimicked in whispers the officer whose crass enthusiasm was all that remained in memory, name and face long forgotten. *We're-getting-the-whiphand-over-the-Jerries*. Then that face of the dying man, almost indistinguishable, blacked with boot-polish in the darkness of the gully.

He came out near the Garden Centre, its pavilions and cafés and amusement arcades mute and deserted, one more of Liverpool's abandoned tourist dreams. The vast car parks stretched below him, acres of asphalt completely empty, spaces for a thousand cars marked out in neat white lines, symbol of the city's perennial optimism and constant, desperately comic disappointment.

Back on Aigburth Road he found a phone box. He had half expected that Slater's number would not be listed but the operator found it for him without difficulty. The house was in Warburton, barely twenty miles from where he was standing. *Over the water*. Thompson too must have enquired, must have checked up somehow.

A woman answered in the impersonal tones of an employee. He gave his name and asked for Mr Slater. There were some moments of delay and then the voice came, well-modulated, brisk without curtness: "Yes, this is Hugo Slater."

Benson gave his name again. "I saw an article about your house in the *Observer* Magazine," he said.

"That wretched article. Yes?"

"Yes. We were at Anzio together, at least I think so. I was

162

in your platoon."

"Anzio?" There was a pause, then without appreciable warmth the voice said, "That is a very long time ago."

"I was in your show," Benson said. "The Beachhead Buddies." He felt a fool, replying to this neutral voice, trying to establish an identity forty years old. He had hoped somehow for an invitation, comrades in arms and so on; but of course people who lived in manors did not respond so easily to claims of acquaintance made from a public telephone. "I was Velma," he said. "When I saw the picture, you know, it reminded me. I wondered how—"

"Velma the Vamp," he heard the other voice say. "Yes, I remember her. Good Lord. How is she getting on these days? Life treating her well, is it?"

"Quite well, thanks. Bearing up, you know."

"That's the spirit. Well, it was nice of you to ring."

"I thought, you know, we might have a drink on it some time."

"I'm rather tied up at present," Slater said after a brief pause. "I'll tell you what, let me have your phone number and I'll give you a ring."

"Right. As a matter of fact, I've got an idea for an article I'd like to write. About the show. But I'd need to talk to you."

"Are you a journalist?"

"Yes," Benson said. "Yes, I am."

"What paper do you work for?"

"I'm a freelance. I've done things for the *Sunday Times*. I've done things for most of the national papers at one time or another."

"I see."

There was a pause, then he heard Slater say, "Little Benson, little Benson," in a thoughtful, considering way. "Yes," he said, "that's right, Benson, it was you and I together who went to ask the major about it, you remember, you asked me to go with you. His name was Burroughs. There was a moon that night. They were shelling the German lines. You came to see me in hospital after the

163

break-out."

"My dear chap," Slater said, "of course I remember you. It would be nice to have that drink after all. Tomorrow would be a good day if you could manage it. We are rehearsing in the afternoon. Why don't you come for lunch? Have you a car? No? There's a train gets into Warburton Station at a few minutes past eleven. I'll arrange to have you met."

"That would be fine," Benson said.

"Until tomorrow then."

The phone clicked. Benson emerged on to an Aigburth Road that seemed in some curious way transmuted by this conversation, by the subterfuge he had practised, not quite a lie – he had done things for papers. He wouldn't have asked me otherwise, he thought. Then by the time I phoned again the woman would have had instructions, Slater would have been occupied or at a meeting or away on a business trip picking up a little something to add to his collection . . .

He had gone some way before it occurred to him to wonder what Slater could possibly have meant by the reference to rehearsing. It didn't seem to fit in with anything else in the conversation.

3

"A writer?" the chauffeur said. He had stopped the car in the middle of the drive. "A book writer?"

"Yes," Benson said. "You know the kind of thing. Hard covers, pages bound together in consecutive order." The flippancy concealed a certain nervousness: he had not much liked this showy halt. Hitherto, he felt, although he had been too talkative, they had both played their parts well: the chauffeur competent and reliable in his dark blue livery; he himself the urbane guest, dressed for the occasion in his old but well-cut grey flannel suit and pale green tie. But on this, the very last leg of the journey from the station, having passed from the main road on to a quiet lane then through imposing stone portals on to this smooth, bush-bordered drive, the chauffeur had suddenly put the brakes on, turned massive shoulders, presented, below the peak of his cap, a broad pale face with excitable eyes.

"I been wanting to meet one," he said.

"Well, I hope you're not going to make me get out and walk?"

But the chauffeur was too much in earnest for sallies of this kind. His stare had taken on a quality of strained significance. "For years," he said. "We could do each other a bit of good."

"How do you mean?"

My own fault, he thought. Entirely. Blabbermouth Benson. I should have known better. If one is being conducted to see a wartime associate after forty years and if that associate has prospered in the interval to the extent of sending a Rolls with a chauffeur called Meredith to meet one, then one behaves in a way appropriate, one does not get confidential, especially since one is not a book writer at all actually, nor any other kind, but more of a stationary mollusc, a silence-encrusted barnacle . . .

"I've had an interesting life," Meredith said. "I've had a *fascinating* life. I don't tell this to everyone but I was John Lennon's bodyguard. I went everywhere with him."

In the capacious, light-filtered, leather-redolent interior of the car the two of them regarded each other at a distance of six feet or so. "We grew up together," Meredith said tenderly. "We lived on the same street. We went to the same school. That's when it started. I used to protect him in the playground. People used to pick on him. Well, anybody could see he was different."

Bordering them on either side was the dense green of shrubbery. Deeper in he glimpsed a dark red mist of rhododendron flowers. Through the open window there came a brief, desultory cadence of birdsong from somewhere in the grounds. Curving away from them the smooth, sunlit drive led to where the house would be, concealed from sight still by laurel bushes and close-growing trees.

"I been in some rough places since, but that was the roughest place you'd want to see. I seen blood flow in the toilets of that school. I was with him the night he was killed." Meredith was thick-necked and heavy and in his present position, half-turned towards Benson, the tunic of his uniform visibly constricted him. His face had taken on a staring, congested look, as if swollen with drama. "I tried to interpose myself," he said, "but I was too late. Eyewitness, see what I mean? I haven't had much of an education. Except in the school of life. That's where you could come in, Mr Benson."

"I really think we should be pressing on," Benson said. "They are expecting me, you know."

"I was with him when he went to see Malcolm X." Meredith spoke with increased intensity, as if Benson had expressed some disbelief. "I know the inside story. We could make a bomb."

"Perhaps we can discuss this matter later, on the way back?"

"You got yourself a deal."

Meredith slowly turned to face his front again. To Benson's relief the car started to move forward. "I met them all," Meredith said, looking at Benson in his driving mirror. "All the stars."

The car swept round a long curve in the drive, came into view of the house, above them on a slight eminence, parkland sloping before it, fields behind rising to a wooded skyline. As they approached Benson took in the long façade, the elegant symmetry of the inward-curving wings, the graceful proportions of the windows. It was the house in the photograph but instead of Hugo Slater, Officer I/C Entertainments, Merchant Banker, standing smiling on the wide terrace at the top of the steps, two women, one in sunglasses, were sitting at a white table with cups and saucers before them.

166

It was a very public arrival. The car drew up at the foot of the steps. Meredith went through his series of chauffeur's actions with impeccable style, moving round sedately to open his passenger's door, even actually saluting, overplaying the liveried retainer – or so it seemed to Benson, who now started mounting to the terrace, injecting as much spring into his step as possible. "Clive Benson," he said, advancing to shake hands.

The woman in the sunglasses made a vague, rather feverish gesture before holding out her hand to him. The white sleeve of her dress fell away from a frail wrist. "I'm Sylvia Slater," she said. "Hugo is about somewhere."

"How do you do?" Benson had a sense of large, languid eyes behind the sunglasses. This was the woman in the photograph, but strangely different, seeming now in disguise somehow, the dark glasses and the screen of hair over the brow making it difficult to get any general sense of her face. With another febrile movement of the arm she indicated the other woman, who was fair-haired and much younger and very good looking. "This is Erika Belmont," she said. "Athelstan's consort."

Some faint edge of antagonism in this caught Benson's attention but he was too much baffled by the reference to think much about it. Could that be her husband's name? She had a Scandinavian look about her. No wedding ring . . . "Oh, yes?" he said, playing for time.

"Do sit down," Mrs Slater said. "Perhaps you'd like some coffee? Mr Benson is a journalist," she said to the younger woman. "He is going to write all about us. If you want some good publicity, darling, you'd better be nice to him."

Erika displayed splendid teeth in a laughing look up at him but said nothing. Still further confused, Benson took the offered place at the table and accepted a cup of coffee, which turned out to be only lukewarm. He was sitting with his back to the long slope of the grounds. Before him was an open french window, a section of carved balustrade and then the central pediment of the house, the points of the triangle marked out with stone balls. Present bewilderment, the unnerving effect of his conversation with Meredith, his sense of being there to some extent on false pretences, all combined now to make Benson feel distinctly uneasy; and uneasiness, as usual, set him talking. "You have a beautiful house here," he said. "Late eighteenth-century, isn't it? That was a good period for domestic architecture, almost everything they built then seems to have this quality of, I don't know, grace I suppose, nothing showy about it, nothing florid. Built on the proceeds of the slave trade of course, like all the big houses of that time round here."

"The present house was built in the 1770s," Mrs Slater said after a short pause, "for a Liverpool merchant named Biggs, Sir William Biggs."

"That's what I mean," Benson said. "A hundred to one he made his money out of the African trade."

There was another, more prolonged pause. Then Mrs Slater said, "Parts of it are Tudor. I don't quite get the connection, Mr Benson. Perhaps you don't intend one. Your mind seems to be running along a track of its own, if I may say so. I'm glad you like the house, but it doesn't seem to me to have anything much to do with the slave trade. The people who designed and built it weren't slavers. I think myself it's better there should be big houses and small ones rather than everyone living in the same type of house and having the same type of mind, which is what some people would want for us, I hope not you. I'm sure I'd feel the same if I lived in a two-up, two-down. And if we waited for untainted money before building we'd all be living in caves."

"That is certainly true." Benson looked at her with respect. He had seldom heard the argument for privilege put better. "I wasn't really intending any connection," he said. He smiled at her, putting as much into it as he could. "Age has made me uncouth."

"You were with my husband in the war, weren't you?"

"Yes," Benson said. "During the Italian campaign, in the

spring of '44. He was our platoon commander."

"And now," Erika said, "after all these years, you battle-scarred veterans meet at another battle. I think it is so romantic." She turned her brilliant smile to Benson. "Old soldiers never die," she said.

Not knowing for the moment what to say to this Benson merely smiled back. There was a curious headlessness about Erika, as if she felt she could say anything. Or perhaps it was simply youth and health. "Young ones quite frequently do," he said.

Mrs Slater allowed another rather long pause to elapse, during which she regarded Erika steadily through her dark glasses. The effect was belittling – it seemed to Benson intentionally so – but Erika looked quite unabashed. He wished now that he had asked for whisky.

"Erika is very romantic," Mrs Slater said at last. "Aren't you, love? Next Sunday is the big day, of course," she added, turning to Benson. "A week tomorrow. Hugo has a hundred and one things to see to. That is why he isn't here to greet you."

"No, don't you remember?" Erika said. "The children are here. He is rehearsing with the children."

"I quite understand," said Benson, who didn't at all.

"It would be a pity to distract him," Erika said. "We should not distract a man from work that is dear to his heart." She raised her head and threw back her long blonde hair with both hands in an exuberant gesture that raised her vigorous breasts and made prominent her forearms, thick-ish but shapely, with glinting golden hairs. It came to Benson that she probably took quite a bit of exercise. From somewhere behind the house he heard a series of sharp, mewing cries, like a gull's or hawk's.

"A man has his work," Erika said. "I can't think anything of a man who does not take his work seriously, can you, Mr Benson?"

"Er, no." Benson felt Mrs Slater's eyes on him. "Well, perhaps a tax inspector," he said. "The same thing applies to women, doesn't it?"

"I can't think even that much of him." Erika snapped her fingers scornfully.

"You don't want Hugo to be distracted at this point," Mrs Slater said. "You don't want to distract a man who is preparing the stage for you. That's only common sense, darling."

The words, though spoken with no particular emphasis, brought the shadow of wrong and recrimination to this sunlit terrace. Erika raised a mirthful face, as if the other woman had made a joke, but she said nothing. After a moment or two Mrs Slater stood up rather abruptly. "I think I'll go and rest for a while before lunch," she said. She looked at Benson. "We have lunch rather late at the weekend," she said. "Around two. I hope that suits you?"

"That's fine."

"I'm sure Hugo will be along soon. Perhaps you'd like a drink now?"

"I'd like a Scotch," Benson said. The alacrity of this reply brought a slight smile to her face, the first he had seen since his arrival.

"Very wise," she said. "Exactly what is needed for dealing with Hugo in the production phase. Or any other phase for that matter. Soda? Ice?"

"Nothing, thank you."

"I'll have it brought out to you here." She smiled again, without glancing at Erika, then walked slowly across the terrace to the open french window and disappeared into the house.

"It must have been great fun, having Hugo as your officer," Erika said, after a moment. "He is so inspiring, so dynamic."

Briefly into Benson's mind there came the picture of Slater as he had last seen him, cap, stick, summer–issue shirt neatly pressed, clean white pips on the epaulettes; vision of neatness and correctness in that long room of bandaged shapes, distraught cries of dreamers, smells of disinfectant and suppuration. "Yes," he said, "enormous fun."

"And to think," Erika said dreamily, "that your paths

have crossed again after all these years."

A middle-aged woman in a dark dress came on to the terrace with a tray bearing Benson's drink. It was a very large Scotch indeed. As she set it before him there came a sudden blast of choral music from some upper room of the house.

Erika grimaced. "That Verdi man again," she said. "She never gets tired of him."

Listening, Benson thought he recognised the *Dies irae* chorus from the Requiem. "Well, cheers," he said. He took a long drink from his glass.

"Hugo drinks very little," Erika said. "He is a dedicated man. Look at him now, how he makes himself responsible for everything. And yet just like a little boy in some ways."

She was looking beyond Benson as she spoke, towards the open parkland below the house. For a moment or two, as she raised her head, smiling with the womanly indulgence of her twenty years or so, Benson allowed his gaze to linger on her smooth throat, in which the words seemed to throb for a while after she had stopped talking. Then the import of the words themselves came to him: Slater must be down there, somewhere in sight. He shifted his chair round sharply. It was the first time he had been able to look out over the grounds; there had been the flurry of arrival, the introductions, the accident of his place at the table . . .

"Where is he?" he said rather wildly, dazed for a moment by the extensiveness of the view. "Is that him? Is that a marquee?"

Beyond the balustrade and the steps and the gravelled forecourt where Meredith had deposited him, lawns sloped away, shading barely perceptibly into meadowland, rising again in the distance to low hills. The downward slope was cunningly landscaped, dotted at intervals with small coppices of oak. Where the ground levelled, a gleaming lake, nakedly artificial, lay like a blade on a green cloth. Beyond this, half-hidden among the trees, was a summerhouse painted in red and gilt, with a roof like a Chinese pagoda.

The whole vista was a dream of ordered and controlled rurality; but to the right of the lake, shattering the illusion, was a very large blue marquee, with the figures of three men standing in a group close to it.

"Is one of those men Hugo?" he said.

"Can't you pick him out?" Erika seemed surprised and somewhat offended.

Benson was visited suddenly by a feeling of dislike for the young woman beside him and a corresponding wave of sympathy for the older one, the wife, who for all her acerbity had been obliged to yield the ground. "How should I pick him out?" he said. "By his air of natural command?" He finished the whisky in a single draught. "If you'll excuse me," he said, controlling the effects of this, "I think I'll walk over and see him. I know a man should not be distracted and so on, but time is passing."

Going down the steps he felt dizzy and it occurred to him that his haste with the whisky might have been injudicious – he had had no time for breakfast that morning; but he made his way at a steady pace over the lawns and as he proceeded he felt better again. He saw the little group break up: one man went round the side of the marquee and Benson saw him a few minutes later near the lake with a wheelbarrow; it seemed unlikely that he would be Slater. The two others had not noticed his approach; they talked for some moments longer, then passed inside the marquee through a square opening in the front.

Approaching the entrance he was in time to hear a childish clamour suddenly cease as a man's voice was raised commandingly. He passed into the cavernous interior and stopped at once, looking towards the far end where on a raised platform some thirty children stood facing him in two ranks, boys and girls, identically dressed in white shirts, blue ties, grey shorts. They were quite silent, standing with their arms by their sides in a position of attention. Benson was not good with children's ages, but he thought these were around nine or ten. One of the men, presumably the one who had called out, was holding up his arms to the children. The other, taller and grey-haired, stood further back, looking towards the stage.

"Second and third verses again, please, Mr Pringle," this man called.

There was a moment or two of charged silence. Then the first man made a sweeping gesture with his arms, throwing them apart and bringing them violently together again. At once, in perfect unison, the children broke into song:

"And did the Countenance Divine
Shine forth upon our clouded hills?
And was Jerusalem builded here
Among these dark Satanic Mills?

Bring me my Bow of burning gold:
Bring me my Arrows of desire:
Bring me my Spear: O clouds unfold!
Bring me my—"

"Stop, stop!" It was the taller man who had shouted. Abruptly the singing ceased. He walked a few paces forward towards the children. "They must mark the change of mood between the verses," he said to the conductor. He turned and began to speak emphatically to the silent children. "In verse two we are questioning things, the movement is slow, rather sad. What has happened to this dear England of ours? What has happened to the dream? That's what we are asking. Then at the beginning of verse three there is an abrupt change. Now we are arming for battle, we are calling for our weapons, we are going to restore Jerusalem, the scent of victory is in our nostrils. You sound at the moment as if you were asking mummy to get you a lollypop."

The children listened impassively. If they had seen Benson they gave no sign. Neither of the men had seen him yet. Standing here in the blueish light amidst the summer smells of sun-warmed canvas and crushed grass, he felt oppressed. The docility of the children, their identity of dress, made them seem like victims in a rite of some kind, initiatory, sacrificial – he could not decide. They seemed burdened; creatures performing, who did not know their own purposes. It was a collective poignancy rendered more acute by individual lapses, the flushed little girl with hair escaping from her headband, a boy whose woollen stockings had wrinkled down towards his ankles.

"You must give all the force you can to the 'bring' at the beginning of each line," the tall man said. "Really sound it out. A clarion call. Then, when you are naming the weapons, just the briefest of pauses before the word, then boom! Open your mouths and belt it out. *Bring* me my *bow* of burning gold, *bring* me my *arrows* of desire . . ." He struck his palm with his fist on the beat of the words. Then he turned back to the conductor. "Let's try it again, Mr Pringle, shall we?" he said. "From the beginning."

This was Slater then, revealed by elementary deduction. But I would have known it anyway, Benson thought, hearing and remembering after forty years the patient encouragement of the words: "Let's try it again, shall we?"

The conductor had raised his arms. Benson was about to leave the marquee with the intention of waiting outside when the man he knew to be Slater turned as if to move back to his former position and saw him. An immediate frown came to his face. Benson walked towards him. As he did so the children broke into song again:

"And did those feet in ancient times
Walk upon England's mountains green?"

"Clive Benson," he said quietly, holding out his hand, raising his eyes to Slater's face: the other was a good six inches taller, something he had not remembered particularly, probably because he was used to being the shorter one.

The frown was immediately replaced by a smile of great charm, crinkling the corners of the eyes and giving the whole face an expression of friendliness and warmth. He felt his hand taken in a firm grip. "Let's go outside," Slater said. "We can't talk in here."

174

To the continuing strains of the choir he led the way out of the marquee. The day seemed almost painfully bright to Benson after the filtered light inside; he blinked at a world that seemed more spacious than before. "I hope I'm not interrupting?" he said.

"No, not at all. Pringle will take them through it. He is their teacher, you know. They've been practising a long time, but this is the first dress rehearsal – it's mainly to make sure they've all got the right turn-out." He gave a brief bark of laughter. "We don't want the boys coming in Hawaiian shirts or the girls in sequins. And then, you know, they've got to get the drill right. At the end of the song they've got to form up and walk down the central aisle two by two, straight out – I don't want them milling around in there, space is limited."

Slater's face was heavier now, the mouth had loosened and the skin below the eyes was pouchy; but the eyes were the same, unfaded blue, level and alert under their straight brows. It was a handsome, well-nourished, confident face, authority unmistakable in it, like an element of complexion. His figure had thickened but there was no stoop and he moved lightly. "Well, well, well," he said. "Little Benson. Over here would be a good place to have a chat."

They bordered the slightly rippled platter of the lake, passed through into a copse of silver birches. Before them now was the summerhouse with the pagoda roof, painted in gold and red, vivid against the pale silver of the birch trees and the water.

"I come in here sometimes when I want to do a bit of thinking," Slater said.

Inside there was a faint, agreeable smell of paint and earth mould. A square window looked out over the lake and a long narrow bench of wood ran along the wall below it. They sat down on this and Slater began speaking at once. "I'll just give you a run-down of what it is I'm trying to do here," he said, "to clear up any misconceptions you may be labouring under. Then perhaps after lunch you could see some of the rehearsals and that will lighten up whatever

175

corners are still dark."

"That sounds like a good plan." Benson felt clear-headed despite the whisky, almost preternaturally alert, watching Slater's face in the clear light from the window, a face so changed, so carnalised as it were, full-cheeked and sanguine, yet with that same intensity of purpose it had worn on the night of the shelling when he had waited through the thunder of the guns to explain his idea. The faintly derogatory tone of his words just now, the imputation of ignorance, had been quite good-humoured – probably habitual, Benson thought, a way of establishing ascendancy. He did not need it with us then, he had his rank. Or perhaps it is simply distrust of the press. In any case quite justified at present – Benson had no idea what he was talking about.

"First of all," Slater said, "to get the terminology right, it is a spectacle rather than a play, a series of tableaus really, with various interludes – like the children's choir for example, which you have just seen in action. I want to make it as nearly as possible like those popular shows they used to take touring round the inns and courtyards and village greens of England. I suppose you know what I mean. Don't you use a notebook?"

"No, no," Benson said, "I have a very good faculty of recall. Training, you know." Since he had only succeeded by subterfuge in getting this audience at all, he was resolved to carry it off with what panache he could muster. The question had sounded suspicious; or perhaps merely impatient – he had probably not given sufficient appearance of attention. In fact, a sort of amazement had been slowly growing in him: he and Slater had never been friends of course; but the other had been his platoon officer, they had lived together through circumstances of hardship and danger, Slater had directed him as Velma, had seen him last quite badly wounded in the clearance ward of a military hospital; yet there had been no word of the past, no word of enquiry, no reference at all – Slater had gone straight to the matter in hand. I suppose that is the mark of the high achiever, Benson thought. "No," he repeated. "I dispensed with notebooks long ago." He glanced briefly through the window, saw a flotilla of ducklings in arrowhead formation on the lake, mother in front. "I bumped into Thompson the other day," he said.

"Thompson?" The frowning expression had returned to Slater's face. It was not a look of incomprehension or puzzlement, but rather as if he had found something in his path, something obtrusive, not envisaged.

"He was in your platoon. The one they called Killer Thompson."

"Oh, him. Yes, I remember him. First-rate fighting man. Invaluable chap to have in your platoon. Inspiring example to the others. Worth his weight in gold, a chap like that."

"He almost was for a while," Benson said.

Slater did not take him up on this. It was clear that he wanted to get back to his project but felt constrained still by these wartime associations. "Getting on all right, is he?"

"Not really." He wondered briefly if he should tell Slater that Thompson might be on his way here too. Better not. "He had the copy of the Colour Supplement with the article about your house," he said.

"That confounded article," Slater said, the frown persisting. "Sylvia making one of those positively last appearances. I wish I had never agreed to it now. Where were we?"

"The children."

"Oh, yes. Traditional songs expressing the unity of England and our great heritage. That is the theme of the whole show – unity. You don't mind a history lesson, do you? Just come over here."

He rose and moved towards the door and Benson followed. They stood together looking out towards the rising parkland, the long grey façade of the house, the rougher, steeper ground beyond, the dark line of woods on the horizon. Benson felt the other man's hand lightly gripping his elbow. "The house faces south," Slater said. "So you are looking due north at this moment. If you struck directly through those woods beyond the house and kept going for about ten miles you would come to the lower reaches of the River Mersey. Somewhere between here and the river is the site of the Battle of Brunanburh. That mean anything to you?"

"Not a great deal, I'm afraid."

"It was fought in the year 937. In that year a coalition of Vikings from Ireland, Scots under their king Constantine and a rabble of Strathclyders came sailing up the Mersey. The Vikings wanted to regain the Kingdom of York to which their leader, Anlaf, had a claim. At least, that was the ostensible purpose – the main thing they were all after was loot. They moored their ships on the southern shore of the Mersey and struck across country, pillaging as they went. They were met by a combined force of West Saxons and Mercians under King Athelstan. They were completely routed and driven back to their ships with great slaughter."

He paused for a moment and Benson glanced sideways. Slater's face was absorbed with the interest of what he was saying; his eyes were fixed on the dark line of the horizon. It was no more possible now to doubt his sincerity than it had been forty years ago, in that cellar below the rubble of Anzio. What had weakened in memory and came back with force to Benson now, as he felt the touch on his arm, was the attractive power of personality the other possessed, the effortless way in which he enlisted you in his purposes.

"Just over there," Slater said, nodding towards the horizon. "Perhaps where those woods are now, perhaps even nearer. The location is disputed but I have gone carefully into it and I am convinced it was on our side of the river. There is a poem commemorating the battle in the Anglo-Saxon Chronicle. The pursuit lasted all day. The fields around were darkened with blood, they say. Five Viking princes died in the battle. Constantine lost a son. People were fighting all the time in those days of course, it was a violent age. But this wasn't just any battle. It was one of the great battles of our history. Athelstan was the first Saxon King to have effective rule over the whole of England. The army he was commanding was an English army – not Mercian, not West Saxon, not Northumbrian. *English*. North and South burying their differences, fighting as one nation to repel the foreign invader."

Slater took some steps forward out into the sunshine and stood waiting for Benson to follow. "I've had the poem translated into modern English," he said. "It will be recited during the performance. My idea, you see, is to celebrate this step in the forging of the English state and nation by dramatising scenes from the life of King Athelstan, very loosely constructed, with interludes and entertainments."

The singing of the choir carried to them from the marquee, a different song now:

"On Richmond Hill there lives a lass
More bright than May-day morn,
Whose charms all other maids' surpass,
A rose without a thorn.
This maid so neat
With smile so sweet
Hath won my right good will . . ."

"They are not getting it right yet," Slater said. "They must give more force to those monosyllables. 'This-maid-so-neat-with-smile-so-sweet.' They are supposed to be singing the praises of an English rose, not reciting their multiplication tables. You may be wondering why I take so much trouble?"

"Well, as a matter—"

"The success of the whole depends on getting all the details right. That was true in the days of the Beachhead Buddies and it's just as true now."

Benson nodded. It was the first unsolicited reference that Slater had made to the past. "The Beachhead Buddies, yes," he said.

"Shall we go up to the house? We could have a drink before lunch."

He continued to talk as they made their way up the gently sloping ground towards the house. "I don't know what

179

your politics are," he said. "That's your business. But you fought to defend this country. Men who have been through that know what unity means. You mentioned the *Sunday Times*. That's a fine newspaper. Increasing its sales hand over fist, I understand, now that they have solved their labour problems."

Despite the express allowance for his own opinions, Benson felt that the pause Slater made here was deliberately interrogative. However, he said nothing. They were crossing the forecourt now, approaching the steps up to the terrace.

"I don't mind telling you," Slater said, "that I've taken a bit of a chance on you, asking you here to my home, agreeing to cooperate in the matter of this newspaper article. But we were in the war together and that means a lot to me. What I am saying is that I'm assuming a basic patriotism on your part. We hear a lot about division these days from the gloom and doom merchants. The North-South divide, all this stuff about two nations. England is one nation, Clive, can't help but be, considering our history. Chains forged like that are not broken by local discontents, or local malcontents either. They are forged in steel."

"Chained to history." Benson was struck by this turn of phrase. It was true – you couldn't open a newspaper without hearing them clank. "You feel that quite strongly in Liverpool," he said.

Slater appeared not to have heard this. He stopped at the foot of the steps, looking back over the grounds towards the lake. "I'm semi-retired now, you know," he said. "I'm sixty-six. I still go to board meetings, of course. I still take care of most of the bank's commodity business and do some investment consultancy work. Most of that I can do from my office here. Meredith drives me down to the City a couple of times a week on average. But I don't take the same interest in the bank's affairs that I used to. There's a time to get out, Clive." He turned and looked directly into Benson's face and said with a sort of smiling frankness that was extremely engaging, "I've got some good years ahead of me yet. I want to get more involved in local matters now. I want to put this place on the map."

The terrace was empty now. They went through the french windows directly into a long, rectangular drawing-room, furnished in Regency style, with walls and ceiling elaborately decorated in moulded plaster, pale grey lined with gilt.

"What can I get you?"

"I'd like a Scotch. No ice, please. Just as it is."

"Just as God made it, eh? My other passion is this house. You won't have seen much of it yet?"

"No," Benson said. "I came directly down from the terrace."

"This room we are in is what the first owners would have called the Saloon. Pity that word has gone out, I always think. It is now only associated with public houses, isn't it? The stucco was done by Pietro Francini. That's the same man who was commissioned by the first Duke of Northumberland to do the Long Gallery in Northumberland House."

"It's very fine," Benson said. This was no more than the truth. The plaster mouldings were the great feature of the room, wrought in graceful, playful patterns of foliation, clustered fruits, curlicues, rosettes, loops, swags, garlands, cornucopias. Winged women with gentle faces and the exuberantly bounding hindquarters of deer decorated the corners of the ceiling. Benson took a drink from his glass and felt an immediate benefit. "Very fine indeed," he said. "There is an attractive incongruity between the rather severe rectilinear form of the room itself and this extravagance of the decoration. I wonder if the designers intended that."

He paused, aware that he had fallen somehow into the role of courtier, aware too that this would be customary with those surrounding Slater, elicited, demanded almost, by the very charm and expansiveness of his manner. He thought he could detect now on Slater's face a shared knowledge of this, a look of faintly derisive alertness, as if his host had noted his malaise, discerned a sensitive spot; not an unfriendly look exactly, but somehow predatory, as if weaknesses emitted a sort of scent, as if within the caverns of personality vanities, follies, exploitable matter, could decay, giving off a whiff for those who had a nose for it.

This impression was confirmed when Slater, instead of helping him with civil assent, merely said drily, "Yes, Francini is generally considered to be rather good," and then began immediately to draw his guest's attention to various of the objects in the room. "The relief over the chimney-piece is a copy of Schiavoni's 'Apollo and Midas'," he said. "The original, of course, is at Hampton Court. The chimney-piece itself has been attributed to Henry Cheers. The painting on the wall over there is a portrait of Sir William Biggs, painted by Reynolds in 1768. He was the first owner, you know. I won't tell you how much it cost me to get it from the family. The commodes by the wall over there are French, of the Regency period."

Benson looked at the portrait, saw a thick-necked slave-dealer in a wig and black tricorn hat. Reynolds should have had better things to do.

"I've tried to keep the general tone of an eighteenth-century interior," Slater said. "The gilt table is Italian, around 1750. Do you see the clock on it, in the walnut case? I'm particularly fond of that piece. It once belonged to Lord Macaulay. The sofa-table is English too, a bit later, turn of the century. It's in rosewood. The wine cistern over by the door is a very rare type, *famille rose*, with dolphin feet, ah, there you are, Sylvia."

Mrs Slater had entered by the double door at the far end of the room. She was dressed in a pale green blouse and cream pleated skirt and no longer wore the sunglasses. Benson was sure now he could remember the face from innocently romantic English films of many years ago. The pale, ethereal prettiness was lined and faded but the large blue eyes were the same as had looked trustfully up at tall hussars and highwaymen. They were slow-moving, the eyes, he suddenly noticed, perhaps myopic, she had to narrow them slightly to keep him in focus.

"You've met Clive already, I gather."

There was a note of genial warning in this, or so it seemed to Benson. He saw her pass her tongue cautiously, like a child, over her lower lip. He realised that after an hour or so of listening to Verdi in her boudoir she was slightly drunk.

"Yes," she said, "we met earlier. Mr Benson had coffee with us on the terrace."

"Did he indeed? You would have done better to send him straight down to me in view of the time at our disposal." The voice was genial still. "I thought that is what I told you to do."

"I don't remember. He had just arrived, Hugo. I thought, after the journey . . ."

Something in the tone of this rather than the words made Benson look quickly at her. It came to him in that moment that she was frightened of her husband. Fortified as she was, mild as Slater's tone had been. "The coffee was extremely welcome," he said, looking at Slater. Suddenly, unexpectedly, he felt the stirring of a revolt perhaps forty years belated. "In fact," he said, "I don't know what I would have done without it, I don't know how I could have coped with the news that awaited me in your pagoda, Hugo."

"News?"

"That England is essentially one nation and that we owe it all to Athelstan."

Slater looked steadily at him for perhaps five seconds. His face was quite expressionless. "Perhaps you'd like another drink?" he said at last. He had himself drunk nothing yet.

"Another Scotch please."

Slater took his glass and went to the sideboard with it. While he was pouring out the drink Erika and another, older woman entered the room and joined him there.

"That's Erika's mother," Sylvia said. "You can't have one without the other, as Hugo has discovered to his cost. I don't think you're a journalist at all, Mr Benson, or at least not a proper one. You don't behave like one somehow. I mean, don't ask me how they behave but you are just not right. You intrude your own opinions. You make quite uncalled-for remarks about the slave trade. You've just offended Hugo, which is a very unwise thing to do, believe me. He didn't show it, but I know him. I don't think he believes you're a real journalist either. He has his reasons for doing things, Hugo always has his reasons, but they are not always what you think. You're not the Clive Benson who wrote *Fool's Canopy* by any chance?"

"Do you mean to say you've read it?"

"I've got a copy. If you really are the author, I'd like you to sign it sometime. It's one of the best historical novels I've ever read. I've always thought it would make a marvellous film."

Benson was so moved by this that he felt the prick of tears in his eyes. "You have just made a friend," he said. There was no time to say more. Slater came back with his drink. He was introduced to Erika's mother, a plump, quick-eyed woman with a vibrant voice. They were joined by a man with a soft face and hard eyes, whose name was Robinson; Sylvia explained in an aside that he was the senior partner in a firm of accountants and chairman of the Constituency Conservative Party. Two more men arrived together just before lunch was announced, one tall and black-haired, the other rather fat, with a full beard. They had driven over from Chester. Benson failed to catch either of their names but Sylvia told him that the tall man was playing Athelstan and the bearded one St Columba, so he thought of them in that way.

The dining-room contained one or two more portraits of wigged worthies and their gowned wives. There was a silver basket on the table, filled with white roses. Benson found himself seated near one end of the table with Erika's mother, Mrs Belmont, on one side of him, Sylvia on the other and Athelstan opposite. He had some soup without much noticing the flavour; then there was rainbow trout and stuffed artichokes – refined and expensive sorts of things such as he almost never ate these days. There was

184

white wine on the table and he had some. He was beginning to feel a certain sense of occasion. He glanced with renewed feelings of friendship at Sylvia Slater sitting to his left at the head of the table. She too was drinking the wine. She sat looking before her with a slight smile on her pale, rather crumpled-looking face. That magazine article had given quite the wrong impression of her, he thought. She was clearly a woman of discerning taste. What was it Slater had said? Positively her last performance. Something like that. Rather an ill-natured remark. She had dressed up for it. She had put on her gold bracelets and her white pyjama suit and tried to make a brave show, tried to do the old-time star, scattering 'darlings' and talking about boudoirs. The only true thing about her in all that rigmarole was that she liked listening to Verdi.

He looked across at Erika, who was laughing at something Robinson had said. She looked radiant, glowing with health. She had dressed her hair on top of her head, leaving unobscured the strong, beautiful column of her neck. She was wearing a white, short-sleeved dress of thin wool, which clung to the lines of her figure. Slater, he saw, was looking at her too.

"This is a beautiful house, isn't it?" Athelstan said, leaning across the table in a stiff-shouldered, man-to-man way. He had very soft brown eyes, like a cow's. "Full of beautiful things," he said. "Mr Slater once let it fall that the creamware dinner service in the cabinet was the personal possession of Josiah Wedgwood. Then there is the *chinoiserie*. Of course, Mr Slater is a collector."

"It's nice to see her happy again," Mrs Belmont said on his right. She had been following the direction of his gaze. "I've been very worried, you know. Erika is so trusting. She gets into some difficult situations simply because of this idealism of her nature. She has always been passionately interested in the stage, of course. Mr Slater recognised her talent at once."

"I thought we'd begin with Athelstan's dream immediately after lunch," he heard Slater say to St Columba.

185

"I should say that this is one of the most desirable residences we've ever had on our books," Athelstan said.

"Are you an estate agent?"

"Yes, I am, as a matter of fact."

"There was this man Gerald," Mrs Belmont said, "just to give you an example. I don't think we ever knew his surname. He said he was an impresario and the silly girl promptly went and fell in love with him. Good address in Knightsbridge. Turned out he had nothing to do with the theatre at all, he was some kind of crook. He kept her more or less locked up in this flat, no furniture in it, just carpet, the floor and walls all covered with beige carpeting. She was very disillusioned. Well, he was mad, but she only found that out when she was in the situation. When she complained he bought her a twelve-foot rubber plant to keep her happy. He knew she loved rubber plants. Of course, it couldn't go on."

"It doesn't sound very promising," Benson said. "I suppose it wouldn't have mattered so much if he had turned out to be a genuine impresario."

"No, that's right. She felt so betrayed, you see. That is what killed her love."

Benson drank some more wine. With something of a shock he saw Meredith, massive in a white jacket, standing at the sideboard. "What was Athelstan's dream?" he said. He had to raise his voice a little – the table was long and his host was at the far end of it. There was an immediate hush as Slater began to reply.

"On the eve of the battle," he said, looking not very cordially at Benson, "St Columba appears to Athelstan in a dream and promises him victory over his enemies. He prophesies that the kingdom he rules over will develop into a great nation of seafarers and inventors and will be the mother of parliaments. He outlines to Athelstan some of the great achievements awaiting England in the future."

"Agincourt," St Columba said, "the Armada, Shakespeare, the Spinning Jenny, the Steam Engine, the spread of Empire."

"You can't possibly bring in the Industrial Revolution," Benson said, "surely, without mentioning the accumulation of capital due to the Liverpool—"

"Liverpool played her part of course," Robinson said. "No one would deny that." He smiled stiffly at Benson. "You're a Liverpudlian, I take it? I like a man who takes pride in his city."

"It's a very important scene," St Columba said. "It's the only scene I'm in, as a matter of fact."

"It's an absolutely crucial scene," Robinson said. "Here you have all the themes summed up in a nutshell, unity through victory, the forging of the nation, the great contributions this small kingdom was destined to make to the civilisation of the Western world. And, seeing it, people will realise that these are not just dim events in history books but things that happened on their own soil, in the case of this battle on their own doorstep. It links people to their past. I should just like to add this, Hugo, while I'm about it, there won't be another opportunity before the event itself and I know it expresses the feelings of us all . . ."

It was clear that Robinson, perhaps by force of habit, feeling he had the attention of the meeting, had settled down to make a speech. "I know that I speak for all of us," he continued, "when I say how grateful I personally feel to you, not only for throwing your house and grounds open, but for the work you have put in, the dedication and the high sense of civic purpose. It's not too much to say that you are continuing the work of Athelstan himself. He had a policy of settling people on the land, as I understand it. You are giving people a sense of having a stake in this country. And that means owning a piece of it, owning your own house, for example."

"Hear, hear!" Athelstan said.

"It means having a stake in the future of this country by being able to buy shares in our great industries. That is what we mean by a property-owning democracy. That was Athelstan's policy a thousand years ago and that is our policy today. Thank you, Hugo. I can assure you of one

187

thing: it doesn't go unnoticed."

"You can see the continuity even in the names," St Columba said. "I mean, my name is Dodsworth. That's pure Saxon. It means the Homestead of Dod."

"Hang on a minute." When he thought of it afterwards Benson could not be sure just what led him to intervene at this point. Alcohol had something to do with it, his obsession even more; then there was Robinson's overbearing manner, the way he assumed he could speak for them all; but it was Slater at the end of the table, dominant even in his modest impassivity, that made the silence of assent suddenly impossible. He felt the tremors of speech in his lower jaw.

"Not quite all of us," he said rather loudly and met Robinson's cold, fishlike stare. "I don't disagree for a moment with what you say about Mr Slater's talents as a presenter of entertainments. I know more about that than anybody here, I should think. No, it's this business of property, of a property-owning democracy. The thing about the notion of a property-owning democracy is that it can come to seem like a definition – only the people that own the property have a share in the democracy, and the more they own the bigger their share. To see it in all its beauty you have to go back to the eighteenth century. As a matter of fact the Liverpool slave trade provides the best example of a property-owning democracy that I know. If you had a bit of extra cash you could buy into it quite easily. A lot of the ships they used were quite small, they could only pack in a hundred slaves or so. These were fitted out by small tradesmen – drapers, grocers, tallowchandlers, barbers, notaries, people like yourself, sir, or Athelstan here. What used to be called the shop-keeping class. Some had as little as a one-thirtieth share – say five slaves. Just a flutter really. Like buying a few shares in British Telecom. I suppose it was what you'd call a volatile market. But if your cargo didn't die you could make a nice little profit."

Benson paused. He was running out of steam. He could feel a slight, continuous quivering of the nerves somewhere within himself. "Enough to buy a bijou homestead for Dod," he said, glancing at St Columba. "Enough to pay Francini for the stucco work and still have something left over for a Chippendale or two."

A hush had fallen over the table. He saw that Erika was looking at him indignantly. Slater was not looking at him at all.

"I understand you are a journalist?" Robinson said coldly.

"Well, not exactly. I've written things for newspapers."

"He is a writer, a novelist," Sylvia said, speaking for the first time. "I've got one of his books." She smiled brightly round the table. "It's very good." It came to Benson that Mrs Slater was enjoying the situation.

"Fiction?" The look of disapproval on Robinson's face deepened.

"I hope you brought your costume," Slater said to St Columba. He still had not looked at Benson. "I want to do a full-dress rehearsal today, you know."

The conversation didn't really pick up again after this – Benson had cast a blight. Quite soon Slater suggested coffee. They went for this into what Slater had called the Saloon. After some brief hesitation Benson sat near Mrs Belmont: obsessed as she seemed with the fortunes of her daughter, she might not have noticed so much how the tone had turned against him. "You didn't finish telling me about Gerald," he said. "You stopped at the point where he bought Erika the rubber plant." Glancing up he met the gaze of Sir William Biggs on the wall; there seemed an extra shade of severity now in the merchant's expression. "What happened?" he said.

He had been right. Mrs Belmont resumed at once, as if there had been no interval. "Oh, well, he behaved quite disgracefully of course. She told him she wanted to go away for a while to think about their love, she tried to be tactful you see, but he lost control of himself completely, he attacked the rubber plant, he began chopping it up with karate blows, knowing full well how much that would hurt her. There was an Alsatian in the apartment and it began to get terribly excited."

But he was destined never to hear the end of the Erika-Gerald story. Slater approached at this point and asked him if he could spare a few minutes. "I thought we might use the study," he said. "Why don't you bring your coffee with you?"

The study was on the same floor, down a short passage. It was done out in mahogany and dark red leather. Slater seated himself at the desk and motioned Benson to a chair. There was no trace of a smile now. "I'm not going to beat about the bush," he said. "I haven't much time – I've got a lot to do this afternoon. The fact is I don't want you at these rehearsals. I've changed my mind about you, Benson. You offended my guests. You practically called Robinson a shopkeeper. You haven't shown the right spirit at all. I want you off the premises as soon as may be."

"I see." Benson looked at the straight-browed, heavy face before him. There was no particular expression there, no displeasure; the face was grave, dispassionate. So might Slater have looked in terminating the account of one of his bank's less satisfactory clients. "I'm just supposed to march off, am I?"

"I thought you were a bona fide journalist." Slater placed his hands together on the table, looked down at them a moment, then back at Benson. "You gave me a false impression," he said.

"It was a confusion." There was a little stack of printed sheets, blue in colour, near him on the desk and in the tension of his feelings he picked one up. "I was thinking of the other Show, the Beachhead Buddies," he said. "You took it for this Athelstan business. That is because your own purposes are so important to you that what is in the forefront of your mind you assume must be in the forefront of everybody else's. As a matter of fact, I don't think you asked me here because you thought I was a bona fide journalist."

"Don't you?"

The voice was very cold now. Benson felt fear of the man before him, so much more powerful and richer than himself, here among the visible evidence of his success, the thick carpet, shining wood and dark leather, the array of books on the shelves. "No," he said, making a conscious effort to control his breathing, keep his voice steady. "No, I think I was a portent for you, I think you took me for a good augury. It must have seemed like that, my phoning just then, after forty years, just when you were putting another show on. Little Benson again. Like a mascot. I was the one you asked to go with you to the Company Commander that night, the night you got the idea for the Beachhead Buddies. You remember, don't you? We had just been relieved. They were shelling the German lines. Then of course, when I came today, you wanted the same loyalty again, because you have to have that, don't you? But I was only a boy then."

"You were a girl, as far as I remember. What do you think you are now?" Slater put his hand flat on the desk preliminary to hoisting himself up. "I've no time for any more of this," he said. "I'll see Meredith runs you back to the station."

"I'm not going yet."

"Not going?" The slight frown had returned to Slater's face, as at something insignificant but obstinate lodged in his path.

"There are one or two things I must ask you about."

"Do you really think I'm going to waste my time answering your questions? You'd better clear off while you can still do so with some dignity."

"It would only take a few minutes." Benson could feel his hands trembling slightly. He put them between his knees. "Supposing," he said, "just for the sake of argument, supposing I did write the article after all, I mean an article about *both* the shows, how I have come back after forty years to find you doing the same thing, still dealing in the commodities market . . ." Nervousness made him lose the thread for a moment. "Sugar and rum, you know.

191

People would make the connections."

"Sugar and rum? What on earth are you talking about? You'd better get out." For the first time a definite note of anger had come to Slater's voice. "I don't think you are in your right mind," he said. "You seemed mad to me at the table just now, as well as offensive, making those pathetically over-simplified analogies."

"Too complicated to understand, is it? Market forces. That's what Hogan says too."

"Who the devil is Hogan?"

"It doesn't matter." The trembling had ceased now. He felt shame at what he was going to say but no longer any fear. "I could say how you used us at Anzio, set us to work for your glory, how some of us were killed or wounded or so on and the gaps were filled with new acts, but you, alone of us – you managed to get out before the offensive, before the Beachhead Buddies were finally shot to pieces, and now I find you doing the same sort of thing. It wouldn't look too good, would it?"

There was a short silence. Slater's face had flushed dark red. His eyes were fixed in a look of furious contempt. "You little shit," he said. "I've a good mind to bounce you off the wall. Do you really think you can threaten me like that, a man in my position? Do you think I'm afraid of that sort of scurrilous rubbish?"

Benson made no reply. He was aware that the threat was a weak one, as well as dishonourable. But he had wanted so much to know. He was about to get to his feet, when Slater said, "I don't need to answer any of your questions, I hope you understand that."

"Yes," Benson said, "of course I understand."

The first flush of rage had left Slater's face now. Benson saw him look briefly away. Then his mouth loosened a little, settled into an expression of more amicable contempt. "Well, since you say it won't take long . . ."

"It's about a man called Walters. You remember him, don't you?"

"Walters, Walters . . ."

"You must remember him. He was in the show too. I was Velma and he was Burlington Bertie. He was killed not long before the break-out. He told me that you had offered to get him a posting to Naples, as part of a new show. He was the only one. I've always wondered why."

The lie agitated Benson, even though he knew there was no possible way that Slater could know it for one.

"Yes, I seem to remember that," Slater said.

"Why Walters? It was a double act. Why not both of us?"

But even as he asked the question he realised that Slater had already answered it – the admission was all that had been needed. Slater had seen how close they were, how they were always together.

"I remember him as being very talented," Slater said. "He was a gifted actor."

"There were others who were talented. Why not them?"

Slater's face still wore the same half-amicable disdain. "I really don't remember now."

"It must have been because you wanted to break us up. You were alone there in your own way. You wanted to divide us." Benson laughed suddenly in release of tension. A distant, destructive impulse, converse of his own jealousy – no more than that. His treacherous tendency to tears again threatened him. "The Beachhead Buddies," he said. "And now your great theme is unity. You must admit there is irony there. Or was it just motiveless malignity, to coin a phrase?"

"You are talking hysterical rubbish."

Slater had spoken coldly and abruptly but the dislike in his eyes was not for the present only and Benson knew in that moment that the other had never forgotten Walters, that the refusal still rankled. He got to his feet. "There's just one other thing. What gave you the idea – in the first place I mean."

"The idea for the Show? That's easy. I always knew there was a need for it, of course. Then that day, that night when we spoke about it, I had been watching a rather ridiculous scene a bit earlier on, before we were relieved. Someone had brought back a German helmet for some reason and one of

193

the men put it on and got dried blood in his hair. There was a Welsh chap whose nerve had given way the night before. I had come over for a runner to go back to Company HQ and I came upon this scene with this lout cursing and trying to wash the blood out and the Welshman gibbering away and that old woman – Baxter was his name – holding forth about how much blood you'd need to make so much powder . . . "

Slater paused. His face had softened with the reminiscence. "It was pure comedy," he said. "I thought what a first-rate sketch it would make. That started me thinking."

The smile faded. Slater looked at him with a sort of contemptuous impassivity. "Well, are you going?" he said. "If you try to write anything about me after this, I promise you I'll make you suffer for it."

Benson could think of nothing to say. He looked for a moment or two longer at the face of the man before him. Into his mind there came the memory of the day Slater had come to see him in the hospital. "It's strange," he said. "The last time I saw you was in the military hospital in Naples. You were on a routine visit to members of the unit – part of your job, wasn't it, though I'm not quite sure how it fitted into the entertainments business. You were very neatly turned out, I remember. The ward was full of surgical cases, some of the men there were dying, some of them were off their heads. I remember all those bandaged, hardly recognisable shapes and you in the middle. I remember thinking, any moment now he's going to start waving his cane about, directing us all."

Do I really remember that? he wondered, going down the steps to where the car was waiting, or did I just invent it as a parting shot? From somewhere above him Verdi was issuing loudly, Aida urging Radames to flee with her.

> "Là tra foreste vergini
> Di fiori profumati . . ."

★

194

"We got a deal then?" Meredith said.

"No, we haven't got a deal. I just said we would talk about it."

"I was present at his wedding. When he got married to Yoko. Keeping the press at bay. She was a one. No inhibitions, Mr Benson, know what I mean?"

Meredith's pale, broad face was full of emotion. His eyes sought Benson's eagerly. A tiny trickle of perspiration had run down from the brim of his cap and stopped at the temple. It was hot here on the station platform, full in the sunshine, and the chauffeur's large body seemed uncomfortable and constricted in its livery. They had walked to the far end, away from the little knot of people waiting for the train.

"I got the facts, you got the gift of words," Meredith said. "We could make a bomb. The title is there already, we wouldn't need to lose any time over that. *I Was John Lennon's Bodyguard*. What do you think of it?"

Benson glanced down the platform at the station clock: a good ten minutes yet before the train; Slater had packed him off early. "It's a good title," he said. "But the fact is, you know, I don't do ghost writing. I wouldn't be any good at it."

It was the third time he had said this and each time Meredith came up with a new offering from his past.

"I was in the army before that," he said now. "Five years in the Coldstream Guards." He looked quickly up and down the platform. "After that I did three years in the SAS. I seen a lot of things, believe you me."

"It's not that I don't believe you," Benson said. "It's just that I wouldn't be the right—"

"Aden," Meredith said, "the Yemen, Northern Ireland. You name it." He had assumed again that congested look, combined result of the intensity of his feelings and the confinement of his tunic. "You're not supposed to say, they make you take an oath. But what the fuck, Mr Benson, if you'll pardon the language, what the fuck? It teaches you to keep your eyes open. I keep my eyes open on this job. A

195

person learns a lot of things driving other people around. He hears things, he picks things up, he puts two and two together."

"What sort of things?"

But Meredith had heard the eagerness in his voice. "We got a deal or not?" he said.

"Listen," Benson said, "I'll be quite honest with you. I'm not the man to do this particular job. I can't even do my own stuff these days. To tell you the truth I haven't been able to write anything for well over two years now. But I know a few people still and I promise you I'll do my best to find someone – someone good – and put him in touch with you. Okay?"

Meredith held out a huge hand. "Shake on it," he said. "I'm a judge of character, I always have been."

"What did you mean just now?"

"She's the only one worth anything. Mrs Slater. She's got human feelings. If it was up to her, I could go into shirt-sleeves. I get heat rash in this uniform. But he wouldn't have it. Full livery at all times. Today is a Saturday but I had to put on full gear – just to come out for you. And look how he treats her. Bringing that woman into the house."

"Erika, you mean?"

"Her, yes. *Actress*," Meredith said with great disgust. "I bet the only acting she done is bum and tit poses for the porno mags. And that mother of hers, looking out for the highest bidder. You know what he's after, don't you?"

"Slater? I imagine he wants to get Erika into the sack."

"Sure, but I don't mean that. He's a man that has never got just one thing in mind. I am friendly with Miss Parks." In spite of the earnest confidentiality of his manner, Meredith managed a slight smirk. "That's the secretary. She doesn't do his accounts, but she does a lot of the correspondence. She once let fall that he's been giving a lot of money to Conservative Central Office over the past five years. And I mean a lot," she said. "Then there's this show he's putting on. He's invited half the county, all the big-wigs. The Lord Lieutenant is coming, the Chief Constable

196

is coming, the Master of the Hunt is coming. He's got people coming up from London. He's asked Sir Geoffrey Howe. 'We're going to put this place on the map, Meredith,' he said to me once. You know what that means, don't you?"

Benson saw the train approaching in the distance. "No," he said. "What does it mean?"

"How many real locals will be there, tell me that? It's by invitation only. It's a society event, Mr Benson. There'll be donations. There'll be caviar and champagne. Why do you think Erika and her mum are so interested? He did more than the agent to get their candidate in last time. Spent a fortune on it. You know what it adds up to, don't you?"

"The train's coming in," Benson said. "What does it add up to?"

"He's after a knighthood. He wants to be Sir Hugo."

Benson got on the train and stood at the window. He was immediately convinced that Meredith was right. That must be why Slater, after the first rage, had been so surprisingly amenable: he hadn't wanted to risk the slightest malodour; preferable to talk for five minutes to this little shit . . .

"He'll get it too," Meredith said. "You won't forget we got a deal, will you?"

"No, I won't forget."

Meredith remained standing still on the platform as the train pulled out. At a distance of some hundred yards or so he made a half-salute. Benson waved. He felt sad to be leaving Meredith alone, dark and bulky on the deserted platform. The train was like a receding tide, leaving him beached there, with his life that was so wonderful to him, in fantasy or fact or their complex blending. Benson wanted to repeat his promise, wanted to shout that he would find someone, but Meredith was too far away to hear him now.

On his way back he discovered in his pocket the printed sheet, much crumpled now, which he had picked up from Slater's desk. It was a programme of events for 'Brunanburh', which was what Slater had called his forthcoming show.

4

On his way to Rathbone's Show he had the impression that there were more people about than usual and more police, especially in the streets running south from Upper Parliament Street; groups of black youths stood at corners, as if waiting for news.

There were empty seats in the hall but not as many as he had expected. A good number of those present would be acquaintances of Rathbone's like himself. Or perhaps clients, he thought suddenly, glancing round. Yes, there were faces he knew, people met on the stairs or the landing. There would be a high degree of suggestibility in this assembly – he wondered idly if Rathbone had implanted the invitation while they were under hypnosis.

All the same there were more people here than could be accounted for in this way and he supposed they must have bought tickets on impulse or for obscure personal reasons. At the far end of the front row he saw a man with a professional-looking camera slung round his neck; probably some friend of Rathbone's on one of the papers. Various of his fictioneers were scattered about the hall. He saw Carter's unmistakable yellow and green sports jacket up near the front. Jennifer Colomb was sitting a couple of rows behind him. He caught her eye and nodded and smiled. She looked flushed and nervous as she did when awaiting his response to the doings of Lady Margaret and Sir Reginald. He saw Elroy Palmer, the creator of Zircon, coming in through the door in his invariable red woollen hat. He felt grateful to these people, who had come here, he knew, purely as a favour to him. By the clock on the wall it was twenty-five past seven: only five minutes to go and Alma had not come yet; perhaps she had changed her mind. He resisted an impulse to go out and look for her – they had arranged to meet inside the hall. When he turned to face his front again he saw that Carter was craning round to look at him and he raised a hand in greeting. In reply Carter lifted his green bag from its place in his lap and held it aloft shaking it to and fro in a triumphant gesture. He was smiling broadly. Benson nodded, resolving to make a quick getaway after the show if possible; it had been a hard day, the last thing he wanted was another dollop of Albert and Sheila to take home with him.

The lighting was not very good; it was not theatre lighting at all, just a row of bare bulbs set at intervals overhead. However, a spotlight had been installed and the white circle of light lay dead centre on the empty stage. There was a wooden box in one corner, about the size of a tea-chest, and in another a hat-stand with a wide brimmed white hat on it, of the sort women sometimes wear in summer. Two upright chairs stood just outside the circle of light.

The audience was quiet, sitting patiently on the hard little chairs. Benson felt anxious about Alma but at the same time he was relaxed and slightly sleepy. His eyes were fixed on the motionless circle of light, within which images formed, swam into focus, fused, dissolved: Thompson raised a blind face, the owl rose into the night, the doomed soldier combed his hair, Walters whispered his mimicry, the suicide leapt from the mild spaces of air, Slater smiled through the noise of the guns. But at the very centre of the circle, where the focus was sharpest, the light was unviolated; there was nothing – these lapping images did not reach so far, did not touch the heart of the light . . .

"Those places free?"

He knew the voice, the loud, strangled-sounding upper-class accent conscientiously but imperfectly flattened. Glancing up he saw Anthea Best-Cummings and Hogan coming down the row towards him. With something of a shock he saw that they were holding hands.

"These are free," he said. "I'm keeping this one on the other side."

"Just made it," Hogan said. "That's what I call good

timing."

He was transformed. Maroon tie, briefcase, business suit had gone as if they had never been; he was dressed now in a tattered blue denim jacket which brought out the colour of his eyes – eyes no longer slow and stricken but full of life and animation; his sparse hair was lighter, soft-looking, free of that sweet balm. Anthea too was changed; she was in her black leathers still but her skin was clear of disfiguring spots and her hair was clean and combed and tied back. She looked extremely happy. "This is a lark," she said. "Never been to a hypnotism show before."

"Well, how are you two getting on?"

"We're living together now," Anthea said. "At my place at Birkenhead. Michael moved in the same day we met."

"We met at your apartment, if you remember," Hogan said. "Lucky day for me."

Anthea turned on him a face radiant with affection. "Lucky for me, you mean," she said.

"I do remember, yes. Well, you are both looking very well on it, if I may say so." He felt pleased, in a gratified, fatherly way, about the change in these two people. "Still writing?" he said.

"I've given up the novel," Hogan said. "Given up thoughts of it, I mean." He paused a moment, smiling. "There wasn't really a novel to give up, was there? But I still want to write. Not stories. I'd like to write down what I see around me, keep myself out of it as far as possible. Sort of reportage, with pictures."

"We thought, you know, that we might start up our own press," Anthea said. "Just a small affair, of course. Bring out a sort of newspaper, real news, try to show what is happening in this city. No pompous bloody comment, no party line. Not really political at all – we just want to show what these bastards have done to the Welfare State." She had spoken very loudly and Benson saw a certain stillness descend on the people in front of them.

Hogan said, "It was seeing these men in Birkenhead picking over a rubbish dump that started me off. There is a big municipal tip up near where we live. You go there early in the morning you'll see maybe twenty fellers picking it over, raking about in it. Grown men, not boys. Unemployed men. Not tramps. Men like myself. Men who feel shame, Mr Benson. Parts of the tip were smouldering and there were gulls and crows picking about in it as well. I want people to see that picture – the dirty smoke, the smell, the birds and the men together in the rubbish. That is the truth, you can go there and you can see it. That is Birkenhead in 1988."

"Michael has had his consciousness raised," Anthea said fondly. "He was identifying with the wrong lot. They kicked him in the teeth then kept him quiet on tranquillisers – same lot of bastards, they're all the same."

"We'd need a camera too," Hogan said.

"But how will you get the money for all this?"

"I think daddy would stump up if I put it to him in the right way," Anthea said.

"I see, yes. Well, I wish you every success with the venture."

"We'll send you a copy of the first issue," Anthea said. "Your friend hasn't come. It's twenty-five to now."

Benson felt her eyes resting on him with a certain quality of curiosity. "Perhaps she couldn't make it after all," he said.

"She may have had some trouble getting through. There's a lot of people about on the streets tonight. Something is—"

She was interrupted by a scattered burst of clapping. The tall, gaunt figure of Rathbone had emerged from behind the curtain at the rear of the stage. He was in a dinner jacket and wore a black turban tied in Sikh style, with a glittering stone pinned to it in the centre of his forehead. On that drab stage he was an impressive sight. In his husky, penetrating voice, which carried easily to every part of the hall, he began to talk to the audience – creating an atmosphere, Benson quickly realised, trying to make up for the bareness of the place, the bleak, unvarying light. He did it rather well.

They were about to see a unique show, he said. One which had never so far been performed anywhere in the Western world. You would have to go back, for the nearest parallel, to the role-playing of so-called primitive societies, during which ancient myths and rituals were acted out. The participants in these ancient rituals were pastmasters in auto-hypnosis. They enacted age-old dramas concerned with the cycle of the seasons, placation of the gods, triumph over their enemies. In the course of this they assumed archetypal roles: scapegoat, healer, trickster, priest . . .

A form of mumbo-jumbo really, Benson thought. It didn't matter how much the audience actually took in, so long as they were softened up. Rathbone had paused for a moment or two; now he began speaking again, moving slowly forward as he did so.

"Now we live in different times," he said. "You often hear people say that a person cannot be hypnotised into going against his own nature. That may well be true, ladies and gentlemen. But what is this nature of ours that we speak so confidently about? Who can claim to know the capacities of his own nature? As an illustration of what I mean I should like to begin the evening's entertainment with what we call in the profession chain-reaction hypnosis. This requires great concentration and I must ask you to cooperate with me to the full."

He was standing now at the edge of the stage. "I'd like to ask for volunteers," he said. "Anyone at all. I don't distinguish between good subjects and bad ones. You are all good subjects to me. I assure you no harm will come to anyone. My methods are tried and tested. There is complete control at every stage."

Nobody in the audience moved or spoke. "Come now," Rathbone said. He looked down, scanning the faces. "What about you? What about you, madam? Can I request you to step up on the stage? What about you, sir?"

The man he had addressed said loudly, "You won't catch me coming up there. I don't believe in it." A rustle of laughter and relief went through the audience. "Lot of

202

hocus-pocus," he shouted, encouraged.

Rathbone stood silent for some moments, looking directly down at the man who had interrupted. Then he said, "Your presence here gives the lie to that." He was smiling but there had been an edge of aggression in his voice. "Real unbelievers stay away," he said. "What about you, madam? That's the spirit. No, bring your handbag with you."

A youngish, stout woman in a green anorak had stood up and begun to make her way to the steps at the side of the stage. She had a heavy, expressionless face, one which he knew, and she looked half-hypnotised already. The audience had fallen silent again, but there was a different quality in the silence now: it was tense, expectant, alert to the prospect of conflict. Rathbone moved across to help the woman up, led her over the stage into the spotlight, placed her sideways to the audience. She stood silent there, a slight, self-conscious smile on her face, holding her large and shiny handbag.

"What is your name, madam?" Rathbone enquired with great suavity. "Will you tell the audience your name?"

"You know her name already." It was the same man, the same voice, loud but without much feeling in it – the voice of a professional heckler. All the same Benson was sure that the accusation was true, he had recognised this woman as one of Rathbone's clients. There had been no laughter this time at the interruption.

"You again?" There was no mistaking now the aggressive note in Rathbone's voice. "Come on, sir, step up," he said, and it was like a challenge to combat. "Come and have a chat with me up here. You are doing your best to ruin this show. The audience has come here to be entertained. If you think I'm a fake, step up on the stage."

It was when the man stood up and began to move towards the stage that Benson began to feel that he might perhaps have misappreciated the situation. But there was no time to think much about it. Another man, elderly and high-shouldered, had risen in belated response to Rath-

203

bone's appeal and was making his way forward.

Rathbone helped this man on to the stage, escorted him over to the box and seated him on it. Then he turned his attention to the heckler.

"Over here," he said. "Come over here to me." This obliged the man to walk the whole width of the stage. "Steady now," Rathbone said. "Where are you going? No, I don't want you here. Over there. Not *there*. I want you on one of those chairs."

"Make your mind up," the man said, but his voice had lost the heckling note and his face was uncertain and sheepish. He was short and poorly dressed, with a bony, sharp-featured face.

Rathbone watched the man retrace his steps, waited until he was in the act of sitting, then said in a sudden loud tone of displeasure, "*Not that one*. That is my chair."

The audience was absolutely silent now, with the unmistakable silence of absorbtion. "Good God, what are you doing?" Rathbone said. The man had stood up hastily and kicked against the chair. It was clear to Benson that he was confused by the stage space, which is both vast and cramped at the same time to those not used to it. And Rathbone's contradictory instructions were confusing him still further.

"*The other chair*," Rathbone said. He moved lightly over and sat opposite the man at a distance of three feet or so. "Why are you looking at the audience?" he said. "Don't look at the audience. *Look at me*."

Benson saw the man's head jerk round. With a sudden change of tone Rathbone said, "That's right, that's good. You don't want to fight, you don't want to argue, I'm your friend, listen to my voice, I'm your friend."

Very quietly, in tones only partially audible to the spectators, he continued speaking, holding the other with his eyes. It seemed to Benson that the man made one or two restless movements with his head at first but after some moments he remained fixed in an attitude of attention. The rather sheepish smile he had worn on his face earlier had gone completely now. Benson saw the lowering of his

204

shoulders.

"You are going down deeper," Rathbone said more loudly. "Deeper . . . deeper. Concentrate on your hands. That's right. Now I'm going to tell you to raise your hands and put the palms together. When you put your palms together, you will go down deeper. Concentrate on your hands. That's good. Now raise your hands, put the palms together."

With astonishment and a sort of uneasy pity, Benson saw the man raise his hands and place them together. Could Rathbone have seen something in the man's face when he looked down at him, heard something in his voice? The bullying had looked genuine enough, unpleasantly so. Could he really have snared the man's mind and will somehow, between a phrase and a phrase?

"You are pressing, pressing, your hands are pressing together. Your hands are chained together. You can't get them apart. I'm going to count to five. When I reach five I'm going to snap my fingers. When you hear me snap my fingers you will go down deeper, you will know that your hands are chained together, you won't be able to move your hands apart until you hear that same sound again."

Rathbone stood up and moved forward to face the audience. "He's saying his prayers," he said. "Long overdue, I expect." The audience tittered, nervous. Rathbone went back to the man, seated himself again and began counting in a slow, deliberate voice. When he reached five he waited a moment or two then snapped his fingers contemptuously under the man's nose – a loud sound in that silent hall. He stood up, fished in his pocket for a moment, then held a hand up to the audience, turning a metal object this way and that. "This is an ordinary tin whistle," he said. "You will observe that I am placing it here, on the stage." He walked forward a few paces and laid the whistle a couple of yards beyond the circle of the spotlight.

The man had remained seated, looking mildly before him, his pale, sharp-featured face set in an expression of placid obstinacy, his hands before him, palms together.

205

Rathbone was standing behind him now, looking down at the top of his head.

"When you hear me snap my fingers," he said, "you will find that you can move your hands apart again, the chains will fall away. But you will have to do one more thing before you can be free. You will get up, you will find the whistle that is lying on the stage. You will pick it up and you will blow on it. Once, just once. When you have done that you will be free."

Again he moved forward to address the audience. "He wanted to be the referee," he said, "so we'll let him, shall we? He can blow the whistle for us." Again there came that nervous, half-unwilling rustle of response. Smiling, Rathbone moved across the stage to the woman, who was still standing where he had left her, near the hatstand. "Look at me," he said. The tone was easier now, quite loud, almost conversational. "Listen to my voice, this is my voice, let yourself relax, let yourself go. You want to relax, your body wants to relax, don't resist it, let yourself go . . ."

This time the effect was almost immediate, confirming Benson's suspicion that this woman had been put under by Rathbone numbers of times before, though what she was being treated for he could only speculate. She had been visibly affected from the start, from the first words Rathbone uttered. Now Benson saw the shoulders relax, the stolidity of the face intensify.

"What is your name?" Rathbone said. "Tell the audience your name."

"My name is Dorothy Spencer." The voice itself sounded tranced – slow, without inflection.

"No, you are not Dorothy, you are Mary, poor Mary. Do you know the song 'Poor Mary lies a-weeping'?"

"Yes."

It must be obvious to the audience, Benson thought, that some of this has been arranged in advance. He must have put her through the song before. Once again he found himself doubting the genuineness of the proceedings. What he didn't doubt was that he was watching one of the most riveting pieces of theatre he had ever seen in his life. Misinformed about owls Rathbone might be, unfrocked therapist, feverish smoker on landings; but tonight he was a magic man. This obscure hall, scene of innumerable humble functions – mothers' meetings, Methodist tea-parties, bring-and-buy sales – was transformed into a place of wonder and terror.

"I want you to stand here and wait. In a little while you will hear somebody blow a whistle. Just once. When you hear the whistle, you will go to the hatstand and you will put on the white hat. When you put the white hat on, then you are Poor Mary, then you can sing your song. When you have sung your song you will be free. You will sing your song and then you will wake up and you will be free."

Rathbone turned to face the audience. "I'll let you into a secret," he said. "In the box our friend is sitting on, there is a frog mask. We are going to see Poor Mary find her prince. I must ask you now for absolute silence. We are entering a crucial phase of the proceedings."

He moved towards the man who had been sitting patiently all this while on the box. Standing before him and looking down intently at his face, he began to speak, but again in a different voice, this time loud and monotonous in tone. He was telling the man to relax, to relax. But what his plans were for this man, what signal he was to make, what he was to do when he heard Poor Mary's song, nobody there was destined to know. Someone, the caretaker perhaps, thinking it too warm inside, had opened the double door at the entrance. While Rathbone was still speaking to the man on the box, the distant sound of police sirens came from the night outside and then, from somewhere closer at hand, a long blast on a whistle. Rathbone, his back to the stage, was concentrating his powers on the man before him and talking loudly. He seemed to have heard nothing.

The woman on the stage turned and went to the hatstand. Quite impassively she took the white hat and put it on. In this summery hat and her green anorak, holding the shiny black handbag, she looked painfully ridiculous. The audience made no sound at all. Slowly the woman began to move forward. Her mouth opened and she began to sing in a soft, rather breathless, surprisingly tuneful voice:

"Poor Mary lies a-weeping,
A-weeping, a-weeping . . ."

Rathbone turned quickly. "Not yet," he said sharply. As he spoke the siren sounded again, very close now, it seemed just outside in the street, a loud, maniacal whooping, terribly startling in that spell-bound hall.

"Good God, what was that?" Anthea said.

The woman's singing had stopped abruptly, either at Rathbone's command or in the shock of the clamour outside. She stood still for perhaps five seconds, then her body shuddered convulsively, she raised her head and broke into a storm of weeping, drawing her breath in long, painful gasps. Benson saw Rathbone move quickly towards her. The photographer had stood up and was taking pictures. The tranced heckler sat motionless with his hands together in prayer. One or two people in the audience were craning to see outside but most were absorbed in what was happening on the stage.

"I think I'll just—" Benson got up quickly. There was a sidedoor immediately opposite him. He went through it into the street and looked up and down. The street was empty but he could hear the receding sirens and from the same direction, up towards Parliament Street, a confused sound of shouts and whistles. There was a smell of burning on the air. Benson hesitated for a short while. He did not want to go back into the hall. Rathbone's show had distressed him considerably and it was in ruins now anyway. Also, he was curious. He began to walk down the street in the direction of the sounds. His view was restricted by buildings to begin with but at the first intersection, glancing to his left, he saw a red glow of fire in the sky, wreaths of black smoke slowly unfurling against it. The noise was louder now, more confused. Two black youths ran past him, going in the same direction. They ran side by side, quite soundlessly, down the middle of the street.

Possessed by curiosity – and against his better judgement – Benson turned left at the next corner, in the direction of the main road. He could smell the fire more strongly now, a reek of burning plastic waste and rubber. The far end of the street was blocked with uniformed figures – he saw that they were police in riot gear, saw gleams from the street lamps on visors and helmets and plastic shields. They were forming up under shouted instructions from the inspector.

Halfway down, ignored by the police, a small knot of people had gathered on a corner. Benson approached them. "What's going on?" he said.

"You can't get through," an elderly man said. "They won't let you through this way."

"We're trying to get across to Edge Hill," the woman beside him said. "I don't know how they think we're going to get home."

"But what's going on, what's happened?"

"They've started fires along Parliament Street. They've blocked the road. The fire engines can't get through."

After hesitating a moment longer, Benson turned and began to walk back the way he had come. He had no desire now to get any nearer to the shouts and fires. He too had to get over to the other side of Parliament Street somehow, if he was to regain his apartment. There wouldn't be buses but he might find a taxi. He began to plot the route in his mind. This was Grierson Street, which ran into Lodge Lane. He could work his way round through the side streets . . .

When he was near the end of the street he heard the smashing of glass. He had been closer to Lodge Lane than he thought. Turning on to it, he saw a crowd of perhaps twenty people around the smashed windows of an electrical goods shop. Men and women were emerging from the shop on to the pavement carrying things, moving off with them, away from the light.

He had an immediate, confused sense of something

travestied about these people. Then he saw that several of them had their faces partly concealed by scarves or pieces of cloth. One black youth was naked to the waist; he had taken off his tee-shirt and tied it across the lower part of his face. A middle-aged woman in a hat with a feather in it came out from the interior carrying a video recorder like a tray. She walked briskly away with it and disappeared down one of the streets on the other side. A tall black man came out hugging a television set, his eyes peering affrightedly over the top.

With a shock of surprise he saw a man in an animal mask come out – it was Mickey Mouse; the light fell for a second or two on the blob nose, the projecting flaps of the ears. A moment later, cradling a variety of small objects in boxes, he saw a grotesque, blubbery-looking Winston Churchill. They must have broken into a shop to get them, he thought, one of the kind that sells novelties and tricks. I should go, I should get back off this street . . . A pop-eyed Margaret Thatcher came out, a hectic flush on her cheeks, carrying a vacuum cleaner in each hand, the flexes trailing behind her. She was followed soon after by David Owen, cadaverous, with something long in a box.

Almost more striking than the masks was the decorous behaviour of the looters. There was almost complete silence among them; no voice was raised; no notice was taken of any oddities of appearance. They hung around the shattered window, dipped in and out, made off with their acquisitions like good citizens. He heard the sound of smashing windows further down: all along the street the shops were being looted. A man stalked past with clothes draped over him, misshapen and strange. Light from the street-lamp fell on his face: it was Neil Kinnock. Of course, he thought, the police will be fully occupied in closing off the main road, containing the riot. They've got their backs facing this way.

He was about to pursue his intention and cross over when, without any warning at all the intent cluster of looters was broken, the crowd round the shop surged across the street towards him. They were joined at the edge of the pavement by another flow from his own side. A moment later he was swept back in a press of bodies. At first he tried to struggle forward against the rush. Then he saw a Black Maria come nosing slowly into the street that ran off opposite and he let himself go with the movement of the crowd. This quickened, he was obliged to break into a stumbling run. The faces around him had a sort of staring exhilaration about them. One man was laughing widely. Benson saw Woody Allen and Stalin and David Steel and Popeye. He was forced back the way he had come for a short distance, then the crowd divided and he found himself jostled forward into a narrow entry between house-backs. His heart was beating heavily. He was powerless to struggle against the tide of bodies behind and around him. He concentrated on keeping his footing. Ahead of him he saw a leaping glow of flame. There was a sound of confused shouting, then a heavy, rattling sound like a roll of drums. A moment later he was out on to broad pavement, in firelight that seemed clearer than daylight. The crowd flowed away, thinned out in this greater space.

In the minute or so that he stood there the scene printed itself in his mind in all essential details – and for ever. He was facing towards Smithdown Road. A barricade of blazing cars blocked the street and there were fires beyond this and within it – he saw that the new branch of Barclay's Bank was burning fiercely, the flames leaping high into the night. Houses on either side of this were alight too, and he saw the movement of flames inside the derelict International Club directly across from him. Soot and sparks showered through the air. Against this lurid light he saw figures of men, mainly young, black and white side by side, bending, running forward, leaping, retreating, in what he took in the first confused moments for a sort of dance. Then he saw the arcs of the missiles rising over the flames, saw them fall among the ranks of the police beyond the barricade. The rattling he had heard before began again – the police were striking with their batons in unison on their riot

211

shields. As they drummed they advanced at a slow run, spread in a line across the street, straight at the volleying stones, the blazing cars. Benson saw a policeman fall and be carried back helmetless, a dark glint of blood on his face. At the barricade they divided, seeking a way through. Then he saw police on his side of the fire, saw batons rising and falling, saw the stoners giving back.

It could only be a matter of time, he knew, before fresh contingents of police, forming behind the lines, came up the way he had come, took the enemy in the flank – and anyone here on the pavement would be the enemy. Escape along the street was impossible – the crowd was too thick. The only chance was to get back down the alley he had come by, even if it meant fighting his way. He had been forced several yards along the pavement in the first surge of the crowd. He was beginning to edge his way back when he caught sight of Alma. She was no more than a dozen yards away but it was a dozen yards in the wrong direction, nearer the police advance. The crowd there could not disperse easily. They were packed too close together. Benson began to push his way through. He was sweating profusely from exertion and from the heat of the fires. He could hear his own panting breaths. Again the fear came to him that he might faint.

She did not see him until he was only a yard or so away, then she began at once to struggle in his direction. She shouted something.

"What?" They were standing up close together and he had his hand under her arm.

"My car," she said. "I had to leave my car."

"Never mind the bloody car."

The crowd was yielding now, flowing back. The recoil of panic at the front was transmitted to them here in a slow eddying motion. Keeping a tight grip on Alma he began to shoulder his way back towards the mouth of the alley. He was aided now by the movement of the crowd and after some moments of effort they reached it, got down into it in the midst of a struggling group of others with the same idea. The coolness and darkness here, as they moved further down, was miraculous almost, better than the thickest shade on the hottest day. Benson was still audibly panting. "Christ," he said, "I'm too old for this."

After that neither of them said anything much. They encountered no police and saw very few people once they had left the alley behind and started to make their way westward towards the centre. Ten minutes' walking took them from all sound and sight of riot. The taxi they stopped wouldn't let them in until the driver had made sure which way they wanted to go.

"Nobody's going across the city tonight," he said through the heavy grid that separated him from his passengers – most Liverpool taxis were fitted with this shield now, assaults on drivers having become so frequent. "Now is the time they will do you," he said, "now the fuzz is busy. They put me in hospital once. This is the second bonfire party in six months. It gets the city a bad name."

5

Back at his apartment Benson went at once for the whisky and poured out two large ones. "What happened?" he said. "Did you get caught on the way?"

She was standing in the middle of the living-room, white-faced but otherwise not showing much disarray. "I was late," she said. "I was visiting some people in Toxteth. I had to leave my car. They wouldn't move out of the way, I couldn't get through. They were taking cars to block the streets." She made an impatient gesture. "Not mine," she said. "But I couldn't get through. They were closing off the streets on the north side of Parliament Street to stop the police going in after them. I spent too much time trying to get the car out. Then I got caught in the crowd. It all happened very quickly. I couldn't get away."

Benson was aware that his hands were trembling. He

213

swallowed some more whisky. "It must have been terrible for you," he said.

"Terrible for me?" She was looking at him with sudden hostility. "Oh, I see, sympathy. And you, what metaphor were you in hot pursuit of? Liverpool as a war zone? A violent acceleration in the heart's decay? It must have been disconcerting for you to be jostled by real bodies."

Benson took a deep breath. He was very tired. His limbs felt weak and powerless after the violent efforts he had been making. In spite of this he felt a rising fury at the perverse quarrelsomeness of the woman. "Why, I wonder," he said, "do you have to be so bloody awful all the time? Couldn't you take a couple of hours off?"

She turned her head sharply aside at this, in anger he thought at first, but then he realised from her stillness and the way she kept her face averted from him that she was weeping.

He advanced awkwardly and put his arms around her. She did not move towards him or away. At once he felt the tears start to his own eyes – tears at her tears, and her struggle not to show them, at the sense of a burden lifted, of being released from something; present anger, previous fear – he could not have said. He felt her body rigid against him and a slow shudder of weeping ran through them both, strangely climactic, like a contraction of love. Then she stepped back away from him. There were tears in her eyes but she made no attempt to wipe them away. "I'm sorry," she said. "I suppose you were just out looking for a sign."

"If so, I found one," he said. "You look exhausted. I don't think you should go out on the streets again tonight, do you? You heard what the taxi-driver said. You are welcome to stay here if you want. You can have the bed and I'll sleep in here." He gestured vaguely towards the sofa.

"I wanted to tell you something," she said. "A story really – in return for the one you told me. Can I have some more whisky?"

"Of course."

Oddly, as though this were some sort of formal inter-

214

view, they both took up positions: he in the armchair, she sitting forward on the sofa.

"Right," Benson said. "Let's have it."

"I know you don't like me much," she began, and this was so wide of the mark and moreover so grotesquely beside the point as almost to cast doubt on anything to follow.

"Liking or disliking has nothing—"

"As a matter of fact I didn't take to you much either. You struck me as shallow and self-centred. Well you are, actually. Self-centred anyway."

"I don't think I'm self-centred exactly," Benson said. "I don't know where my centre is, I always feel on the periphery. On the other hand, of course, I don't deny that I am intensely—"

"Just a minute," she said. "You are providing a pretty convincing proof of what you are setting out to deny. I'm supposed to be telling *you* something, remember."

"Sorry, so you are. Go ahead."

"I was born in this city, you see. Yes, yes, I know, on the night of the break-out. In Great Mersey Street, Liverpool 5. In a bed on a landing – there was only one bedroom and I already had a brother and a sister. My mother had seven children but one of them died before I was born and another when I was three. I've still got a sister living here, in Toxteth, my youngest sister. I had been at her place tonight when I got caught up in that mess. Her husband's been out of work for three years now. He's not a bad guy but he's given up. She's got three kids and no money. I help them a bit but life is much the same for her as it was for our mother fifty years ago in Great Mersey Street."

Alma paused, drank some whisky. "Not that much different," she said, "not when you think we've had forty years of the Welfare State since then. Of course Bill smokes, that's the husband, and they rent a television set, and it's true that the kids could have a bit more protein if they didn't, but that's not a choice people should have to make, people who've got nothing in a society where others have

215

so much. I was the lucky one, I was good at writing essays, I got an education. But that wasn't what I wanted to talk about. Tonight made me think of an incident in my childhood concerning my father. He worked in an abattoir as a slaughterman – he used to bring home meat for us under his jumper. He was quite illiterate but he was good at making things. He used to make plaster of paris statues of the Virgin Mary and Christ on the Cross and sell them – he made his own rubber moulds. We were Catholics, you know. Then his health began to go. He'd had a hard life and a terribly poor childhood and when his youth went his strength seemed to go with it. Of course they sacked him at the slaughterhouse. A week's notice. I don't know what standards they applied to the cattle but they had no time for a slaughterman with a bad chest. He had worked there for twenty years.

"At first it was all right. That winter, when the gas and electricity were cut off, he found an old combustion stove on a tip and pushed it home in a ramshackle pram. He knocked a hole in the ceiling of the back kitchen, got a bag of coke from somewhere. We were marvellously warm – I still remember it. They moved us out of there for damaging the property. After that he began to give up, like my sister's husband. He had always liked to drink but he started going out all the time whether he had money or not. He would rake the tips for what he could sell. He would sing for coppers in the street. He sang in the pubs too and people stood him rounds. People liked him. He used to drink himself silly night after night.

"One night I was alone in the place with my two younger sisters. My mother was spending the night with Katy, that was the married one, she was pregnant again. I was seven years old. I got my father his dinner and he went out. I put my sisters to bed and I went to bed myself. In the middle of the night I woke up. There was a smell of burning rubber, a very strong, acrid smell, I've never forgotten it – there was the same smell tonight. I went down to see what it was. My father was asleep in the armchair by the fire. His feet and

216

legs were in the fire. His trousers were smouldering. He had come home drunk and put his feet up against the fireplace and his legs had just slipped down into the fire. The fire was nearly out but the embers had charred his trousers and they were burning him – I could smell the scorched flesh.

"I couldn't wake him and I couldn't move him. He was too heavy, I wasn't strong enough. I wrapped cloths round my hands and lifted his legs out of the fire, one after the other. I could see the red burn marks on his legs through the holes in his trousers. The soles of his shoes had melted – that was the smell of burning rubber that woke me up. I put the guard on the fire. I couldn't think what else to do – he wouldn't wake. There was no one to ask. I went back to bed.

"When I came down in the morning he was still asleep but he was groaning. His face was white as death. He heard me moving about and he opened his eyes and said, 'Get us a cup of tea, love,' in the same way he always said it. He didn't know yet what the pain was, where it was coming from. Just then my mother came in, she had caught the early bus. 'What's going on here?' she said. I started to cry now she had come. 'Dad's burned himself,' I said. 'Dad's burned his legs.' She took in the whole scene in one glance. I'll never forget her face, the way she looked at him. Not anger, not concern. No expression at all. 'Let him be,' she said. 'Let the sod be'."

Alma made a grimace which might have been intended as a smile or might simply have registered the last of the whisky. "I'm talking too much," she said. "I won't go on much longer. You could say of course that my father was feckless and a drunkard and my mother an ignorant drudge who should have used contraceptives, that they were simply a 1950s version of those undeserving poor who are always with us – they're enjoying a resurgence today, aren't they? But the fact is that they were good people, both of them, valuable people. My mother was strong and sensible and my father was creative. They were both generous-hearted. And they had loved each other. Perhaps in ways I couldn't see as a child they still did. But what I remember now is that insensibility, that deadness – the stupefied man and the woman with a face like a stone. My parents. Now I see my sister going the same way. Anything is better than letting yourself be ground down like that, anything at all. Throwing stones at the police, burning down Barclay's – or half the city for that matter – is infinitely better than having all the energy and hope drained out of you by an inhuman system. It's so much better that it's not on the same plane of comparison at all. I know the people to blame are somewhere else. But it's still better. Those people tonight were *fighting*. I thought it was marvellous."

Alma appeared to flag for a moment then she said with sudden, vehement energy, "Yes, I do blame the system, I don't care if you think I'm a solemn lunatic, that's what you called me in the pub that day, don't imagine I've forgotten it—"

"You called me an Alliance voter, which some might think worse."

"And I don't bloody care about your oh so world-weary view of the people's struggle. Fighting is *better*, that's all. That's why, you know, when you said that about its being terrible for me, well, first of all there you were, grey in the face and shaking, dishing out comfort to the weaker vessel, and then I thought, no, he is missing the whole point, it wasn't terrible, it was marvellous."

There was no ambiguity about the smile now. It was direct and friendly as she looked at him. "It's taken me a long time to get round to it," she said, "but I'm trying to say I'm sorry for snarling at you like that. And thank you for getting me out of it the way you did. It was marvellous but I was extremely frightened."

"You didn't show it."

He was silent for a while, not knowing quite what to say. As she was speaking he had felt the last remnants of his belief in her as a muse depart for ever; she was a muse for heroes perhaps, but not for him. Her story had meant something different to him but he could not tell her so because it was hers. The father had inflicted the burns on himself, the mother had choked her own love. Brutalised people turn against themselves like suffering animals. Who had they been hurting tonight? The police were simply performers, uniformed slaves. They were burning themselves, he thought, stoning themselves. Even the looting – that street of poor shops . . .

"At first," he said, "just for a moment or two, when I saw those people throwing stones, the movements they were making reminded me of a dream I once had, black people dancing on the deck of a ship."

He stopped again and looked at her. It came into his mind that vulnerable as she was now, softened by the intimacy of their talk and the emotions of the night, she might be willing to sleep with him if he asked her. He wanted her; but it was a kind of opportunism repugnant to him, in conflict with the conditioning of his generation – scruples she would think of as sexist no doubt; and he was so much older, perhaps not attractive to her, he needed stronger indications than any she had so far given. As they regarded each other in these moments of silence it seemed to him that he could see some similar kind of speculation on her face too. But he remained silent and the moment passed.

"It's a bit complicated," he said at last. "The dream, I mean – and everything else. I'll tell you what I mean another time. I'm dead beat and I suppose you are. We'd better get some sleep, don't you think?"

Later, on the narrow sofa, as he drifted into sleep, he was not sorry. She would be still there next morning, he reminded himself. She was there now, in his bed, asleep already probably, her slight form under his sheets, all that anger dissolved. She would leave of course, but she wouldn't have to rush away – it was Sunday. They could have breakfast together. Had he the necessary ingredients for breakfast? Eggs, butter, bread, marmalade, coffee . . . Was there milk? He could nip down to the shop on the corner and get some. She wasn't the Muse but he liked her.

219

He would take care not to bore her, he would be amusing, he would disguise his egotism and his obsessions. He would not refer to his block, or Anzio or the slave trade . . .

6

"So there was no way of telling how much of it was genuine," he said. "But the woman broke down and I was sure she wasn't acting. I don't know what I'm going to say to Rathbone next time I bump into him, I can't feel the same about him anymore, what he did up there on the stage was evil. But he has a great future."

"Evil? What does that mean?"

"Ah, I see, not in your vocabulary. I mean he corrupted the solidarity that should exist between the members of the human race. As I say, I can't think of him in a very friendly way now. But it was one of—"

"Solidarity?"

"We seem to be having trouble with terms this morning. What I mean is that he made us consent to the business, with himself as ringmaster, conducting—"

"Yes, I understand what you mean. It's just that I don't happen to think there is such a thing as solidarity in that general sense at all. It's a political word. There can't be solidarity between men and women, for example."

"Are you saying there couldn't be solidarity between you and me?"

"Never. Among men, yes. Among women, yes. That's why I say it is a political word."

"Good God," Benson said. "And you accuse us of distorting the language. What I'm trying to get to is that Rathbone is a kind of genius. It was one of the most gripping things I've ever seen in my life."

"I missed something then."

"Yes, you did, but I'm actually not sorry you missed it."

"I appreciate the sentiment," Alma said, "but I like to

220

make that kind of judgement for myself. Anyway, perhaps you'll be able to use it in a book."

"Highly unlikely. I haven't been able to write anything for a long time now. The Liverpool slave trade was to have been the setting for my next book but it has defeated my imagination. Somewhere in the process I have fallen sick. And then, you know, it went on so long, I couldn't think of it just as an historical episode. I couldn't deal with it and I couldn't leave it alone."

"I know what you mean. That's how it was with my marriage. Of course you get out in the end, otherwise you'd die. It's how they're supposed to catch monkeys, isn't it, put a banana in a little cage with a very narrow entrance, the monkey puts its hand in, gets hold of the banana, but he can't get his hand out while he's holding it and he can't let go, so he just sits there."

"Hm, yes." Benson had not much cared for this comparison. "Anyway," he said, "that's why the meeting with Thompson was so important. The war was a kind of slavery too. The essence of slavery is having a role imposed on you, being made to perform. And I see now that that is true of everything. The meeting with Thompson made me think again about Walters, that's the chap I told you about, the one I got killed. I found something out from Slater, you know, I tricked him, really, into an admission, and it changed my whole feeling about Walters's death. After all these years. Walters transcended the condition. He died as himself. It may not sound much, put like that, but it is terribly important to me. It doesn't make me less to blame but it makes him less to be pitied."

"To tell you the truth, it always seemed to me that there was more of pity than blame in that business. Who is Slater, by the way?"

It was a brilliant morning. Sunlight lay across the table, over the remains of their breakfast. Benson had opened the window and they could hear the squabbling of sparrows in the eaves outside and see swifts wheeling high above the city in a cloudless sky. A faint, acrid smell of smoke came

221

drifting in on the mild air, only sign of the previous night's disorders. She looked at him across the table with a sort of ironical patience which he felt marked a deeper acquaintance between them. Her face still had some of the softness of sleep on it, but the eyes were as dangerously bright as ever.

"Of course, there hasn't been time to tell you," he said. "He's been so much in my mind, I was assuming he must be in yours." He was silent for some moments, then said rather awkwardly, "I was going to make some more coffee. But I suppose you have a lot to do . . ."

"I haven't got anything to do. It's Sunday, isn't it? I'll have to go and see about my car later on."

He glanced through the window at the bright day. It was undeniably Sunday. "I'll go with you, if you like," he said.

From the kitchen, busy with the coffee, he told her about his visit to Brampton Manor, the forthcoming show, his talk with Slater, Meredith's revelations. "He'll do it, you know," he said. "He'll get to screw Erika. He'll get his knighthood. Just as he got to be Officer i/c Entertainments, just as he has made a packet out of the commodity market. It's monstrous, really. I wish I could put a spoke in his wheel somehow."

"Perhaps you could," he thought he heard her say.

"What?"

He was advancing towards her with the jug of coffee when the doorbell rang. He put the jug down on the table and went to the door. He found himself confronted by Dollinger, massive in a dark suit, holding a long white envelope.

"I hear you lit a fire in your grate," Dollinger said in a deep, deliberate voice as soon as the door was opened.

Benson gaped at him. Did the envelope contain his notice to leave? It was three months now since that votive fire. Had the greater fires of last night finally moved Dollinger to action? In this dawn of riot he had judged the time ripe.

"I wanted to make an offering . . ."

222

But a wrestler would not be interested in that aspect of things. Was he now, with Alma looking on, about to be subjected to the Crab or the Boston Whip? "It was a cold day," he said.

"Mrs Dollinger informed me about it."

This was redundant, something they both knew, a sign of weakness then, to state it now. Benson looked for a moment into Dollinger's eyes. They were deep brown and amazingly gentle. Within their depths he saw the ordeal of a sensitive soul. This was a man who abhorred altercation. Dollinger had not come in wrath to throw him around. He was here because the implacable Mrs Dollinger had finally nagged him into it. Three months he had resisted; now, in his Sunday suit, after Mass, he had been able to resist no more.

"It is true, what I hear?" he said.

"By God, yes." Benson said, with experimental boldness. He saw wavering and dismay on the other's face at this defiance.

"It's all right," he said quickly. "I'll apologise to Mrs Dollinger in person, this very day."

Dollinger nodded slowly. "Thank you," he said. "Do not forget to do it." He held out the envelope. "This came for you. In the night they brought it. I found it downstairs on the mat."

"Thanks."

Dollinger's face broke into a sad smile. "Good, very good," he said, "we have understood each other, no?"

"Yes." With a strong sense of sympathy Benson returned the smile. He watched Dollinger retreat down the stairs. As he went back towards the kitchen he opened the envelope and took out the folded sheets. He recognised the handwriting at once: it was Carter's.

He took the pages back to the breakfast table. "Will you excuse me a moment," he said, "while I have a quick look at this?" Out of long, self-protective habit, he began reading at the last page.

Albert was squeezing her breasts inside their gossamer-thin

casing, seeking by the urgency of his handling of them to make her
equally desirous of him as he was for her. He had already removed
her briefs and he was hoping with a hope as clamorous as his need
for her, a need that had grown so mighty and potent that he could no
longer contain it, that she would remove his, because he knew that
in so doing she would be elated by her own audacity and so more
ready to give of herself. She, knowing his desire for a love
uncluttered and unhindered, hastened to meet his wishes because
now the time had come for both of them to abandon reserve and
reward themselves and each other for the strength and constancy of
their love.

With a strange smile on her face, half dreamy, half self-
conscious, she uncupped her breasts one after the other as her
brassière sprang below. Albert brought his mouth to them, exciting
her to a pitch almost unbearable. "Oh, my love," she said between
a groan and a sigh, and "Marvellous, marvellous, Sheila," he
kept repeating and now as their passion mounted she eased the
implement of his power into the deepest fronded recess of her being.
On her face he saw an expression he couldn't read, abstract, as if
she were looking at something far away. Then he was surfing
home on a gathering tide of ecstasy all rhythmic to her throbbing
convulsions and so there came to Albert and Sheila after all their
long tender trials the supreme oceanic floodings of saturated and
seraphic completed love . . .

Benson raised a delighted face. "Thank God, they've
finally done it," he said. There was a disturbing touch of the
Black and Decker in the description of Albert's member and
that faraway look of Sheila's was a bit ambivalent, as if she
might have been imagining it was Clint Eastwood. But
they had got there, they had broken through.

"They've done it," he said again. Waving the papers he
performed a brief impromptu dance. He remembered now
Carter's triumphant gesture of the evening before. He must
have been intending to hand it over then, but the riot had
delayed him; delayed, not prevented: he had come through
a battle-torn Liverpool to drop this long-deferred consummation on the mat.

"They have finally fucked," he said, unconsciously

employing in his exhilaration Carter's favourite stylistic device.   "Albert and Sheila have finally fucked."

"Who are they, friends of yours?"

"Not exactly. I'll tell you. But first, what did you mean just now? Did I hear you say you thought I could do something about Slater?"

"Well, you could, if you really wanted. You said you had a programme of next Sunday's events."

"Yes, that's right."

"How is your memory these days? You said you had a good memory for landscape, details of ground and so on."

"Yes," he said, "but that was in the war, you know."

"This is a war, too. You can't really stop people like that, short of revolution. What I have in mind is a token, something symbolic – it should be just up your street. And I think it would be good for you."

"Good for my character you mean?"

"Your character is beyond saving. No, good for your spirit. Do you remember the lay-out of the grounds, where exactly the marquee was and so on?"

Benson thought for a moment or two. He could see the exact curve of the drive, the house on the rise with the wooded skyline beyond, the long slope of parkland, the lake, the summer-house, the marquee. "Yes, I think so."

"How easy would it be to get to the marquee on foot from the road without being seen?"

"Well," he said, "it would be a question of leaving the drive at a certain point and going through the wooded part of the grounds. Of course it's difficult to be sure. There was a hawthorn hedge not far behind the marquee, I don't remember how far exactly . . ."

He stopped, looking at her with sudden awe. Her eyes were glittering.

"Yes," she said. "Of course it would depend on how my car has fared overnight. We'd need a get-away car. And we'd need recruits. Two at least. Young and active, if possible."

225

7

"That type of hat," Carter said, "does it mean something?" His smile was false.

"I don't talk about it," Elroy said.

With a sense, yet again, of coming to the rescue, Benson raised his glass. "Here's to the Old Brigade," he said. "Never say die."

The Disbandment Party was not going at all well. In fact it was edging towards disaster. Fundamental differences in world-view kept rearing jaggedly up among the Fictioneers and his own nervousness made him slower on his feet, less adroit than he might have been at smoothing things over. He was heavily aware of ulterior motive, this recruiting business which with Alma's battle-bright eyes upon him he had charged himself to undertake. To be disbanding and recruiting at the same time was something that life had not prepared him for. There was the fear too that Elroy, in spite of cautioning, might let it out that he alone was being persisted with, thus wounding and alienating all the others.

"Well," he said, "I'd like to wish you every success in your future labours. It's a hard trade, as we all know."

"The pursuit of excellence," Carter said from his arm-chair. "That is what it's all about."

"You really have been marvellously helpful," Jennifer Colomb said, looking as usual close to tears. "I really don't know how I shall get on without you."

"Hear, hear!" Anthea said loudly, throwing back her head and taking a bacchanalian gulp at her rosé. "It was here that Michael and I met," she informed the others.

Hogan, in his born-again denim jacket and jeans, sat beside her smiling gently. "Lucky day for me," he said, feeling all eyes upon him.

Benson smiled back but could not help wondering what

fate held in store for these two. If only people would drink at the same rate, he thought, we might whip up a bit of conviviality. But the Fictioneers were as various in this respect as they were in their literary concerns. Anthea was getting boisterous already, with Jennifer Colomb still on her first glass of pale dry sherry. Elroy, it had emerged, did not touch alcohol in any shape or form. Carter was putting away the beer at a fairly steady rate. He had been rather silent so far, except for the odd discordant remark, but looked as if he might be gingering up for something more, perhaps an analysis of the Quest Novel or a paean to Thatcher's Britain. Benson was keen to prevent this. Besides, he had suddenly glimpsed a way of working round to his object and possibly rescuing the party at the same time. If he could present the thing as work in progress somehow, put it to them in the guise of fiction . . .

"I don't think of this as an ending, you know," he said. "Of course, I am giving up my consultancy, so it is natural in a way to talk about endings and strike a valedictory note and so on, but there are no real endings any more than there are real beginnings. There are accidents and there are pauses, that's all. Stories are made from the pattern of these, sometimes very intricate. Our lives too – if you start thinking of your life as a narrative, these are the pegs you hang it on to. Without accident there could be no events, without pauses no perception. I'm thinking of those moments when you realise something or gather yourself for something further."

"I think that is so true." Jennifer was leaning forward tensely, her pale fingers clasped together. Her eyes behind the gilt-rimmed spectacles had the look of pleading Benson remembered from their sessions. "Birth and death are at the limits, aren't they?" she said. "We make sort of parallels for them, closer within the confines, accidents, as you say. Arrivals, departures, the idea of a journey. That is why I am finding this section of my novel so utterly absorbing, you know, this journey of my two characters through the wildwood."

"Through the what?" Anthea had begun frowning in an exaggerated fashion, but the speaker – and it was a danger signal – neither answered nor turned her flushed face.

"The wildwood" Benson said quickly. "Some more wine?" Anthea was not usually so disagreeable but she had some of the attitudes of the escapee – he suspected that Jennifer had all unwittingly struck an echo from the submerged past in Surrey.

"Yes, please. Jolly good, this wine. What on earth is the wildwood?"

"It is the ancient woodland of England," Carter said suddenly. "There is forest in this country that has been in continuous growth since the Middle Ages with its plant and animal life quite intact. I'm surprised you don't know that, young lady." He paused, then said to Jennifer with ponderous courtesy, "That's right, isn't it?"

"Quite right." Jennifer gave him a smile of tremulous radiance.

"Very good idea." Carter was clearly encouraged. "Journey of life. Characters riding through these ancients woods at a steady pace. Of course, you've got to have a sense of history for that. We go back a bit further than the Beatles, you know," he said to Anthea, catching her in the midst of another swig at her wine.

The tone had been jovial enough but Benson saw Hogan's smile thin down a bit. He tried to think of something to say, but nothing came to mind. His recruitment plan had gone astray among skirmishes and alien literary concerns. Carter winked at him, as if to include him in the circle of the older, wiser ones.

"A bit further, yeah," Elroy said, breaking a sombre silence. "Depends where you sitting. Sitting on a horse in among some old trees, that's one thing. But you on your backside in this street, you don't go back so far, mister. Liverpool a one-horse slum place till you found out where the black man lived. Left your visiting card in them wildwoods."

"Now we're getting this homeland business," Carter

said. "You were born right here, mate. Like me. Do you think I don't know that accent?"

It was Jennifer's obsessiveness that for the moment prevented graver discord. "I've introduced a new character," she said to Benson eagerly. "I should so much have liked to hear your opinion. His name is Jasper Schulberger, he is a money-lender."

"They meet a money-lender in the wildwood?" Hogan said. "Bit improbable that, isn't it?"

"Of course they don't meet him in the wood," Jennifer said crossly. "As they are riding along they are both thinking of their lives. Lady Margaret is wondering whether her fiancé, Sir Denis, is really a strong enough character for her and Sir Reginald is thinking about his crippling debts, he is a very extravagant person – so the reader is introduced quite naturally to Jasper Schulberger."

"Excellent device," Carter said. "Stream of consciousness." He and Jennifer exchanged smiles again. A natural alliance was forming between these two.

"Aristos, are they? I'll tell you what," Anthea said, and in this earnest moment she forgot to disguise the confident modulations of her upbringing – the voice, if not the sentiments, could have been her mother's – "you should have the oppressed peasantry dig a pit for them with sharpened stakes in it, cover it over with brushwood. One moment they are riding along, thinking their over-privileged thoughts, next moment oop-la! they are impaled on the stakes. Wait a minute though, that wouldn't be fair on the horses. You could have them dismount first, perhaps, you know, for a spot of—"

"I have absolutely no intention of impaling my characters on stakes," Jennifer said. She was flushed and there was a slight but perceptible quiver in her voice.

"Endings must be left to the author, I think," Benson said hastily. "All the same, it is surprising how often we follow these archetypal patterns. There must be something to carry the charge of meaning. It might be a single, crucial act, as in Elroy's book. Elroy's hero arrives, breaks the

229

mould, departs. His action has momentous consequences, it liberates a whole people. This corresponds to the belief in significant action which most of us cling to against all the evidence. The whole meaningless or at least confused welter of our lives is brought into the order of a single shape. Then another ending is the type Harold uses – the climactic moment. Death itself, the moment of dying, can be used in this way and so can orgasm – or, in romantic fiction, the final embrace which is its prelude. As a matter of fact, I've run into a bit of a problem myself as to how to end my, er, current enterprise."

But it was no use: Jennifer had been too badly mauled. She had finished her sherry now and he noted the look of mild determination on her face, the small changes of posture that indicated impending departure.

"I was hoping," he said, "for some constructive—"

"I don't think all that much of Harold's type of ending," Anthea said. "I don't think simply screwing, *per se*, is a good way to end a novel. I mean, that is an on-going process, isn't it? I mean, it's open-ended. I always think, well so what, they'll be doing the same thing tomorrow and the next day, then after a while they'll settle down to twice a week."

"You are missing the whole point." Carter had leaned forward. "It is what it means to the characters that is important. I know this is the so-called permissive society, but we haven't all got your attitude to sexual promiscuity. I belong to a generation that was brought up to think that sort of commitment between a man and a woman is important."

"I didn't mean it isn't important." Anthea seemed genuinely surprised by this suggestion. "I wasn't talking about promiscuity. It's just, you know, I don't think you can make an art form out of aspiring and contriving to have a fuck, not these days. You started on about generations, otherwise I'd be too shy to use such a word, but just because it wasn't readily available when you were eighteen is no reason to think it is the road to Mecca now."

"What do *you* think the road to Mecca is?" Carter said. "A spot of hash? Lying around on social security? No wonder this country is in the mess it's in. I know more about the road to Mecca than you ever will. I've had to work on the road to bloody Mecca since I was fourteen years old. With pick and shovel at first, then I worked my way up. Do some people good to roll their sleeves up, get down to some work."

For the first time in his experience Benson saw Elroy's face split into a smile of pure amusement. "Haw-haw," he said. "Do me some good, show me where it's at."

This laughter of Elroy's seemed to be the last straw for Carter, who now stood up rather abruptly. "You wouldn't see it if it was under your nose," he said. "You'd be too busy thinking about your identity or Haile Selassie. Well, I'll be getting along."

"I must be going too, I think," Jennifer said, fluttering with handbag and scarf. "It was really nice of you to ask us," she said valiantly to Benson.

Farewells with the other Fictioneers were not marked with much cordiality. Aware that they had not had a very nice time but helpless now to do anything about it, Benson saw them down. This might be the beginning of something too, he thought, watching them walk away down the street conversing indignantly together.

Returning to his three remaining guests he was struck by the way things had worked out for him: the Fictioneers had divided themselves along lines of age and ideology; it was the active service unit that awaited him now. He resolved to lose no more time. Still, however, he felt the need to be circumspect in his approach. He gave Hogan and Anthea more wine, saw that Elroy's orange juice was topped up.

"I didn't mean to offend her," Anthea said rather unhappily. "She reminded me of an aunt of mine, as a matter of fact."

"That guy got hang-ups," Elroy said. "He is *festooned* with them."

"Never mind that now," Benson said. "There is another

231

kind of ending that I didn't mention before, which could broadly be called the symbolical. This often takes the form of some natural phenomenon like a rainbow or a flood, or a symbolical action like forging your swords into plough-shares or running up the Union Jack. I've come across a bit of a problem myself, as I said, in my current enterprise, as to which kind of ending to adopt, either the moment of realisation or the symbol type. Perhaps you can advise me. If it won't bore you too much, I'll tell you something about the story so far."

"Fire away," Anthea said. Hogan folded his arms as a mark of full critical attention. Elroy, gravity restored, nod-ded slowly. They were interested, they were pleased that for the first time he was discussing his own work with them.

He told them then the essentials of the plot, blocked and wandering hero sees old buddy-killer singing in the street, recognises the birthmark, tracks him to his lair. He told them about the conversation between these two old soldiers, the finding of the magazine, the visit to the merchant banker, what the hero discovers there.

"I could end it at that point," he said. "He has discovered something, he has found something out after all these years, a small thing in a way but very significant to him. He has understood something about Walters, this man I call Walters in my book, something about his refusal to be shipped off to Naples like a slave. It's to do with slavery because that has been so much in my mind. It isn't com-pletely clear to me yet but I know it will be important for the rest of my days. Important for my hero, I mean of course. It is bound up with slavery you see, he wanted to write a novel about the slave trade. He can't do it but even this failure doesn't matter so much because he has been brought to see a kind of truth, and that is that slavery is as much to do with unity as coercion, the unity, or perhaps fellow-feeling is what I mean, that is our best guarantee of survival and which all forms of slavery practise to subvert. And then, of course, he sees that this man, the one who put on the show at Anzio, has the mind of a slave-owner too. As

I say, it could end there . . ."

In spite of all efforts, his voice had not remained quite steady through this. Glancing up, he saw Anthea's eyes fixed on him with the same sympathetic curiosity she had shown on the night of Rathbone's Show, when she had remarked on the empty place beside him. Despite her headlong style there was a perspicacity about Anthea older than her years, evidence of suffering in her own life perhaps.

"But he's having this new show," she said slowly. "He is doing the same thing again, this man I mean, who was your platoon commander, or I mean the platoon commander of your character in the book. Were you in the war?"

"Yes, I was."

"Were you at this Anzio place?"

"Yes."

"What's his name, by the way?"

"Who?"

"The hero of your book?"

This question, which he ought to have foreseen, took Benson completely by surprise. He paused for too long. "Bingham," he said at last with a terrible sense of falsehood.

There was a short silence among the Fictioneers. Then Hogan said, "You have to do something. You have to show which side you are on. I've found that out from my own experience."

"You got to strike a blow," Elroy said.

"But if he strikes a blow, what about my unity idea? Bit of a paradox, isn't it?"

"Unity made by striking blows." Elroy looked sternly before him. "Like a anvil," he said.

"He knows he could subvert this show," Benson said. "That would be the symbol. He has a plan, which I haven't worked out in detail yet. He can't put a stop to this man but he could turn the show into a fiasco. The thing is, he needs recruits, he can't do it alone."

"How many people does he need?"

"Two or three."

"Two or three here," Elroy said, looking down with what seemed sudden shyness.

"Cut the ropes." Anthea held out her glass. "Can I have a spot more of that wine? Cut the ropes on them, bring the whole issue down on their heads."

"Cutting ropes is no good," Hogan said. "This marquee is out in the open, you said. Big tent like that, you don't bring it down so easily. All four of us would have to be cutting ropes at the same time. We'd be certain to be seen."

"Set fire to it," Anthea said recklessly. "It's you, isn't it? This is real, isn't it?"

Benson looked from one face to another. He had come to it somehow. "Yes," he said. "I'm afraid I practised a bit of deception on you. I'm sorry, but I didn't know how you would feel. I know now, I think. The fact is, I can't do anything without your help."

"This got to look like a battle," Elroy said.

"Why?"

"They celebrating one nation, aren't they? We need smoke bombs."

"Smoke bombs?" Benson felt now the beginnings of that dismay which was to accompany him through all the planning stages, the sense of things moving much too fast. "Where could you get smoke bombs?"

"Don' you worry," Elroy said. "I can get smoke bombs."

"And jumping crackers to simulate gunfire." Anthea ran her hands excitedly through her hair. "My God, what terrific fun it's going to be."

"Now wait a minute—" Benson began.

"No good smoke bombs and jumping crackers if they can run straight out," Hogan said. "We must secure the entrance somehow, give ourselves time to get away." He thought for a moment, then smiled broadly. "Safety pins," he said. "Good strong safety pins."

234

8

The most perilous moments of the approach phase were on the first hundred yards or so of the drive. There was no way off it, the hedge grew close and thick on either side; and they were an odd-looking group for anyone to come upon, Benson in grey flannel, the binoculars slung round his neck, Hogan in his business suit – trappings of servitude briefly resumed – Anthea in combat kit, a baggy brown boiler suit and green wellies, Elroy in his fringed jacket with the equipment in a rucksack on his back – he had been persuaded to abandon his red woollen hat and now had his dreadlocks tucked under a black beret. The original idea had been that they should all dress as far as possible like guests, so as to avoid notice, merge into the background if necessary; but Anthea hadn't been keen on this and Elroy had refused point blank – there was no disguising him anyway. It had been a question of principle really, but a rather unfortunate confusion had resulted. Hogan had turned up in his suit, making him, on this festive summer-afternoon occasion, extremely conspicuous.

It was the only demur they had made – the rest had been all enthusiasm; the eagerness of his Fictioneers to cooperate in the enterprise had surprised and touched Benson and – increasingly – alarmed him.

On the drive itself fortune favoured them. They heard a car turn in through the gates but they were at the bend by then and so had time to get in among the trees and conceal themselves till it was past. From here, in single file behind Benson, treading softly, they made their way through the wooded part of the grounds. As he had remembered, the woods on this side extended as far as the lake and some way beyond. When they reached the edge, still under cover, they stopped again. To their right, through the screen of trees, they could see the blue of the marquee. There was another, smaller, white one beyond it now – the refreshment tent, presumably. Benson was dismayed to see people moving about at the front of this – he had hoped everyone would be inside the big marquee. However, by good fortune the white tent was set back a little, no one standing at the entrance to it could actually see the entrance to the other. You would have to walk forward twenty-five yards or so to do that, he thought. Unlikely. He licked dry lips. His nervousness was increasing. The marquee was a hundred and fifty yards away, and quite in the open – he had known there was no getting to it that way. Immediately before them, however, less than ten yards beyond the last of the trees, even nearer than he had remembered, was the tall, rather straggling hedge of thorn trees that marked the limit of Slater's property on this side. Beyond it there was a field of half-grown wheat, bright in the sunshine.

Leaving the others where they were, he moved cautiously forward to the outer edge of the trees. He had taken something of a chance on this hedge, not quite sure whether he was relying on last Saturday's memories or more distant ones. Old hedges of this kind, used to mark land divisions, were usually banked up. That would mean a slope on the other side too, no more than a couple of feet probably, but enough – dead ground, they had called it in his army days. Peering forward through the trees, he saw at once that he had been right; there was a short bank on the near side. Cautiously he rejoined the others. "It is 1454 hours now," he said. "Would you please check that your watches are synchronised with mine."

"We done that already," Elroy said. As zero hour approached he had shown a tendency to question orders.

"I'd like you to do it again, please. We are slightly ahead of time. We shall have to stay put here until 1500 hours. I think we'd better run through the O.P. again."

"What's the O.P.?" Since Elroy already knew the answer to this, his gravity held more than a hint of satire.

"Operation Plan." In his anxiety, all the inherent superstition of Benson's nature had come out, the faith in magic

236

formulas, spells, potent phrases. There was dire need of them, he felt. The concept, the grand strategy, was all Alma's, but the tactical disposition had been left to him; and there were too many unpredictable elements, too much that could go wrong. Left to himself, prey to scruples and misgivings, he would have abandoned the project long before it had reached this operational stage; but with the Fictioneers once enlisted there had been no going back: their enthusiasm, their loyalty, his fear of disappointing them, had driven him on step by remorseless step.

"At 1500 hours precisely," he said, "Anthea and Elroy start off towards the hedge, keeping close to the ground. When you reach the hedge you go straight through to the other side, then you crawl under cover of the bank until you are directly opposite the rear of the blue marquee. Stop at the nearside corner – don't go right behind it or you won't see my signal. I have allowed two minutes for you to get into position. The marquee will then be about six yards away, on our side of the hedge of course. There is no cover for those six yards but you are not in any field of view as far as I can determine it. The final phase, once you are at the marquee itself, shouldn't take more than a minute – in fact it must on no account take more than a minute. Speed and surprise and exact timing are the essence of the plan. Remember for Christ's sake not to move for one and a half minutes after seeing my signal. You must give Michael time to get across and secure the entrance flap. As soon as you have discharged the smoke bombs and crackers into the marquee, you retrace the route exactly, get back here, make your way to where Anthea has left the motorbike. You remember the signal, don't you?"

Benson fumbled in his trouser pockets and brought out two handkerchiefs, one scarlet, the other white. "The red one is the signal to launch the assault," he said. "The white one is the signal to abandon the operation and adopt the escape procedure immediately. That is clear, isn't it?"

He looked from one face to the other. They nodded without speaking. Both showed signs of tension. They were on alien ground here, behind the enemy lines; and they were about to disturb the peace in a very definite manner. Anthea's face wore already the fixed, staring look of exhilaration he had seen on the night of the riot. Elroy's lips were compressed and his eyes were glowing in their deep sockets. So might Zircon have looked at the utmost limit of his lethal laughter.

"Now you, Michael," Benson said, wondering what his own face looked like, "you stay on here. You keep a watch on the entrance to the marquee. At approximately 1504 hours you'll see someone crossing over from the house – I don't know who, perhaps the secretary, someone. You can't see the house from here but you'll see her when she comes into your field of view. She'll go into the marquee and after thirty second or so she'll come out again with another woman – that will be Mrs Slater. I know this is a complication but, as I have explained to you, Mrs Slater is my friend, I want to get her out. Forty-five seconds after they have left you'll see my signal. They'll be out of sight by then, on their way back to the house. As soon as you see the signal you stroll directly across from here to the marquee. When you get to the marquee all you have to do is close the canvas across the entrance. Have you got the pins?"

Hogan fished in his jacket pocket for a moment, then held them up silently. They were thick steel safety-pins, about three inches long.

"Good. As soon as you have done it you follow the escape procedure we have agreed on, make yourself scarce. I'll see you back at the rendezvous with Alma and the car."

A sudden loud burst of clapping carried over to them from the marquee. "This will require a bit of nerve on your part, Michael," Benson said in the silence that followed. He was unhappy about Hogan's suit.

"You can count on me." The voice was quite untroubled.

"I know it."

Benson looked at his watch again: it was a minute to three. "Quick drink?" He took the flask from his hip pocket

238

and passed it round. "Power to the people," Anthea said.

"Off you go then. Good luck." He watched anxiously as Anthea and Elroy crawled out through the trees, covered the few yards of open ground and disappeared behind the hedge.

"I'll leave you then," he said to Hogan, but for some moments still lingered indecisively. He was deeply troubled about Hogan, who had to stroll a hundred and fifty yards across open ground, secure the flap, stroll back, all in that conspicuously inappropriate suit. He would look as if he had strayed from a business convention – a rather shabby one, Benson thought, noting now the slightly frayed look, the shine of use on the lapels. Three years of trying to keep up appearances. It had not been a good-quality suit to begin with. He would stand out like a sore thumb . . . Suddenly the solution came to him. "Michael," he said, "we shall have to exchange clothes. You are bigger but not all that much and this suit of mine is fairly loose-fitting. I can't let you go like that. Hurry up, we've only got half a minute."

Hogan uttered no word of query or protest. With solemn haste the two of them stripped off jacket and trousers, made the exchange. It took longer than Benson had thought because they had to remove their shoes before they could get their trousers off. Hogan looked a bit cramped about the shoulders and the trousers rode rather high but he was passable.

"Right then," Benson said. "Christ, we've lost thirty seconds."

"My pins."

"What? God, yes." He dug in the jacket pockets, found them. "The handkerchiefs," he said. "I nearly forgot the handkerchiefs. No, in the trousers – thanks. Now don't forget, Michael, wait for my signal."

After half a dozen stumbling paces through the trees he had to stop to roll up his trouser bottoms. He made his way to the observation post he had selected, midway between Hogan's position and the point where the drive began to curve towards the house. From here, armed with his binoculars, concealed among the rhododendrons, he could survey the whole field of operations, the marquee and the refreshment tent with the lake beyond, the red and gold roof of the summerhouse effulgent among the birches. By moving the binoculars through an angle of forty-five degrees he could command the final few yards of the drive and the level area immediately below the house, where ranks of cars were gleaming.

It was a brilliantly sunny day with no breath of wind. Benson swept the glasses slowly through a world that was arbitrary and intense, disconnected, vivid green of the lawn, deep blue glow of the canvas, glittering sections of the lake, woods a depthless tangle of sunlight and leaf. Slater had been lucky in the weather: he found himself hoping fervently that it would be the limit of Slater's luck that day.

Another burst of clapping came from the marquee. He glanced at his watch: 1503 hours. Anthea and Elroy should be in position by now. They would have to wait there for six minutes, but if they kept their heads down they would be safe enough, between the hedgebank and the half-grown wheat. He was more worried about Hogan. He raised the binoculars again: there was nobody outside the white tent now, but he could make out the forms of people moving within it. They would be busy with the refreshments for the interval at half past three, not much to worry about there . . .

Nevertheless his nervousness mounted. As he slowly moved the binoculars once again across the field of view, he could feel the palms of his hands getting moist. He felt strange, loose, in his borrowed jacket. The sweet smell of Hogan's erstwhile hair-oil rose to him from the collar, troubling him further. A spot of Scotch would be in order. But his hand encountered nothing in the hip pocket but some loose change: in the haste of the moment he had forgotten to claim his flask . . .

From the marquee, quite clearly and distinctly he heard the children's choir break into the opening verse of 'The

240

New Jerusalem'. Dead on time. The next item was Athelstan's Dream – scheduled for a rude awakening . . . His eye caught a flicker of movement near the summerhouse, flashes of white among the trees. He trained the glasses carefully on the spot. For a moment there was nothing. Then with terrible clarity a bearded man in a white robe sprang into focus among the sharp silver of the trunks. It was St Columba. A moment later, at the side of the summerhouse itself, he saw two men in horned helmets and leather jerkins standing together. Then he understood: they were using the summerhouse as a changing room. Of course, the house itself was too far away . . . This was something he had completely failed to take into account. He tried desperately to calculate the route they would take. Between the lake and the rear of the white tent almost certainly – that was the nearest way. Anyone approaching from that angle during the sixty seconds that Anthea and Elroy were at the back of the marquee could not fail to see them, catch them red-handed with the canisters and the crackers. Benson was swept with terrible remorse at having exposed his Fictioneers to this risk. They had trusted him with their literary work, they had committed their bodies to his selfish and vindictive purposes. Should he signal the retreat? They would despise him . . . He strained to listen to the choir.

"Shine forth upon our clouded hills
And was Jerusalem . . ."

Second verse: forty seconds a verse then, roughly, then the applause – say thirty seconds. They should finish by 1506 hours. That would leave three minutes for the change-over. Time enough, surely. Athelstan's Dream would be well on the way before Anthea and Elroy came out of cover. It was four minutes past now. Alma should be at this moment making the phone call, purporting to come from a hospital spokesperson, urgently demanding that Mrs Slater be fetched to the phone without delay. This complication of sentiment broke all the known rules of tactics – Napoleon wouldn't have done it, he knew. His eyes were burning and his mouth and throat were completely dry. Why wasn't the secretary or someone beginning the trek to the marquee? Could Alma have failed somehow? They had checked the phone, she had occupied it well in advance . . .

A middle-aged woman in a black dress and a white apron appeared below the terrace. It was not the secretary, it was the woman who had served at table the previous Saturday. She was walking very quickly indeed – in fact, she was almost running. Another miscalculation. He had forgotten she would be possessed by haste; he had allowed two minutes for her to get there; she would do it in half of the time.

> "I shall not cease from Mental Strife
> Nor shall my Sword sleep in my hand . . ."

They were coming to the end. The woman was halfway there. Hogan would have seen her by now. There was a prolonged burst of clapping from the marquee. He waited. Why didn't the choir come out? Then a terrible thought struck him: what if Slater had changed his mind, allowed the children to stay inside during the intervals between their songs? The little girl with hair escaping from her headband, the boy with wrinkled stockings . . .

The dryness of his throat had become painful, like an inflamation. It wasn't only the children. He felt like a man awakening from a trance. He had done it again, the same thing, exactly the same, in forty years he had learned nothing: he had tried to make the ground conform to his conception, wrench the reality of things to a metaphor. Not vindictiveness or any real desire to hurt Slater, not Alma's eyes, not the zest of his Fictioneers – it was the beauty of the ending that had led him on. But they were people down there, not elements of narrative pattern. A high proportion of nasties the marquee would doubtless contain; but some there must be whose only offence was to be on Slater's invitation list. Some old buffer with high blood pressure, a dowager with a weak heart . . .

He must signal the retreat. Which pocket was the white one in? He thrust hands into both trouser pockets, found a handkerchief in the left one and in the other nothing but a gaping hole – Hogan's right-hand trouser pocket had no bottom to it. With a sense of foreboding he pulled the handkerchief out: it was the red one. Frantically he searched through the other pockets. The white handkerchief was nowhere on him, it was nowhere on the ground near him. It must have slipped down, fallen somewhere between Hogan's position and his own – there was no time now to look for it. Shirt? It was dark pink. Underpants, he couldn't remember. He checked quickly: they were blue. He had no means of signalling the retreat. The Fictioneers had no instructions about what to do in the event of no signal at all; they might embark on a death or glory attempt. He couldn't risk it. Benson raised his face to the hot sky above him. At least let the children come out . . .

The choir in their grey and white and blue emerged from the entrance with Mr Pringle at their head and trooped sedately towards the summerhouse. At the same moment he saw Erika, dressed in a long red gown and with a sort of diadem on her head, come out from among the birch trees into the open, followed by St Columba, bearded and bare-headed in his white robe, and then by lanky Athelstan, sober in a black skullcap and a dark-coloured kaftan. They met the children at the lakeside and went on past them towards the marquee. The woman was at the entrance now; he saw her go inside.

They would have to go through with it now, come what may. He kept the entrance in steady view through the binoculars. Thirty seconds to find Mrs Slater, explain, extricate her. Forty-five seconds more would take the pair of them far enough away. Then he could give the signal, set Hogan in motion. Ninety seconds after that, zero hour.

The woman emerged. To his utter consternation she was accompanied, not by Mrs Slater, but by Slater himself, in a fawn suit with a pink carnation in his buttonhole and on his face a look of strong displeasure. The two of them started off towards the house, side by side at first, but soon Slater was several yards ahead.

Benson lowered the glasses. He felt breathless, as if he had just received a physical blow in the region of the chest. How long would Alma be able to hold him on the phone? If he gave the attack signal now and Slater started back within the next three minutes, he would see the smoke, he might go round to the rear of the marquee to investigate or he might catch Hogan strolling back towards the cover of the trees. Slater was a big man, still strong and active. He might be too much for Hogan. They couldn't wait till he was back in place, the time was impossible to calculate, the interval was approaching. Slater would have to be delayed somehow. There was only one way . . .

A certain calm descended on Benson. Slowly he got to his feet, slowly he waved the red handkerchief back and forth three times. He waited until he saw the figure of Hogan emerge from the trees and begin to walk at a moderate pace towards the marquee. Through the glasses he scanned Hogan's face for a second. It was quite untroubled. Then, without further pause, he turned and began to make his way rapidly through the grounds towards the drive. He would have to keep Slater talking while the Fictioneers pressed home the attack and made good their escape. Three minutes was all that was needed. He would say he had come to apologise, he would humble himself, anything to save his troops. Once they were clear there would be nothing to connect him with the devastated marquee. I can say the binoculars are for bird-watching, he thought.

He came out on the drive and turned towards the house. No sign of Slater yet. Alma couldn't still be on the phone, she would have to be back at the car by now, something else must have claimed Slater's attention. As he approached the terrace he heard opera issuing at full blast from an upper floor, the great aria from the last act of *Tosca, E lucevan le stelle*. The volume was enormous. Of course – he ought to have thought of it: Sylvia hadn't been in the marquee at all, she had shut herself away here with music, on this day of

Erika's triumph. Booze too, probably. Hearing knocks she would simply have turned the music up. Or she might have passed out . . .

Crossing the terrace he stopped for a moment to look back. The marquee was closed. Hogan was twenty yards or so into his leisurely return journey. No one seemed to have noticed anything.

There was no sound of activity inside the house. He experienced some wavering of purpose. Entering would make him definitely an intruder, a trespasser. Need he do anything? In ninety seconds or so from now all the Fictioneers would be on the escape route.

Peering uncertainly into the interior he noticed with vague surprise that a small circular table had been over-turned in the middle of the room. Flowers and pieces of the vase that had contained them lay scattered round it. There was something else too, lying alone on the carpet. He moved a little nearer to the french windows. It was a knife with the hilt on one side like a bayonet. The short, broad blade was not gleaming, as when he had seen it last, but dulled by some stain.

His new position allowed a better view into the room. On the floor, some way beyond the overturned table, he made out a pair of legs in fawn suiting sticking out from behind an armchair. They ended in blue socks and up-turned shoes of the moccasin type set at a relaxed angle.

Still conscious of not much more than surprise he entered and went along the side of the room until he could see past the chair. Slater was lying on his back, eyes closed, face set in an expression of stern repose. His jacket lay open and the upper part of his shirt front was covered with a red that made the carnation in this buttonhole look pale. He had brought Lord Macaulay's clock down in his fall and frag-ments of china lay around him. In the warm, still air of the room there was a clinging, fetid odour, one Benson immediately knew – from sense, from memory, from a sudden conviction of necessity. Thompson had made it over the water. The signals had got crossed again. He had come creeping down the drive to ask for his bit of capital, found no one, entered. Surprised among objects of plunder, he had gone back to the Wadis. In Slater's grip, in that crazed struggle to get the knife home, he had shed his smell about. It must have happened now, the scent was fresh, perhaps half a minute before. While I was coming up to the terrace. There had been no crash, no sound of struggle – the loud yearning of the music had muffled it. He could hear the aria continuing as he stood there. *O dolci baci, languide carezze.* No more than thirty seconds ago. He must be still about. Crawling somewhere, looking for a safe trench, at the last gasp himself or he would never have left his cherished knife behind.

The recentness of it, the sense of Thompson's proximity, gave Benson his first real stab of fear. These two looters had killed each other. He must get away, there would be people here soon. He took a last look at the dead face. This blood-dabbled bulk among its litter, what price the knighthood now, where was the caviar, where the champagne? With a shock of fear and surprise he saw Slater's eyes open, saw him look up fixedly at the rococo extravagance of his ceiling as if pondering a reply to these questions. Then an arm came up with an inch of immaculate shirt cuff showing. Slater pawed the air for some moments, then grasped strongly at the arm of the chair. Slowly he began to hoist himself into a sitting position, making slight motions of the head. In seconds he would be on his feet, he would turn his terrible, his inextinguishable gaze about the room.

It was this, not fear of detection but the horror of meeting Slater's eyes, witnessing his resurrection, that brought the panic rising to Benson's throat. He went shuffling back the way he had come, the trouser bottoms again impeding him. As he crossed to the steps he was momentarily struck by the vastness of the sky. He saw smoke, dark curls and plumes of it, drifting up from the foot of the marquee, hazing as it rose, shot through with sunlight, slowly in the windless air enveloping the whole structure. There were no sounds of shouts – they were drowned by the great sobs of lost love still coming from Cavaradossi upstairs; but he thought he heard the staccato crackling of the fireworks. People were running from the summerhouse and from the refreshment tent towards the smouldering marquee. He saw figures, small in the distance, come squirming and crawling from under the canvas, like creatures expelled by fumigation.

In his haste to get down the steps and away he was tripped by his trouser-bottoms and almost fell headlong. He had to stop and roll them up again. He went through the trees at a stumbling run. The car was waiting on the road, engine running, Alma at the wheel, Hogan already ensconced in the back. As they gathered speed Benson let out a single sobbing breath of exhaustion, distress, relief.

Alma was smiling. "What held you up?" she said.